THE EX-WIFE

SALLY RIGBY

AMANDA ASHBY

Boldwood

First published in Great Britain in 2023 by Boldwood Books Ltd.

Copyright © Sally Rigby and Amanda Ashby, 2023

Cover Design by 12 Orchards Ltd

Cover Photography: Shutterstock

The moral right of Sally Rigby and Amanda Ashby to be identified as the author of this work has been asserted in accordance with the Copyright, Designs and Patents Act 1988.

Every effort has been made to obtain the necessary permissions with reference to copyright material, both illustrative and quoted. We apologise for any omissions in this respect and will be pleased to make the appropriate acknowledgements in any future edition.

A CIP catalogue record for this book is available from the British Library.

Paperback ISBN 978-1-80483-511-1

Large Print ISBN 978-1-80483-507-4

Hardback ISBN 978-1-80483-506-7

Ebook ISBN 978-1-80483-504-3

Kindle ISBN 978-1-80483-505-0

Audio CD ISBN 978-1-80483-512-8

MP3 CD ISBN 978-1-80483-509-8

Digital audio download ISBN 978-1-80483-503-6

Boldwood Books Ltd
23 Bowerdean Street
London SW6 3TN
www.boldwoodbooks.com

1

PRESENT

'Right, time to go.' The officer opened the door to the cell. He was young. Probably only twenty-five judging by the smooth skin and straight spine. The older officers walked differently. Like the job had beaten them down. Hardened them up. Given them a filter through which to view the world. But this one wasn't quite there yet.

All the same, his eyes narrowed into a glare. Alice flinched. She still wasn't used to people disliking her. After all, she'd successfully managed to get through the first forty-five years of her life without too much drama – if you didn't count the divorce. Even then, she'd been well-mannered. She never let Cassie see her cry. Never called Mark in the middle of the night begging him to take her back.

Because I'm Alice Hargraves. Not the kind of person to make a fuss.

Yet here she was. About to go to court and be tried for a murder she didn't commit.

It sounded like such a cliché. The lament of every person who'd ever been arrested. And maybe she'd think so as well, if she hadn't just spent the last six months of her life locked in a cell. No bail for her. Too much of a flight risk, according to the prosecutors. She wanted to tell them she threw up on ferries and couldn't even fly to Spain without taking sleeping tablets. But they stopped listening to her long ago.

Ever since they found the knife.

Ever since she stopped being a relatively unknown children's book illustrator and instead became the nation's most hated monster. The ex-wife who'd killed sweet, nurse Norah Richmond two weeks before her dream wedding.

The tabloids had already conducted the trial. This was just a formality.

It was for the best. Cassie was better off living with Mark. That way she wouldn't be tainted by the infamy the case had created. And prison hadn't been that bad. No more sleepless nights worrying how to pay the bills. No more fighting against the outgoing tide of her dying career. Just white walls and silence.

The same calmness spread through her now, and she almost smiled. Everything was so much easier when you accepted fate. She wanted to tell her younger self to stop trying so hard. Stop fighting reality. It was never going to bend to your will. Not in the end.

That's why she wasn't scared. Because she'd finally given in to the inevitable force of life, letting it do with her what it wanted.

'I said it's time to go,' the officer repeated. His mouth twisted, making it obvious he didn't appreciate her lack of panic. *Remorseless.* That's how they'd described Alice in the paper.

She stood up. A cramp shot up her calf muscles from lack of movement, but she ignored it. Not enough potassium. Not enough anything, really. She gritted her teeth to ignore the pain and stepped out into the corridor.

The navy suit her lawyer had collected for her swam on her hips, and the shoulders of the jacket drooped. She had no idea how much weight she'd lost, but it wasn't a diet she'd recommend. The officer bustled her through security and into a police car to transport her to the Liverpool Crown Court. The drive was silent as they sped along the M56, past the oil refineries of Runcorn and back into Liverpool proper.

From there she shut her eyes, not daring to look out the window in case it brought back memories. It wasn't until the car came to a halt and she was pulled out of it that she dared peer around. Her stomach sank at the crowds of reporters and onlookers waiting for her, and she bowed her head as they led her inside and through to the court.

There were stairs. Alice counted them as she went. Eight, nine, ten.

Her shoes clipped against the concrete, the leather tight and unforgiving. As if they too were determined to take their pound of flesh. In front of her, the officer's gait was uneven. Had he been in an accident? But the thought evaporated as the door to the court opened up.

There were people everywhere, making the low-level noise that came from repressed energy. But as soon as she stepped across the threshold, as one, they all turned to stare.

Like she was the bride.

Except she didn't have a white dress, or a glow of happiness. She was just a middle-aged woman in an ill-fitting suit.

She scanned the room for the one face she didn't want to see. Her daughter hadn't spoken to Alice since the arrest, and while it had left her broken and in tears for the last six months, today she was pleased. No eighteen-year-old needed to see this.

Everywhere she looked, hostile eyes stared back at her. The animosity filled the room, so thick that it pressed against her skin like heat on a summer day. God. She swayed on her feet, and another officer prodded her in the back to move. Lowering her head, she shuffled forward.

They reached the dock and the officer nodded for her to sit down, before taking his own seat next to her, as if worried she might run away. The irony scraped down her insides. Even if she could run, she had nowhere to go. She'd only ever wanted one life, with Mark and Cassie. But that was gone, and while she'd once hoped Mark might change his mind, might fall out of love with Norah, and back in love with her, that hope was no more.

Whoever killed Norah Richmond had effectively killed Alice as well.

Maudlin, she knew. But she'd had over five months to try and figure out who was behind it. Why someone would want to frame her? It was a puzzle that refused to be solved. A tangle of threads destined to stay as they were. There were no answers. Only more questions. Which was why she'd accepted what was about to happen.

Her barrister shuffled some papers. Cameron Lyle was about her age with pale blue eyes and a wool suit sleeve poking out from under his black robes. He turned and gave her a thin smile, but defeat sat around his shoulders like a mantle. She didn't blame him. He'd tried his best to build a case, but he hadn't been able to fight the media interest that had turned the nation into a swarm of amateur lawyers, all convinced they knew the truth.

Someone coughed, and the energy of the room shifted, causing Alice to finally raise her gaze. Once again everyone turned to the back of the court, like it was a Wimbledon match.

'All rise for the Honourable Judge Heath.' The bailiff's sombre voice was followed by a scraping and shuffling of feet as the crowd stood.

Alice stood as the judge swept past, black robe trailing out behind her. A woman. Cameron said that might be a good thing. But Alice wasn't so sure. She'd attended a same-sex school and had seen the damage girls could do to each other. It was why she'd insisted Cassie go to the local comprehensive.

Judge Heath waited until everyone seated themselves before leaning into the microphone. It hissed and then settled down as she called in the jury.

Alice watched them come in. A young woman, three middle-aged men, a couple of older women, one with a sharp haircut and the other with what looked like a wig. On they came. Twelve in all. And each of them pausing to look at her as they took their seats.

What did they see?

An insipid mother of one? Someone so beige that they'd never even notice her if she wasn't in the courtroom? Or were they already seeing the character the media had created? A bitter woman, scorned in love and jealous of the younger, more beautiful rival who'd broken up their marriage?

Once they'd settled, the judge called for the prosecution barrister to address the jury. He was well over six feet tall, and with his black gown and wig, he seemed to fill the entire room.

'Members of the jury, I appear for the prosecution in this trial and my learned friend Mr Lyle for the defendant, Alice Hargraves. I would like to explain to you the prosecution's view of the case. On the sixteenth of May at ten in the evening, the police were called to North Road, Grassendale, after Norah Richmond's body had been found by her fiancé, Mark Hargraves. As part of the investigation, the police had cause to search the house of Mrs Alice Hargraves, and during this search they found the murder weapon, a knife. This...'

Alice zoned out as he talked to the jury, arms wide, like an actor. This wasn't about the law. This was about him putting on a show. She was just collateral damage. On and on he went. The jury stared at him, as one, like they'd been swept up by the deep, compelling baritone notes in his voice. *Means and motive*, Alice could almost hear them think. *She had them both. Look at her. She's inhuman. A monster. She killed someone just because she was jealous.*

Finally, he lowered himself back into his chair. The room was silent, and Alice's throat burned, like all the air had been sucked out, leaving behind only some kind of deadly gas. She was drowning in it, and once again she longed for the solitude of the white-walled cell. No more eyes on her. No more accusations. Just peace.

Soon it would all be over, and she could sink into her new life, safe from hurting the people she loved the most. Because that was the secret truth. She might not have killed Norah Richmond, but she was guilty of other things. Just as bad. This was her karma.

The judge turned to Cameron, and he stood up. At five foot eight, he seemed like a minnow compared to the prosecution. Someone coughed, and there was a shuffling noise as he opened his mouth. *It's okay*, she reminded herself. *I've accepted my fate.*

Cameron stammered his way through the opening statement and Alice finally allowed herself to study the courtroom. It was smaller than she'd imagined, but still, there must have been at least forty people all crammed in.

In the third row sat a girl with long, caramel-coloured hair. Alice's heart pounded, but then the girl turned towards her, displaying a wide mouth and different nose. Long and aquiline. Not Cassie. Thank God. Towards the back she spotted an old man from the end of the road, who'd always smiled when Alice walked Hugo in the park. He wasn't smiling now.

Part of Alice longed to explain that she was a victim too, but she'd always been accused of having resting bitch face. She suspected that any smile she gave would be chilling.

Sighing, she was about to withdraw her gaze when a man on the fifth row suddenly ducked his head to study his phone.

Which was when she saw them.

Right behind the space where the man's head had been. A familiar face. Her gaze drifted down past their collarbone, and ice slammed through her body. There it was. A tiny flash of gold, from a pendent that she'd know anywhere.

A golden circle with the figure of a ram inside it. For Aries.

Such a tiny thing, yet so achingly familiar that the tranquil calm that had been engulfing her for the last six months retreated, leaving only a sea of nausea. Spots flickered across her vision and pain stabbed at her brow. She was going to be sick.

She jabbed her nails deep into the flesh of her thigh. It would bruise later, but at least it stopped the nausea from rising up to her throat. As the pain subsided, her mind continued spinning as she finally pieced everything together. How could she have been so stupid? How could she have missed what was right in front of her eyes?

All the tiny parts settled into place now. Like an ambiguous picture that held an extra image, just waiting to be perceived. She finally understood everything.

But there was no relief for finally knowing who was behind Norah's death and her own impending trial. Because now that she knew who it was, she also knew *why* they'd done it.

They were still staring directly at her, mouth upturned in a satisfied grin. Clearly delighted that Alice finally understood what was going to happen. And if she was found guilty – which she surely would be – there wouldn't be a goddamned thing she could do to stop them.

But she had to find a way. Because there was nothing Alice wouldn't do for her daughter.

2

SIX MONTHS EARLIER

Alice dabbed the brush down onto the paper, trying to repair the smear of blue, but it was too late, and what should have been a delicate cornflower now resembled a bloody bruise as it spread out across the paper. She swore and put the brush down. Sometimes it was better to just cut her losses and start again.

She carefully peeled back the tape that held down the page and crumpled it into a ball. Such a waste. Before the divorce, she'd only had the rainforests to worry about when she made a mistake. But now even paying for the supplies was problematic. Lawrence, her agent, had suggested she start working digitally. But after attempting to learn a few programs, she'd quickly retreated back to her watercolours and overpriced paper.

Thinking of Lawrence caused her heart to pound. After the debacle of the last picture book, he'd told her she couldn't afford to miss this deadline. He didn't need to say anything else. Despite the consistent sales of her Mr Crow series, there was no guarantee of getting more work. It was her own fault. He'd been warning her for years to spend more time on social media.

Grow her following, maybe do some book festivals, and start offering an online course. But she'd ignored his advice. It wasn't like she needed the money.

Not when she had Mark.

She gritted her teeth and chanted a mantra.

'*The past is behind me. The past is behind me.*'

Her therapist said she needed to interrupt her thoughts every time they tried to take her back to the darkness of when Mark first left her. Alice wanted to laugh hysterically at the idea of forgetting what had happened. She just needed to look around her to be reminded.

Gone was the detached Edwardian house in the Liverpool suburb of Grassendale, with the top-floor studio that caught the afternoon light, and the tranquil gardens where she'd spent hours with her sketchpad. Now she and Cassie were in a two-up, two-down in Aigburth, surrounded by people and noises and eyes, all intruding on them, as Alice tried to paint in the tiny, converted loft that was simultaneously too hot and too cold. The skylight let in some natural light, but there were no windows for her to peer out of, no way to escape the captivity of her new life.

All while another woman lived in Alice's old house. She could have contested it. Her lawyer had told her it was within her rights, but the house had belonged to Mark's great aunt, and she couldn't bring herself to make a claim on it. And he'd been generous enough, helping her with a deposit for a new place. But there were still bills to be paid.

And no money to pay them.

Rising heat crawled up her throat as the lump of anger that constantly sat in her belly tried once again to escape. It was like a festering wound that kept trying to take over her life. Correction. It *was* her life. Every waking moment seemed to be consumed with the fact that Mark had left her.

The front door slammed, and Alice managed to swallow it back down.

Cassie.

She got to her feet and listened for the sound of voices, but there were none. That meant Scott wasn't with her daughter. In a day of disasters, it was a small victory. He was the first boy that Cassie had ever brought home, and Alice hated him with a visceral intensity that scared her. He made her skin crawl. And he'd created a minefield between them, with Alice never sure what would happen from one conversation to the next. All the books kept reminding her it was a phase all teenagers went through. And that she had to sit tight and trust the old, loving Cassie would reappear. Alice hoped they were right because at the moment it was bloody awful.

Not that Cassie cared. Ever since the divorce, her daughter had been spending more and more time with Mark and Norah. As if they were her real parents and Alice was some distant relative to be endured. Maybe her next picture book should be the story of the invisible mother?

Sighing, she walked across the room to navigate the ladder-like contraption that was the only way of accessing the loft.

Hugo greeted her at the bottom step. He was a rescue dog with tufts of black and rust-coloured fur, and large brown eyes that were full of outrage. In the past he'd always curled up near her chair while she worked on her latest painting. But she could barely navigate the attic ladder with a cup of tea. No way could she carry a twenty-pound dog up there.

'Sorry, boy.' She patted him on the head, reaching for the space between his ears. He let out a little snuffle and followed her down the narrow staircase to the ground floor. Cassie was in the kitchen, fridge door open, staring into it, as if hoping to find something fresh and delicious. Except Alice had forgotten to go shopping, which meant there was only stale bread and a tub of hummus.

Her daughter's long caramel hair was tied back in a thick ponytail, which had been teased, making it look like a squirrel's tail. Her navy eyes were ringed in liner, and a tiny gold stud glistened from her stub nose. Her lips were set in a grimace.

'Hi, love, have you had a good day?' she asked in what she hoped was a casual voice. Their latest fight was about a gap year Cassie wanted to take. A trip to Europe and Asia with Scott. Alice had refused outright, trying to ignore the fact her daughter could legally do whatever she wanted in a few short months. But there was another reason Cassie was asking. Because she had no money, and the generous allowance she received from Mark had always been frittered away on clothes and concerts. For once Alice was glad that her daughter had been unable to save.

At least Mark had agreed with Alice, and despite his fortune, he'd also refused to fund the trip.

'Same as usual. It was school.' Cassie didn't bother to turn around as she shut the fridge with a dramatic sigh. It was obvious Alice hadn't been forgiven.

Hugo loitered by the wall where the dog leads hung. In the past he'd tried to paw them off, but today he stared at them before turning back, dark eyes mournful. It had been Mark and Cassie who'd wanted a dog. She was more of a cat person, but they'd both insisted, so Alice had agreed, with the caveat that she wouldn't be left doing all the work.

'Will you take him for a walk?'

'I'm going to Deb's house to study.'

'Please, Cass. I'm on a deadline and someone has to take him out.'

'Well, I can't.' Cassie opened the top cupboard and extracted two new packets of biscuits, the good ones that Alice saved for visitors. Cassie stuffed them into her backpack and pushed past.

'What are you doing with those?' Alice called after her.

'Snacks while we're working.' The front door slammed shut.

Alice sat down on one of the mismatched kitchen chairs, resting her head in her hands. How had everything got to this? Was Cassie really going to study? Alice could call Deb's mother and ask, but that would only get her daughter's back up. Frustration churned in her stomach. Cassie was so bright, and up until a year ago had been looking forward to studying anthropology. But these days she kept talking about what a waste it was to do a degree.

Once again the simmering rage churned in her chest. She hated that Mark's betrayal didn't just affect her; it had affected their daughter as well. And it wasn't Mark who was paying the price. It was Alice. Somehow she'd become the monster. The bad cop. The one to be treated like shit.

A burst of screeching guitars filled the room and Alice jumped before twisting around to the bench where Cassie's iPhone was sitting. It had a broken screen, and stickers were peeling off the back of the case, making it look like a relic rather than the latest model. She raised an eyebrow. Cassie never went anywhere without it. Alice walked over and picked it up. Scott's name flashed across the screen and part of her longed to accept the call.

To tell Scott that she'd met his type. That he was bad news, and that he needed to stay away from her daughter. Because Alice knew all too well how these things ended. Her sister,

Jasmine, had gone from a sweet teenager who loved nothing more than reading Jaqueline Wilson books to suddenly dating one no-hoper after another, first getting hooked on alcohol and later crack.

By her second year of university, she was dead.

And it had all started with a boy just like Scott. Dark, brooding, and with the kind of dangerous charisma that had stripped Jasmine of her own free will. The darkness of having to identify her sister's lifeless body had taken Alice into a void that she still struggled to get out of. And the idea of history repeating itself was more than she could bear.

The front door groaned open, and the sound of boots echoed out. Alice put down the phone and dropped back into her chair as Cassie reappeared.

'You just missed a call,' she said helpfully, but Cassie just tucked the phone into the back pocket of her jeans and left the room again. It was getting hard not to take it personally.

Hugo let out a snuffling sound and Alice reluctantly stood up. She'd been hoping to get another hour of work in, especially since she was now an extra page behind. But Hugo wasn't the only one who needed some fresh air.

Sensing that his hard work had paid off, Hugo gave a little bark and trotted towards the front door. She shrugged on a jacket and picked up the lead, with its small tube of disposable bags dangling off it, before pocketing the door keys. The house was just off Lark Lane and Hugo gave a bark as he expertly weaved through the strollers and school kids spilling out all over the pavement.

Alice wasn't originally from Liverpool. She'd never even been there until after she and Mark started dating. They'd been living in London at the time when he suggested a trip to his hometown to celebrate a bank holiday. She grudgingly agreed, while secretly wishing they were going to Paris. But from the minute she stepped off the train at Lime Street, into the clatter of a city filled with Georgian buildings, Victorian dockyards and the cacophony of scouse accents, she'd fallen in love.

And she'd been happy there, up until last year when Mark had ripped her heart out of her chest. Blindsiding her by doing the one thing that he'd promised never to—

The past is behind me. The past is behind me.

She cut herself off as they reached Sefton Park. Hugo tugged violently and charged forward. Alice had to jog to keep up and her cheeks were warm by the time they reached the palm house. It was April and the place was alive with the famous daffodils that turned the park into a sea of yellow. She really needed to get down here with her sketchpad.

Hugo dragged her forward until they reached a large field, then stopped to be let off his lead. She did so, and he immediately raced towards a discarded stick and carried it back to her. Alice picked it up and tossed it. He gave a little bark and darted after it.

It took an hour for him to wear himself out and they could return home. She'd just slipped out of her jacket when the doorbell chimed. Hugo, now curled up on the floor, didn't bother to raise his head as she walked back down the hallway.

It was one of the women she did yoga with, and they'd become friends since the divorce.

'I'm so glad you're home,' she said. 'I've had the most God-awful day you can imagine. Have you got any wine? I could really do with a drink and a chat. Unless you're busy. You're not, are you?'

Alice closed her eyes, trying to summon up the energy to explain that just because she worked from home didn't mean she was always available. But she thought of the evening ahead.

No husband or daughter to cook for, only the unfinished water-colours waiting for her in the stuffy loft, and her own thoughts for company.

'A glass of wine sounds perfect.' She opened the door fully and ushered her friend inside. Having a drink wouldn't solve her problems, but it certainly couldn't make them any worse.

* * *

'Christ, they're animals,' Scott said. 'I can't think why I'm friends with them.'

'Because they're your cousins.' Cassie sank deeper into the old grey couch that ran along the wall of the apartment. It belonged to Aaron and Ned, who were currently lying on the floor, surrounded by biscuit crumbs, after having devoured both packets that Cassie had brought with her. At nineteen, the twins were two years older than her and Scott and were now laughing hysterically as Aaron tried to roll yet another joint.

'They're still feral,' Scott complained, the softly rolled Rs giving away his Cornish accent. He'd moved to Liverpool when he was ten and even though that was seven years ago, there was still something so mysterious and exotic about him. 'Sorry we couldn't meet at my place. My parents are getting it fumigated.'

'It's fine,' Cassie said, though it wasn't strictly true. What she really would've liked was to be in Scott's bedroom. Alone. Together. Instead, they were cooped up in Aaron and Ned's apartment, in a shitty part of Smithdown Road. Still, she supposed it was better than the park, where her mum might see them.

'Hey, Cass. Want some?' Aaron held out the lopsided joint but before she could answer, Scott tensed and leaned forward.

'I told you she doesn't smoke. Don't be a dick.'

'Calm down, it's just weed.' Aaron's eyes were glazed.

Next to her Scott stiffened, and Cassie quickly put her hand on his arm.

'I'm fine,' she said. Aaron just shrugged and passed it back to Ned, spilling ash onto the carpet in the process. Her brow started to pound. She'd read about passive smoking. Could she get high just by being in the room?

'Stupid twat.' Ned rubbed the ash in before laughing hysterically. Cassie ignored them and turned back to Scott. He didn't smoke weed now but he had done in the past, and he'd told her how much it had fucked with his mind. And while he did drink on the weekends, it was way less than either of her parents. Yet her mother acted like he was one step away from prison. Typical Alice. Accuse first, ask questions later. It was probably why her dad had left. Not that Norah was much better.

Familiar anger curled through Cassie's gut. At her mother. Her father. Norah. All of them.

Why were adults so fucked up?

'You okay?' She pressed her shoulder against his and some of the tension left his body.

'Yeah. They're just a couple of tossers.' He blew out a long breath and moved closer, mouth brushing hers. His lips were soft and warm. God, he was a good kisser. Too soon he pulled away, but his fingers remained curled around hers. Heat filled her, and she pressed her leg into his.

He wasn't tall. About five foot eight with a lean body and a smile that made her insides melt. Grudgingly, Cassie probably owed Alice for the fact they'd met, since her mother had insisted on the local comprehensive rather than a private school.

She'd seen Scott around, but they'd never spoken until a year ago. She'd been in the student lounge when someone had literally pushed Cassie out of the way as they barged past, sending her flying into Scott's arms. What should have been the most embarrassing moment of her life became the most important one. Because he'd looked down at her, green eyes fringed with thick lashes and pale blonde hair that hung down to his shoulders. He was so different to the other lads at school, with their footballer fades and gold chains.

After that they'd become friends. He told her about his parents, who were always on his case. Trying to convince him to go to university, not caring that his dyslexia made it almost impossible for him to study. And how they ignored the fact he loved music and was already getting DJing gigs around town, doing weddings and club nights in local pubs.

In return she tried to articulate the rage she felt about her mother's need to be liked. Always worrying what other people would think. How she'd pushed Mark away. And how Mark had become such a cliché, falling for a younger woman, suddenly buying clothes that made him look ridiculous.

Their relationship had just been as friends until Cassie had turned up at a pub where he was DJing. And oh, God, but he was amazing. The place was filled with half-drunk punters who probably still listened to ABBA, but once Scott had started mixing his beats, they'd all started to sway, getting drawn into the hypnotic set, until the crowd all moved as one.

She'd waited for him in the corner until it was over, and he'd let out a soft groan, like he could no longer contain himself. When he kissed her, all the anger and frustration she'd been feeling about her parents was swept away by the heat of his mouth and the press of his body on hers. He anchored her. Kept her sane. Saw her for who she was, not for who someone wanted her to be.

He was literally the best thing that had ever happened to

her. An original in a sea of copies, and for some reason he thought she was too.

As if reading her mind, he tugged at the sleeve of her shirt and pulled her close for another kiss. It was deeper this time, and she was about to press against him when Aaron made a snorting noise. Christ, he was gross.

They pulled away, but Scott didn't look at his cousins; instead, he kept his gaze on her. She loved the way he did that. Making her feel like she was the only person in the room.

'Did you ask your mum about the trip?' he said, referring to the gap year he was planning to take. Her stomach roiled at the reminder of the fight. Alice had said Cassie wasn't mature enough to go overseas, and as for Scott...

'She's being a bitch about it.'

His green eyes darkened. The muscles in his arms coiled with restless energy. He was smart enough to know what Alice had said, and sensitive enough to be hurt by it. She ran a hand up his arm, trying to press down the rising emotions. It worked, and he let out a deep breath as the darkness passed. It's why they were so perfect together. She could reach him when no one else could, and it was the same for her.

'Whatever. So, what now? Will you talk to your old man again?'

'I'm staying there tonight.' She nodded. Her dad was rich. He'd grown up in a massive place in Formby and gone to Merchant Taylors', a posh private school, and then to Oxford before starting up his engineering company that made him loads of money. Problem was he didn't want to hand her every-thing on a plate because, quote, she wouldn't realise the value of things. That was fine, but she bet her grandparents had forked out for his trip over to Europe after he'd finished his degree, and he seemed to understand the value of it.

Besides, why couldn't they see how lucky she was to have met Scott? How great it was that he'd asked her to go with him? *Wanted* her to go with him. It was the opportunity of a lifetime.

'Good, because I need to be in Portugal by August,' he said as Aaron and Ned started wrestling on the floor. They rolled against the coffee table, sending a half-empty bottle of lemonade spilling out onto the filthy carpet. Scott winced. 'No way am I staying here in this shithole and turning out like those two.'

Cassie's stomach tightened at the idea of him leaving without her. She tried to imagine trudging to the bus stop every morning and squeezing onto it, before being deposited at the university to study something that wouldn't even give her a job at the end of it. And doing it all without Scott. Besides, the trip was going to be epic. He'd arranged a DJing slot in a club in Portugal, and then backpacking on to Asia. Cassie had suggested the rest of Europe as well, but he'd scoffed and explained that Asia was better for his music and it would be cheaper to live there.

Perhaps indefinitely.

It sounded perfect, and no way was he going without her.

'I'll get the money,' she said firmly. 'Whatever it takes. I'll get the money.'

3

Cassie walked along the street where she'd grown up. She'd asked Scott to drop her at the corner. It was stupid really, but the first time he'd seen her childhood home she could feel him pull back from her. And it wasn't like his own house was bad. A terrace house on the other side of Sefton Park. But this detached house was so much bigger, with a large garden, and more bathrooms and bedrooms than they needed.

She trudged up the path, noting that her dad's latest model Range Rover was in the driveway. The front door was locked but thankfully the security lights weren't blinking, which meant she didn't need to stab in her code. Her dad had had the system installed a month ago after he'd found footprints all through the garden beds, suggesting that someone had been there. Possibly casing the house with the intention of coming back to rob it.

A couple of other houses on the street had been broken into so he had a point. All the same, she was pleased she didn't have to interact with the high-tech system. Next it would want a retinal scan.

She unlocked the door, and let herself in. It still felt weird not to hear Hugo's snuffles as he raced to greet her. But Norah was allergic to dogs and so Hugo had moved out of the house, along with Alice. Out of all of them, he seemed to handle the new arrangement the best.

A moment of guilt went through Cassie that she'd refused to walk him earlier. She'd take him out tomorrow, and not because of Alice's nagging, but because she loved him.

The long table in the hallway was filled with what Cassie supposed were normal items considering the wedding was only a few weeks away. A vase of tulips and sweet peas and other flowers she didn't recognise. Four cane baskets, a glass jar filled with dried rose petals, a seating plan, as well as a pale gold tiara perched on top of a stack of bridal magazines.

She ignored them all, just like she'd ignored the request to be a bridesmaid. Please. The clang of pans came from the kitchen and Cassie frowned. She hadn't seen Norah's car in the drive, but since her dad wasn't the kind to potter around in the kitchen, it could only mean one thing. Crap.

The faint scent of essential oils drifted into the room and a woman appeared. If Norah hadn't been engaged to her father, Cassie probably would have liked her. She was tall with loose blonde curls and a wide smile that was accompanied by a set of dimples. She was also only thirty-eight, compared to her dad, who was fifty-one.

Her dislike wasn't out of loyalty to Alice. But she'd rather her parents had stayed together, because it was easy. It made sense. She knew how the world worked when Alice and Mark were one unit. And she knew for a fact that she would've convinced them about the gap year. A simple process of divide and conquer. But since the divorce her parents had built a strange new alliance. Plus, Norah was a new entity and had changed the dynamics completely.

It was unnerving.

'Cass, so great to see you.' Norah gave her a warm smile that reached her eyes. She was originally from London but had moved to Liverpool seven years ago and worked at Alder Hey Children's Hospital. 'How was school?'

Cassie only just resisted the urge to roll her eyes. 'Fine,' she said as her dad emerged from the direction of his home office.

He was tall with dark hair and even darker eyes, and he hadn't gone to seed like some of her friends' fathers. It still didn't mean he should be wearing the tight jeans and pink Ralph Lauren polo shirt Norah had fitted him out in.

'I didn't know you were coming around tonight.' He crossed the room and gave her a big bear hug. 'How's my little princess?' he said in her ear.

'I'm almost eighteen,' she said, pulling out of his hold. 'Don't keep calling me that. And I only just decided to come around. Alice was being a cow.'

Her dad flinched. He hated when she used her mother's name. Cassie ignored it and wandered into the kitchen, beelining straight for the fridge. Unlike at Alice's house, it was always stocked with fresh fruit and vegetables, not to mention her favourite vegan cheese. Norah only bought it to try and get on Cassie's good side. And while it would take a lot more than cheese, at least she was trying.

She took it out and went to the cupboard in search of crackers. Her father followed her in. 'Dinner's in an hour; should you really be eating?'

'I'm starving. I haven't had anything since breakfast,' Cassie retorted.

Her father shrugged. 'So, what was the fight about?'

'Guess.' Cassie sliced off some of the cheese and pressed it down onto the cracker. The smile on his face faltered and he let out a sigh.

'She's just looking out for you. And she has a point, Cass.'

Frustration climbed up her throat. 'Her only point is that she doesn't like Scott. Which is bullshit. She's hardly spoken to him. And I'm not saying I won't go to university. I just want to see a bit of the world first and figure stuff out. It's better than wasting loads of money doing a degree that I don't even like.'

Her cheeks were heated by the time she finished, and her hands were shaking. Why couldn't her parents respect her decision? It made total sense, and it wasn't just about Scott. It was about her, and what she wanted. For a moment her dad was silent, as if waiting for her to calm down. It only pissed her off more.

'You won't know if you like it or not until you try,' he said in a maddening voice.

'You're not listening to me,' Cassie said, then turned to Norah. 'You took a gap year before you studied nursing.'

Norah's usual smile faltered as she looked from Cassie over to her father, as if trying to weight up her options. Then she pressed her lips together. 'It was a long time ago and things are different now.'

'Not *that* long ago,' she said, irritated that Norah was happy enough to buy vegan cheese but totally backed down the one time Cassie needed help. Duly noted.

'That's enough.' Her dad's mouth tightened. 'Your mother and I have discussed it. You're too young. Go to university first and then take a year out. You'll be twenty-one then and much better equipped to go.'

'I'm going to be eighteen soon and don't need your permission.'

'I know. But you do need my money, and if you want it then you'll have to wait until you finish university.'

Another wave of irritation flared through her. Her other option was to get a job, but she'd tried that a few weeks ago. It hadn't gone well, and from the upmarket boutiques down to the local chippie, they had all given her the same response. *Come back when you have experience.*

'But... Dad.'

'Sorry, but it's not up for negotiation.'

The doorbell went, breaking the tension, and Norah quickly darted towards it. No doubt relieved to have an excuse to leave the room. Cassie pushed away the rest of the crackers and folded her arms, while her dad raised his hands, as if trying to silently apologise.

Not accepted.

She was just considering whether to go back to Alice's house, since at least Hugo would be on her side, but before she could make her escape Norah reappeared with her brother, Felix, in tow.

Cassie had met him a few times and he seemed okay, though a bit lame. Like the kind of adult who thought they were still 'down with the kids'. He was a few years older than Norah, so Cassie guessed he was about forty. They didn't resemble each other that much and while Norah was fair, Felix had dark hair and a square chin. Tired of London, he'd moved to Liverpool a couple of years ago after visiting Norah, and now ran a restaurant on Bold Street.

Felix held an old leather-bound book in his hand, which he passed to her father. 'Mark. Thanks for this. Great read. I loved it so much that I made a note of all of my favourite passages.'

Her father, who collected British history books, went pale. Even Cassie, who'd grown up knowing the bookshelf in the study was out of bounds, gasped. Then Felix gave a rueful chuckle.

'Relax. I'm joking,' Felix said. It was a moment before her father realised he'd fallen for it.

'God, you almost gave me a heart attack. Remind me not to let you take home my Churchill books,' he said as he reverently put the early edition down on the table.

'Definitely no more books until after the wedding,' Norah said in a stern voice, though there was no malice in it. 'Do you want to stay for dinner?'

Felix gave her a reluctant smile. 'Wish I could, but I've just had a text from Melanie. She's bloody quitting, and Friday's her last day. Which means I need to hustle to find someone before the weekend. Christ, do you have any idea how hard it is to get reliable staff right now?'

Cassie blinked, wondering if someone had secretly been reading her mind. 'You need someone to help in the café?'

'I need about three people.' He sighed, combing a hand through his hair. 'Why, do you know anyone?'

Her dad went to open his mouth, but she beat him to it, giving Felix a wide grin.

'I sure do. And even better, I can start as soon as you like.'

Once upon a time, Alice had liked Sundays. It was the one day of the week she didn't need to leave the alarm clock on. Back then Cassie had always been happy to help herself to cereal and watch cartoons, leaving Alice and Mark to lounge around in bed. Sometimes they'd turn to each other to have languid, easy sex, before one of them would stumble downstairs to make the coffee and retrieve the papers. Then at some stage the three of them would head out for brunch or lunch, depending on the time, and perhaps a walk along the Mersey before heading home for a night of leftovers and gentle conversation, immune to the pressures of the coming week.

But recently her Sundays had become a punishment. An endlessly long day that she couldn't fill with phone calls or shopping or dropping something off to the post office. She had no family in Liverpool, and her friends here all had families of their own. As for Cassie, after their fight the other day she'd only been home twice.

Alice's irritation grew. Despite Mark agreeing with her about Cassie not taking a gap year, it was Alice who'd come out as the villain, while Norah was the hero because her brother had offered Cassie a job. She'd heard about this phenomenon from other single mothers, of course. They all talked about the cool stepmum who didn't need to discipline. But coming up against it in real life was like a bitter stake in Alice's increasingly shitty life.

The unfairness of it whipped through her like a tornado.

Norah wasn't the one who'd gone through all the years of broken sleep, helping with the homework, and worrying about every little skin rash and cough. That had all been Alice. The invisible side of mothering that no one saw. Not even her own daughter. And now Norah was the hero. The one who'd not just found Cassie a job, but who'd also single-handedly destroyed all the work Alice had done, trying to prevent Cassie from making a huge mistake.

And now Cassie – who'd previously seemed indifferent to her new stepmother – kept talking about how great she was. It was infuriating.

Even Hugo didn't seem interested in spending time with her any more.

But after spending the last twenty-four hours stuck at her desk working on a painting of Alfred the Rabbit and friends having a tea party underneath an old oak tree, the idea of staying still any longer was unbearable so she retrieved the lead and rattled it. Hugo immediately cocked his head from his basket by the cupboard.

Fine, he seemed to say as he got to his feet and padded over. *If you insist.*

Alice gave him a grateful tickle, not sure when her life had managed to become so very small. She shrugged a jacket over her shoulders and left the house to make the five-minute walk to Sefton Park. It was a mistake. The park was packed with families and couples, all out and enjoying the early spring sunshine.

She turned to leave, but Hugo, who was now thoroughly awake, let out a howl and sat down on his haunches, refusing to budge. 'I swear we can come back later when it's not so busy.' *When I don't have to look at quite so many happy families and couples.*

Hugo barked in reply and didn't move.

Tears stung in her eyes, but she swiped them away. These days she didn't allow herself to cry. A little wallowing, maybe, but no crying. She let out a sigh as something barrelled into her legs.

'Ouch,' she yelped, sticking out her arms to stop herself from falling over. The thing that had charged into her was a dog, who let out a bark – obviously just as surprised as she was. The dog was dripping wet and covered in mud, and there was a lead dangling from the collar, suggesting that they'd managed to run off and discover one of the muddy puddles that dotted the path.

'Hetty, come here, girl. Where are you?' a voice called out in the distance and Alice raised her eyes at the little dog as she reached for the lead.

'Let me guess, you're Hetty?' She looked down at the soft linen trousers she was wearing. They now had a dog-shaped mark down one leg where Hetty had hit her. The dog answered by shaking her fur, sending out a sprinkle of wet mud onto the other leg of her trousers. She let out a groan as she clutched at the lead. 'Well, at least they match now.'

The dog gave a little bark, as if acknowledging her good work, and Hugo appeared from behind Alice to see what was going on.

'It's okay, Hugo,' Alice said in a firm voice and Hugo stayed behind her, watching the new dog from a distance. Hetty seemed friendly enough, but Alice wasn't taking any chances until she met the owner. It didn't take long as a flustered-looking woman jogged towards them. Hetty wagged her tail, as if to prove ownership.

Alice handed her the lead and the woman took it, before dropping to her knees.

'Hetty, hello, my darling.' She patted the dog, her voice warm and soothing. After a couple of minutes, she stood up and gave Alice an apologetic smile.

'I'm so sorry. We were trying to avoid the muddy puddles, which Hetty obviously took as a personal challenge,' she said as her eyes swept over Alice's mud-splattered trousers. 'I swear this dog is going to bankrupt me with dry-cleaning bills.'

'Please don't mention it. And don't worry about the trousers. Nothing that a good soak won't get out,' she said as Hugo inched his way forward, as if reminding her there might be a possible friend for him to meet. 'Not this time,' she said in a firm voice and Hugo sat back down on the ground by her legs. She patted his head.

'Thanks. I've been trying to teach her that she can't be friends with every dog we meet. But obviously I first need to teach her to come back when I call,' the woman said. She was tall, maybe five nine with muscular arms and a freckled face. Her hair was cut in a short bob and there was a hint of a tattoo peeking out from under one sleeve of her T-shirt.

'Tell me about it. It took me weeks to get Hugo to sit,' Alice said as Hugo made a snuffling noise at the mention of his name. 'I'm Alice and, as you can probably guess, this is Hugo.'

'Nice to meet you. I'm Belinda and this is Hetty-the-dog-that-isn't-mine.'

Alice raised an eyebrow. 'You're not dog-napping are you?'

'If I was, I'd be doing a pretty bad job of it.' Belinda made a rueful sigh. 'She belonged to my ex. But she got a promotion down south and decided that a dog wasn't part of her plans. She didn't seem to care that a dog wasn't part of my plans either. I never even wanted one in the first place and now I seem to be expected to wait on her hand and foot. Where's the justice?'

'Exactly!' Alice couldn't hide her surprise. She'd forgotten how nice it could be to talk to someone without having them scream back. 'My ex-husband and daughter insisted on Hugo, yet I'm the one left walking and feeding him, and then having to watch the way he practically throws himself at them every time they're near.'

'Hetty refuses to go to sleep unless she has my ex's T-shirt in the basket. It's like rubbing salt into the wound.'

'Ouch. So rude,' Alice said as a bubble of laughter rose in her throat. It felt foreign. Like she was learning a new language. Probably because it had been a while. 'And get a load of this, one of the few friends that didn't side with Mark after the divorce actually told me that I was lucky to get Hugo, since at least I wouldn't be alone.'

'Damn. That's harsh.' Belinda raised her eyebrows. 'I take it the divorce was messy?'

Alice let out a bitter sigh. 'The truth is it was quite clinical. He met a younger, more gorgeous woman and decided that he'd prefer to spend the rest of his life with her, instead of the vision in front of you – complete with crow's feet, a saggy middle and varicose veins down one leg,' she said with a swing of her hands to take in the mud-splattered trousers and tousled hair. 'He got the house, I got a mortgage and a pissed-off daughter who somehow blames me for it all. And not even enough money to buy the good plonk to help drown my sorrows. Bastard.'

Belinda gave an understanding nod. 'That sucks. If it's any consolation, it's not just you. My break-up with Melanie was brutal. She should've been a surgeon with the way she cut herself out of my life.'

'I'm sorry to hear that,' Alice said as they spent the next ten minutes exchanging war stories.

Alice wondered why there was such comfort in finding out she wasn't the only one whose life had been upended. Not to mention the deliciousness of being able to talk about Mark's betrayal to someone who hadn't heard the story before.

Her therapist had warned about falling into the role of victim, just to support her narrative, but since the therapist was happily married, Alice had decided she was just being smug. Next to her, Hugo got to his feet and nudged her, as if suddenly remembering there were sticks to be chased.

She sighed. As nice as it was exchanging war stories with Belinda, she needed to let Hugo go for a proper run or he'd drive her crazy all night. But before she could make her farewells, a flash of blonde curly hair caught her attention. *Norah?*

Her whole body went rigid. No. She was just being stupid. It was just her annoyance at talking to Belinda about what had happened.

All the same, she turned to have a proper look. Just to make sure.

It had started after being introduced to Norah in an awkward encounter in Tesco. Mark's mouth had been a tight line, and he'd looked almost as if he'd been forced to introduce them. She couldn't even blame him. It must've been like a before and after photograph having to look from Alice – who had light wrinkles around her eyes and mouth, a spare tyre around her middle, and owned more pairs of tracksuit bottoms than she cared to admit – and then back to Norah, the new model. Who... well... wasn't any of those things.

Ever since that encounter, Alice had been hypervigilant. At first just looking at every blonde woman she saw, but then she'd started walking past the old house to see if there were signs of Norah, and on occasion even going into the garden itself to peer through the windows at a life that was no longer hers.

Not the healthiest post-divorce habit to have picked up, but it wasn't one she could stop. Still, it wasn't like she managed to see much – just tiny glimpses of Norah's life as she came and went from the house. Like bringing in the upmarket deli-catessen bags and passing off the overpriced trays of lasagne as her own. Doing yoga on the lawn in an oversized Take That T-shirt, and sometimes coming home with slightly blonder hair, and better-shaped brows.

But that was all Alice watching her from the house. This was the first time Alice had seen her out in the wild, so to speak. Her heart pounded with the combination of adrenaline and guilt. She swallowed it down.

If Norah didn't want Alice watching her, then she shouldn't have stolen Mark and put a target on her very flexible, yoga-enhanced back.

The woman hurrying around the path that led down to the boat lake was most definitely her. She was wearing wide-legged jeans and an oversized cardigan with a plain T-shirt under-neath, making her look like a sickeningly perfect influencer. Hugo barked, and Alice realised she'd been holding the lead too tightly. She immediately loosened her grip.

'Is everything okay?' Belinda studied her, eyes curious.

Sure. Just my ex-husband's younger, fresher fiancée walking past to remind me that my life is shit.

'I'm fine,' Alice said, resisting the urge to track Norah. 'I just remembered I have an appointment, so I'd better go.'

'Of course,' Belinda quickly agreed. 'And again, I'm sorry about Hetty. Deep down she's very, very contrite.'

'Don't give it another thought,' Alice said, keen to finish the conversation. She gave the lead a wriggle. Hugo quickly responded by barking, and Alice used it as her cue to leave. There was no sign of Norah, so she followed the path down to the lake. The Sunday afternoon crowds had increased, and she had to weave past families and strollers, all while Hugo tugged on the lead.

Fishermen wearing expensive-looking gear were dotted around the shore and kids played around the old-fashioned rotunda, but there was no sign of Norah. Disappointment stung Alice's throat, leaving behind a sour taste.

Which was stupid. What was she going to do if she *did* find her? It wouldn't be a confrontation. Alice was far too polite. She should just turn around and go home to an evening of Netflix and overeating on the couch. Then she could mentally think of all the things she wanted to say. Words to make Norah feel the thousand tiny pains that had become Alice's life since Mark had left her. The anger she felt at her crumbling relationship with Cassie.

Her fury at the woman who'd ruined her life.

'God, I hate Sunday,' she muttered just as a blonde-haired Norah bobbed up from behind one of the trees that lined the bank of the lake. The cascade of blonde hair hung down her back in gentle curls, while her skin was smooth and radiant, without any make up apart from the salon enhanced perfect brows. Alice's stomach churned with irritation, making her realise how useless it was to keep slapping on all the vials of oil and creams in her bathroom drawer. At the most they were merely holding back the tide of middle age, compared to Norah.

Her study was interrupted by the appearance of a man suddenly stepping out from the same clump of trees that Norah had just left. His face was red and lined, as if he'd spent most of his time in the pub, and his thinning hair spiked up in the air.

Curious, Alice leaned forward. He looked nothing like Mark or any of his friends, or the kind of people that Alice imagined Norah would spend time with. In fact, he looked like the kind of person that Mark and Norah would usually go out of their way to avoid. So why was she meeting him in a dark corner of Sefton Park on a Sunday – the one day that Mark always went out to play golf?

The man called out something. Alice was too far away to hear anything, but whatever he'd said had an immediate effect on Norah, who stopped walking and slowly swivelled back to face him. The man began to speak. Norah's shoulders were stiff and when she answered, her eyes flashed. Even from a distance there was an energy between them. Like the aftermath of a storm.

It was an argument.

Alice stiffened.

And did Mark know?

Suddenly Norah held up her hand in front of the man's face and walked away, back along the path she'd first been on. The same one Alice was standing on. Shit. She quickly stepped behind a father who had a young boy balancing on his shoulders. It would be so embarrassing if she was caught spying. Not that she was spying, exactly. It was just that her legs seemed incapable of listening to reason. It was like she was punishing herself for losing the one man she'd ever loved.

But Norah didn't even glance up as she swept by, and she certainly didn't notice Alice following behind her, with a small dog in tow.

4

'It's glorious.' Norah's dressmaker let out a soft sigh and stepped away from the flowing white dress, stopping only to tweak one of the embroidered winter roses on the skirt. She was right. The dress was beautiful. Simple, and fitted with billowing sleeves. The bodice was silk with tiny pearl buttons that ran down the back. It had cost a fortune, but Mark had insisted she get exactly what she wanted.

And it *was* what she wanted. The dress. The ceremony. The baby she was hoping to soon have. All of it was going to be perfect because she was about to marry the most amazing man alive. Tall, brilliant, sensitive. A wonderful lover, who made her feel like she was the only woman in the world. Except it wasn't quite true. Because Mark also came complete with an ex-wife and a surly teenage daughter who seemed to think that Norah was a homewrecker of epic proportion.

Cassie wasn't exactly wrong.

Familiar guilt caught in her throat. Norah hadn't known Mark was married when they'd met at a hospital fundraiser. They'd been seated next to each other on one of the tables, purely by accident. A friend of hers had been due to go, but had come down with the flu, and asked Norah to take her place. There had been no ring on his finger, so they'd talked nonstop all evening, and when he'd asked to see her again, she'd said yes.

It was the following date that she'd discovered the lie.

Not a lie, he had protested in his gravelly voice that had twisted her insides from the first moment she'd heard it. *My marriage has been over for a long time. We've only stayed together because of Cassie. But as soon as I saw you at my table, I knew you were the one. That's why I took my ring off.*

True to his word, he filed for divorce the next day. All before they'd even slept together. But still, it was there. The questions. If she *had* known he was married, would she have leaned in so closely that first night? Would she have let him push away the strand of hair that kept falling from behind her ears? Would she have brushed his arm with her hand as she'd slipped on her jacket?

But she *had* done those things and had fallen unequivocally head over heels with Mark Hargraves. And now here she was, eighteen months later, staring at herself in a white dress, trying to pretend she hadn't been the other woman. Husband-stealer. Bit on the side.

A shrill hum rang out and Norah let out a sigh. Following her thoughts usually ended up in a dark place that she didn't like visiting. Her phone was on the gold and glass coffee table that was covered in bridal magazines. She carefully climbed down from the plinth, ignoring the dressmaker's hand of assistance.

'I'm fine,' she said, gathering her skirts and reaching over to pick up the phone. It was a text message from Felix.

Your carriage awaits, Cindy.

She smiled. He'd been calling her Cinderella ever since the engagement, saying that at least one of them had been lucky in love. Not that her brother seemed in a hurry to settle down, since he never dated anyone for more than a month at a time. She typed:

I'll be out in ten minutes.

Then she remembered the tiny buttons on the dress.

Make that fifteen.

It was actually twenty-five minutes later when she stepped out of the Mossley Hill bridal shop, with the dressmaker promising to finish off the last of the alterations by the following Monday. The dull morning had given way to a brightening sky and a very faint easterly. With her wedding less than a month away, she'd been following the weather as feverishly as a fisherman.

People had warned her against a May wedding. It was too risky. Beautiful one day and sodden the next. Not to mention the old wives' tale. *Marry in the month of May and you'll surely rue the day.* But there was also a magic to spring. It was all about new life and new beginnings. Not to mention that she could have peonies, which were her grandmother's favourite flowers. A little reminder that not all of her childhood had been terrible.

Besides, considering the way the summers had been lately she was doing people a favour by not making them stand around in the sweltering heat. And so every day that the meteorologists got it right increased her confidence that Saturday 20 May really would be warm and sunny, with only a gentle breeze.

Felix's Mini was parked across the road, but her brother wasn't in it. She scanned the area until she caught sight of him sitting outside a coffee shop, nursing what looked like a milkshake. She hurried over. He'd offered to come with her, but she hated the idea of anyone seeing her in the dress until the big day. Call her superstitious, but she couldn't help it. Besides, both their parents were dead so Felix would be the one walking her down the aisle. It would be fun to see his face at how well she scrubbed up.

'Hey.' He stood up and kissed her cheek. 'Any last-minute dress disasters?'

'No. But sorry I'm late.' She slipped into the seat across from him. She had an afternoon shift at the hospital but had arranged to meet him for help with her wedding vows. And it wasn't something she could exactly do at the house with Mark around.

'Let me guess. The buttons?'

She laughed. 'I'm afraid so.' She pulled out a notebook and asked for a coffee when the waitress came up to the table. Felix ordered a scone. He waited until the girl had gone back inside the café before turning to her.

'So, have you forgiven me yet?'

'There's nothing to forgive,' she said. It hadn't been his fault that he'd walked into the house mid-argument and unknowingly offered Cassie a job, but all the same she wished it hadn't happened. Mark's mood had been frosty all evening, while Cassie had blasted music from her bedroom, letting it run through the house like a victory lap.

Besides, that hadn't been the real problem. What bothered

her most was being dragged into the argument. Norah had never regretted her own gap year, but she could hardly say that without upsetting Mark. And having met Scott, she could easily understand why Mark and Alice were so against the idea.

Scott had a pasty complexion, and his mouth was set into a permanent smirk, as if he'd set a bomb somewhere and was waiting for it to go off. She had no idea what Cassie could possibly see in him. But unlike Mark and Alice, Norah had been able to keep her opinion about him to herself. Until last week.

The look on Cassie's face had told Norah that all her efforts to build a relationship had been undone in that moment.

'At least I can discreetly slip in a good word for you,' Felix said, as the girl reappeared with the drinks.

'She'll see straight through you.'

'Are you doubting my charm?' He took the scone and gave the waitress a dazzling smile, as if to prove his point. Norah ignored him and poured milk into her coffee. 'Okay, I won't convince her to vote you stepmother of the year, but tell Mark to stop worrying. I pay my staff well, but it's hardly enough to let her travel around the world for a year. It might just about get her to Calais.'

Norah had told Mark much the same thing. 'I know. And now, we need to stop talking about Cassie. I still have a mile-long list of things to get finished before the wedding, including these vows. And my shift starts at three.'

'My poetic skills are at your disposal,' he said, not bothering to mention her job. They'd had several discussions on why she was still working, when it was obvious Mark could afford for her not to. But she was adamant. Not only did Norah love her work and her patients, but Alice had never been ambitious, and Mark had once said it was part of what drove them apart. That she was content to just drift along instead of challenging herself. Norah wasn't going to be anything like that. 'Show me what you have.'

She pulled out a neatly folded list and handed it over to him. 'This is everything I could think of.'

Felix nodded, his eyes scanning the page before finally looking up at her. 'You sure you're not tempting fate by saying what a great father he'll be to your future children?'

Norah swallowed. She'd always known she was meant to be a mother. It was as much a part of her as her nose or the tiny mole on her arm. But during her early thirties she'd taken it for granted. Her boyfriend at the time kept promising that they'd start trying the following year. Except it had never been the 'right' time and it wasn't until he'd left her childless, with her best fertility years behind her, that she realised just how much she'd assumed it would happen.

It was another reason she loved Mark so much. Because she'd been upfront with him from the start. That she was thirty-eight, and considering IVF. He hadn't even blinked. Instead, he'd promised to be there every step of the way. Which was good. Because she had no plans to be sold down the river again. This time she was taking things into her own hands.

But the process was still tediously long, and while she'd already had her own fertility test, his appointment wasn't for another two weeks.

And then they'd be able to start IVF.

'You don't think I'll get pregnant?'

'I didn't mean it like that. I just don't want you getting disappointed, if...' He ran a hand through his hair. 'Well... would life really be so bad without having a kid? I imagine Mum thought that quite a lot about me over the years.'

'She loved you in her own way,' Norah said quickly. And

while it was true that Felix had been a handful when he was a teenager, their mother had had her own demons that she'd faced via an ongoing battle with alcohol that eventually killed her. That had been eight years ago. 'And she would have been proud of how far you've come.'

'Debatable. But she totally got it right with you. And I'm sorry for trying to rain on your parade. You and Mark will make great parents. While I will be an extraordinary uncle. Hey, we should include that in the vows.'

'Let's just stick to the list for now.' Norah raised her eyebrows and he grinned.

'You're the boss, sis.'

An hour later, the vows were done. A poetic and powerful statement of everything that Norah had been trying to convey. Even though her brother hadn't finished his degree in English literature, he had never lost his love for language. She gave him a grateful smile as her phone beeped with a text message. It wasn't a number she recognised.

I saw you.

A second later her phone beeped again. It was from the same phone number, and this time it was a photograph of herself. She was wearing her favourite cardigan and was standing next to a lake.

The blood drained from her face and all the happiness of the day disappeared.

It was Sefton Park. When she'd gone to meet *him*.

'Hey, everything okay?' Felix asked; his voice dragged her back to the present. His gaze was studying her face, concern playing out across his dark eyes. Her pulse thrummed in her ear, and she took a shuddering breath, trying to calm herself down. She hated lying to her brother, but she knew how protective he was. How much he'd worry if she showed him the text. And how he'd step in and make things better.

Besides, they both thought that time in her life was over. *It is over*, she corrected herself. She'd left all that behind and that's the way she intended to keep it.

'I'm fine.' She closed her phone and got to her feet. 'One of my patients has just been admitted to the ward. I really need to see them.'

'Anyone tell you that you're too dedicated?' he said, but his eyes gleamed with pride. 'Go do your thing. I'm heading to the wholesaler's anyway.'

He stood and gave her a kiss on the forehead before crossing the road towards the car, his long confident stride catching the attention of a couple of women walking by. Once he'd pulled away, Norah sat back down on the chair and looked at her phone again.

The photograph danced in front of her vision. It had been taken from the very path that she'd walked along. But how? She'd been so careful to make sure no one had followed her. Or so she'd thought.

I saw you.

Her heart pounded, the thump, thump, thump ringing in her ear. Someone had seen them together. Which meant that they also knew her secret. *No.* How could it be? She was so close to escaping that part of her life and this could potentially ruin it all.

Her hands shook as she hit reply.

What do you want?

There was no answer.

* * *

Cassie walked down Bold Street, trying to ignore the wind whipping through her hair. It was her first official day at work, and she regretted not wearing a hat. Now she'd look like a freak. She finger-combed it down as she reached Felix's restaurant. The Blue Radish had been there for several years, but Felix had taken it over two years ago. It had a large glass window and a blue door, which was flanked by tubs of bright spring flowers.

The walls had been stripped back to brick and the wooden floorboards gleamed with polish. Down one side was a food cabinet for the lunch rush, which was filled with vegetarian and vegan rolls, salads and pastries. Menus were stacked on the counter for those who wanted something fresh from the kitchen. There was also a bar with beers and wine, and an evening menu. Or so Felix had told her yesterday when she'd come in to discuss the job and work out her roster.

'You made it,' Felix called out, smiling at her. 'I'm glad I didn't scare you off.'

'Definitely not.' She headed over to him, the heady scent of garlic filling the air.

'Great. I find it easier to give everyone a proper induction before they start; that way, you're not going in with your eyes closed.' He tidied up the pile of accounts he'd been working on. After coming in yesterday, she'd realised there was more to Norah's brother than she'd thought. He'd left university early and trained as a chef, but had then started his own restaurant in London, before moving to Liverpool.

It had given her a new-found respect for him, and while she

didn't want to own a restaurant, it did prove she didn't need to go to university to be successful. Not that her parents would believe her. Neither of them had been happy about her taking the job, but at least her dad had just shrugged and said Cassie would need to wash a lot of dishes to pay for a year away. Cassie, who'd come to the same conclusion, didn't bother to argue. Besides, her real plan was to show her father how responsible she was so that he'd change his mind about helping her out financially.

Then she wouldn't have to put up with Alice trying to control her life any more. No more telling her what to study or who to date. It was suffocating.

'So, what would you like me to do?' she asked once she'd put her bag in the staffroom and donned an apron.

'I've got Tamsin on coffees until eleven thirty, and then I'll move her over to table service. You can shadow her and learn the ropes.' He nodded to a girl with spiked green hair who was standing behind the coffee machine, her face framed by the steam off the espresso.

'Alright.' Tamsin gave her a friendly smile and beckoned Cassie over. 'Are you here full time?'

'No. I'm still at school but I don't have classes today,' she explained as Tamsin twisted something out of the espresso machine and emptied the grounds into a long cylindrical container.

'I'm at John Moores, doing design,' Tamsin said as she picked up the next order. 'So, what's the deal? Are you related to Felix or something?'

'God no. Well... not exactly. His sister's getting married to my dad.'

Tamsin's eyes widened. 'Norah's going to be your step-mother? That's insane. She comes in all the time to see Felix.

We were all shocked when she announced she was getting married, especially after what happened with—' Tamsin broke off, and colour stained her cheeks.

Cassie's eyes widened, and she leaned forward. She hadn't met anyone who knew Norah apart from a couple of women from the hospital who had come around a few weeks ago for a glass of wine, and they'd acted like Norah was some kind of saint.

'What happened?' Cassie said, not able to hide her curiosity. But before Tamsin could say anything, Felix reappeared.

'Can you take these drinks to table number eight, over by the window?' Tamsin thrust a tray of drinks at her. 'It's a long black and a pot of tea. Once you've given them their drinks, bring the number back and put it next to the register.'

'Sure.' Cassie carefully balanced the tray as she walked out from behind the counter. It was for a young couple with lots of piercings, and after she managed to pass out both the drinks without spilling anything, she picked up the number and headed back to the counter, just as Tamsin finished another set of drinks.

'Table five. It's a green juice and a hot chocolate, plus two scones.'

'Got it.' Cassie gave her a nod and took the next tray, just as another customer walked up to the counter. The rest of the day flew by, and it wasn't until two thirty that Cassie even looked at the time on her phone.

Felix, who'd been out in the kitchen, covering for the chef, reappeared. 'So, how was the first shift?'

'I loved it,' Cassie said. 'Though I'll hopefully get faster.'

'Then we'd all better watch out,' Tamsin said before turning to Felix. 'This one's alright. Good choice.'

'High praise indeed,' Felix said as Tamsin disappeared into

the kitchen with a stack of dirty dishes. Once she was gone, Felix went over to the cash register, so Cassie took a cloth and bottle of spray and started cleaning down the tables like Tamsin had shown her.

'Hey, Cass.'

Scott? She turned around to where a familiar figure was sitting at a table by the window. His bleached hair was pulled back from his angular face, and the black jacket and white shirt gave him a Byronic vibe. He flashed her a smile that made her stomach flip, but before she could return the smile, a clatter of cutlery being tipped onto the bench dragged her attention away. She turned to where Felix was polishing a handful of knives, his gaze firmly fixed on Scott, who was studying the menu, oblivious to the attention.

Felix's eyes were narrowed, and the humour that usually lurked there was gone. But why? So far today Tamsin's girlfriend had come in three times, and they'd even made out in the corner during a break. Yet Felix hadn't batted an eyelid. So why was he staring at Scott like he had a disease?

Her confusion turned to annoyance. Norah. Of course. No doubt she'd had a great old chat with her brother about Scott and what a bad influence he was. Irritation prickled her skin, but she turned away before Felix could notice. Cassie swallowed and threaded her way over to the table where Scott was sitting.

'What are you doing here? I don't finish for another hour.'

'I know, but I wanted to see how your first day was going.'

'I can't talk in case I get in trouble.' She kept her voice low, knowing that Felix was probably still looking at them. But Scott didn't seem to notice. Her annoyance increased. It was so unfair. Scott hadn't done anything to Norah, yet that didn't seem to matter.

'I'm a customer – of course you won't.' He leaned back in the chair, legs splayed out. 'Just pretend you're taking my order.'

'You order at the counter and then we bring it over to you. Why don't you go down to Burger King and I'll meet you there when I finish?' she said, hoping he wouldn't figure out why she was trying to get him to leave. It didn't work and Scott just grabbed her hand and gave her a pleading look.

'I hate that place. Besides, I came to see you. Can you get me a free drink?'

'No freebies for friends,' another voice said as Felix appeared from somewhere behind her. He was carrying a pile of papers in one hand and a coffee in the other.

Shit. Cassie swallowed and turned to face Felix. His eyes were still boring into Scott, but his voice sounded calm.

'I-I wasn't going to,' she stammered, not daring to look at Scott.

'Great. Then we won't have a problem,' Felix said but before Cassie could answer, Scott stood up, his eyes remorseful, as two balls of colour worked their way up his cheeks. He hated that he blushed, but she kind of loved it, because it was her way of knowing what he truly felt.

'Sorry. I was being a dick. Don't blame Cass; I was just messing around.'

Felix shrugged. 'It's cool. If I had a pound for every time a friend asked for a drink, I'd be able to retire to the Bahamas. But just remember that Cassie's here to work.'

'Sure thing, man.' Scott raised his hand to give Felix a fist bump, then grinned as Felix returned it. 'We good?'

'We're good,' Felix agreed as he walked to the table and spread out his papers. Once he was out of earshot, Scott rolled his eyes.

'Sorry, babe. Didn't realise the brother was as stuck-up as the sister.'

He's not, Cassie wanted to say. But if she did, she'd also be admitting that she suspected Norah had given her brother a heads-up to watch out for Scott.

'It's okay, but you'd better go before he changes his mind.'

'No problem. I'll swing by in an hour and pick you up. My folks are out, which means we have the place to ourselves,' he said before blowing her a kiss and heading outside.

Cassie returned to the table she'd been working on and finished stacking the plates. But the whole time all she could think of was how unfair the world was. No wonder Scott wanted to leave Liverpool so badly. Because no one seemed interested in giving him a chance. They just looked at him and saw a rebel.

'Right, that's me done for the day.' Tamsin appeared at her side, wearing the same cute denim jacket Cassie had been admiring last week at the markets. 'But looks like we're on a shift together tomorrow, so I'll catch you then.'

'Definitely. And thanks for all your help,' Cassie said, too late remembering the comment Tamsin had made earlier about Norah. It had completely slipped her mind, but now she made a mental note to find out what Tamsin had meant. Because if Norah was hiding something, Cassie wanted to know what it was.

Then her soon-to-be stepmother might think twice before trying to spread rumours about Scott. Not that Cassie knew what she'd do with any information she found out, but, like her dad always said, forewarned was forearmed.

5

Norah yawned and resisted the urge to rub her eyes. She'd just applied mascara in an attempt to make herself appear human. She'd been sleeping even less than usual, thanks to the text messages she'd received two days ago.

There hadn't been any more, leaving her jittery and on edge. Someone was toying with her, and she was helpless to do anything but try and figure out who was behind it. But her mind was blank. Who knew about what had happened? And who wanted to make her pay?

She tugged on her uniform and covered it up with her favourite hoodie before heading down to the kitchen. Mark was already there, his glasses perched on the end of his nose as he read the paper. His hair was ruffled, and his face tanned from hours in the garden. He was gorgeous.

What would he think if he knew the truth?

'Morning.' He stood and wrapped her into his arms. His mouth found hers and some of the fatigue left her body. Kissing him never got old. She breathed in his cologne before they finally broke apart. 'You sleep okay?'

'Not too bad.' She yawned and looked over to the marble breakfast bar, but instead of the pottery mug he always used for her morning coffee there was a large porcelain teacup and the lemony scent of Earl Grey drifting from it. He seemed to read the horror in her eyes.

'Slight problem with the coffee this morning. Blame your brother. Cassie was practising her barista skills last night and went a bit overboard. But I do have tea. What do you say?'

Norah swallowed. In a very un-English quirk, she hated tea. Especially Earl Grey. Not to mention that the insipid taste wouldn't blast away the brain fog. But she forced herself to smile. She was an oncology nurse who worked with dire situations every day. This was hardly a disaster.

'Tea would be lovely.' She splashed some milk into the cup to hide the taste of washing-up liquid. 'Hmm, this is good.'

A bemused smile danced on Mark's mouth. 'You're going to buy a coffee on the way to work, aren't you?'

She wrinkled her nose. 'Is it that obvious?'

'The gagging gave it away.'

'I didn't gag,' she protested. 'Okay. Maybe a little. But I'm down to one cup a day now. It's my only indulgence.'

'It's very impressive,' he agreed in a supportive voice. She'd read that caffeine could affect fertility so had forced herself to reduce her four-cup habit down to a solitary long black. 'It's going to pay off. We could even try right now.' His hand slid across her flat stomach. Flutters of desire went through her, and her own fingers searched out his waist. Then the alarm on her phone beeped, and she reluctantly stepped back.

'Rain check? I've got to go if I want to miss the traffic.'

'I can be quick,' he said in a hopeful voice.

'Sorry. Besides, it might be good for you. You need to start saving your sperm for your fertility test,' she said.

'I think I'd prefer the dentist.' He gave her a pained look. Though considering Norah had been menstruating since she was thirteen, not to mention her own fertility tests, smear tests, and all that IVF and pregnancy would involve, it was hard to feel too sorry for him.

'One cup and a magazine of your choice,' she said, while planting a kiss on his cheek.

'I'd rather have you.' He wrapped her up in his arms for a moment before finally releasing her. 'I'll try and look forward to it.'

'Thanks, and don't forget we're meeting the wedding planner after work.'

'Eight o'clock at Nina's,' he confirmed. 'Where we will taste wine and work out a contingency plan for if Aunt Enid goes a bit overboard on the G&Ts.'

'We both know that your aunt's a complete angel,' she said, but all the same loving the gentle way he joked about his family. So different to her own family life growing up. Still, soon she would be part of it. Her alarm beeped again, reminding her of the time. 'I need to go, but I'll see you tonight. Love you.'

'Love you too.' He returned to his newspaper and Norah headed for the door.

The traffic along Queens Drive wasn't too bad and, even with a detour for a takeaway coffee, she reached Alder Hey twenty minutes before her shift. It was an impressive place, having been built several years earlier on the park next door to the old hospital site. In a nod to the younger patients, children and young people had been involved in the design and long wings spanned out like petals.

She reached for the reusable cup and took a long sip. Caffeine flooded her system and she hurried towards the hospital proper. The usual mill of staff, patients and visitors snaked around her as she reached the entrance.

When she'd moved from London, she'd trained as an advanced nurse practitioner and had been working in the oncology unit ever since. Her office was small with just enough room for a desk, and two extra chairs. There were several emails about prescriptions, and numerous messages. She managed to return all of them just as a head appeared around the door. The girl was ten years old with stick-thin arms and a Beyoncé-style wig almost twice the size of her tiny frame, the curls cascading over her shoulders. But the girl's smile was wide as she stepped into the room.

Rose. Norah shut down her screen and smiled.

'I'm here,' Rose announced with a dramatic fling of her arms, as her mother appeared behind her. Ruth Jenkins was twenty-seven but the thick worry lines made her look older. Then again Norah would probably be the same if she had to watch her own daughter go through the gruelling treatment Rose had been through. There was a husband somewhere in the background, but Norah had never met him, and Rose always went stiff if his name was mentioned.

'Remember you're meant to wait out here until your name's called.' Ruth gave Norah an apologetic smile as she draped a bright pink backpack over her shoulder and clutched at a pink coat.

Rose made a disgusted noise. 'Norah doesn't mind. I'm her favourite patient.'

'Favourite person,' Norah corrected with a smile. She had always hated the word 'patient' and preferred to think of everyone she worked with as a friend. And while she knew it was bad to get attached, she admired Rose's unflappable spirit. 'And come in. I'm all ready for you.'

Rose immediately walked around the desk and picked up the heavy circular paperweight that had always fascinated her. It was a glass dome with spirals of pink running through it. She sat down in the chair while her mother took the other one by Norah's desk. The white blood cells in the latest test results hadn't been what Norah had hoped for, and now she had to break the news.

'What does that mean? Should we try chemotherapy?' Ruth said fifteen minutes later as she dabbed at her eyes.

'I think we should move her on to Tasigna.' Norah explained how it worked and the details of how to take it. Ruth nodded along, listening intently.

'Thank you.' Ruth blew her nose as Norah updated the file on her computer. There was a thud from the other side of the room and they both swivelled around. Rose was sitting on the floor, using the paperweight as a giant marble, trying to roll it across the carpet. She'd somehow managed to get it under the chair.

'I did it!' She squealed with delight and crawled under the chair before they could stop her. 'Hey, look what I found. A letter.' She wriggled back out, the paperweight in one hand and a thick envelope in the other.

'I'm so sorry, Norah,' Ruth said as she plucked both objects out of Rose's hands. 'You know you shouldn't be playing around like that.' She put the paperweight back on the desk and passed the envelope over to Norah.

It was a plain blue and there was nothing written on the front or back of it. She frowned. It wasn't unusual for her patients to give her cards and artwork, but when they did, she treated them all carefully, grateful that they'd taken the time to think of her. She had no idea how any card could've ended up under a chair.

She slid a nail under the fold and opened it up. There was a photo inside. It was of her and Mark at New Year's Eve when they'd dressed up for an Art Deco party. Mark had been in a striped gangster suit and she'd worn a beaded flapper dress along with a tiara that his mother had lent her. She'd been transfixed by it and Mark had teased that she wanted to get her hands on the crown jewels.

Norah, who'd been a little tipsy from the champagne, had rubbed against him until his hardness had pressed into her leg and whispered that she was definitely interested in his crown jewels. They'd ended up having sex in a dark corner of a guest room and had spent the rest of the night giggling about it. As a joke she'd had the photo framed and kept it on his side of the bed, to remind him of it.

Smiling at the memory, she lifted the photo out, too late noticing that only she was in it, and where Mark should have been had been torn away, leaving behind only a rough, jagged line. Pain lanced through her, so sharp she leaned forward. Why would someone do that? And how had they got the photograph to begin with? Her hand tightened on the envelope, suddenly spotting there was a second piece of paper in there. But before Norah could pull it out, Ruth coughed.

'Is everything okay, Ms Richmond? You look pale.'

'Y-yes, of course.' Her stomach churned as she forced herself to smile. 'It's a party invitation,' Norah lied. It must have worked because Ruth gave a weary smile. Norah quickly finished her notes as adrenaline surged through her veins. She printed out a new prescription and passed it over, desperate to know what was on the piece of paper. 'R-right. Here you go.'

'Thanks, love.' Ruth stood and reached for Rose's hand. They both gave her warm smiles before leaving the office. Once the door was closed, Norah turned the envelope upside down and shook the contents out on her desk.

The torn pieces of the photograph tumbled out. First Mark, then herself, followed by a plain piece of A4 paper that had been folded up into a neat little square.

Her hands shook as she opened it up to reveal a grainy photograph of a familiar-looking box of tablets. Fentanyl. Oh God. Norah's stomach churned and bile rose in her throat. Fentanyl was a synthetic opioid painkiller that was often used to relieve chronic pain. But in recent years it had been making its way onto the streets, and the increase in demand had made all hospitals tighten their security.

She stared at the photograph of the drug. It looked like it had been downloaded from the internet. And underneath it someone had scrawled:

5 boxes by tomorrow.

Was it from the person behind the text messages?

But she already knew the answer. Of course it was. Why else send her a threatening text message if they didn't want something from her. But who was doing this to her? Who could possibly know her well enough to follow her to the park, and to somehow get the photograph from inside her bedroom?

And how had she missed it?

Fear ran up her spine.

She knew that some people travelled through life making enemies, but that wasn't her style. She got on well with all her colleagues and friends, and even Mark's family had eventually warmed to her. Well... apart from his ex-wife. But Norah couldn't really blame Alice for being angry. She also couldn't believe that the woman Mark had lived with for over fifteen years would be capable of something like this. Then there was Cassie. But again, Norah could understand why Mark's daughter might be standoffish.

So who else was there?

She didn't move. It had always been like that. When their mother would drunkenly throw things, Felix would be the one to act. To yell at her to stop, while Norah just watched on, paralysed. As if trapped in her own body.

That's how she felt now. Numb.

But while her legs wouldn't move, her mind raced.

If she ignored it, what would happen?

Mark would find out the truth about her past. Would he forgive her? Would he understand? Guilt and shame spiralled through her body and up to her throat, pressing down on her windpipe until she could hardly breathe.

No. She leaned forward, finally breaking the hold her paralysing fear had over her. Air rushed down into her lungs and she coughed. Once her panting subsided, Norah forced herself to stand up. She couldn't risk Mark rejecting her. Not when it wasn't her fault. And why should she? Why should she destroy the one good thing that had ever happened to her?

Her mouth was dry, and she grabbed her water bottle before stepping out of the office and looking around. How long had the envelope been there? She scanned in each direction but there wasn't anyone who looked out of place.

She headed for the dispensary. The rubber soles of her shoes squeaked against the floor and the rhythmic tapping of her ID badge against her shirt pounded out like tribal drums. She needed to act like it was any other day. She'd heard plenty of stories over the years of drug theft. From swapping out medicine and replacing it with water, through to under-medicating existing patients. But Norah wasn't sure she had the poker face for either of those things. At least not with such little notice.

Five packets by tomorrow.

Sweat gathered around her breastbone as she finally reached the door. She pressed the number on the keypad and breathed a sigh of relief when the door clicked open.

There had been talk of cameras being installed so she scanned the corners before walking over to the far shelf. She reached in and pulled out five boxes of fentanyl. She had no idea what the street value was, but she knew how dangerous drug addiction could be. Not to mention how necessary it was to help relieve the pain of so many of her terminal patients.

Shuddering, she slipped them into her pocket.

I'm a thief.

The words echoed through her skull like a roaring avalanche that kept compounding as it went. But she pushed it back. She shouldn't be defined by a single mistake. She deserved a future with Mark.

She swallowed and walked back to the door. Almost there. The corridor was empty, and she quickly stepped out and took a long drink from her bottle.

'I hope you're not hitting the hard stuff.'

Norah jumped as Norman, one of the porters, appeared next to her, pushing an empty trolley. Adrenaline surged through her, and if she was a cat, she probably would've shed all her fur. She forced herself to stand still and breathe.

'Sorry, I was miles away,' she said, hoping he couldn't hear the thump, thump, thump of her erratic pulse. That had been way too close. What if it hadn't been Norman? It could have been a doctor, or one of the ward sisters, who might think twice about what she was doing in the dispensary. Or worse, decide to check her pockets.

'I can see that. Penny for them.' He'd been at the hospital forever and was coming up for retirement. He was part of the furniture, and if you wanted to know the gossip, he was the person to go to. When she didn't answer, he patted her arm. 'Your upcoming nuptials, I bet.'

'I'm panicking that there isn't enough time to get everything done,' Norah lied, pleased there was something she could latch on to. Except it didn't help calm her nerves.

'It'll all happen exactly as planned. Just try not to worry. I remember my wedding as if it was yesterday. The heavens opened the moment we stepped into the church and stopped straight after the service. My Nancy looked beautiful. And I'm still the luckiest dog in the world to spend every day with her. It will be the same for you.'

'Thanks, Norman,' she said, hating the way the drugs were burning a hole in her pocket. She needed to get them safely into her car before her afternoon meeting. 'Anyway, I'd better go.'

'Don't let me keep you.' He smiled. 'By the way, did you get the congratulations card? Someone was looking for you earlier. I left it on the chair in your office.'

'That was you?' she yelped, before dialling it back. 'I mean thank you. I was wondering how it got there. Though they didn't leave a name. Do you remember who gave it to you?'

Norman rubbed his chin. Hours passed. Or so it seemed. Finally, he gave her an apologetic shrug. 'Sorry. She didn't give me her name. I probably should have asked.'

'It was a woman?' Norah said, clinging to the first tiny clue she'd had. Her mind whirled, trying to tease out any memories she might have. But nothing came to mind. Except the most obvious one, of course. And yet, they would hardly blackmail her, since they had even more to lose than she did. So, who was this woman? 'Can you remember what she looked like? I'd love to say thank you to her.'

He shook his head. 'Sorry, I didn't pay much attention. I feel like a stupid old git now.'

'Don't feel bad. I know how busy you are. And I appreciate the favour,' she said, though the words were like ash on her tongue. 'If you see her again, do let me know.'

'I won't let you down.'

'Thanks. I'll see you around.'

'Not if I'm a-square,' Norman quipped before turning his attention back to his trolley. He was still chuckling as he disappeared down the corridor. One of her colleagues walked past in the other direction with a raised eyebrow.

'Thinks he's a regular Ken Dodd, that one does.'

'He's harmless enough.' Norah tapped at her wrist, to indicate she was in a hurry. Her colleague nodded in understanding and Norah all but ran to the car, not bothering to tighten her jacket against the light drizzle of rain that had been forecast. She fumbled with the key fob and yanked open the door.

It wasn't until she was inside, with the doors locked, that she finally let the tears fall. This wasn't her. She wasn't the kind of person who stole. But it had been an impossible choice. If she hadn't agreed to do it, Mark might find out the truth and never forgive her. But now that she had done it, she'd crossed an invisible line, and if the hospital ever found out what she'd done, her entire career would be ruined.

Norah swallowed and wiped away the tears. She needed to pull herself together. She hadn't been caught, and as soon as she'd given the blackmailer the drugs, she could pretend that it had never happened. After all, that was something she'd become better at doing over the years.

She picked up her phone and pulled out the text message she'd received the other day.

I've got it.

* * *

'Back off, love,' an old woman said before snatching the last of the baked beans from the shelf. Alice stared at her, but the woman didn't notice. Or, more likely, didn't care. Instead, she pushed past Alice and clattered away, talking loudly to herself as she went.

So, this was her life now. Battling it out with pensioners for canned goods. And losing. The worst of it was she didn't even like baked beans. But she'd read somewhere that they were high in fibre, and were a lot cheaper than the sushi she'd once indulged in. She sighed and grabbed a packet of baps, a jar of Branston Pickle and a bag of Quavers. Breakfast of Starving Picture-Book Artists. Still, it wasn't like there was anyone but Hugo to judge her. Cassie had only been home once to grab clean clothes, and even then, she'd hardly said a word.

Her daughter was clearly no closer to forgiving her about the gap year argument.

It didn't help that Alice was tired to the bone. She'd been staying up late trying desperately to paint fields of spring flowers to match the breezy tone of the picture book that had been due yesterday. Except it was proving difficult to be breezy when her life was falling apart. Alfred the Rabbit's fun jaunt through the country was looking more like a surreal journey through Dante's seven levels of hell.

She reached the checkout and laid out her paltry items before taking a deep breath and pulling out her carrier bags. The staff all seemed to be in training for the Olympics with the way they scanned everything at lightning speed, then glaring when Alice couldn't get it all packed and paid for within a ten-second interval.

'Hurry up,' the same old woman who'd taken the beans chimed from behind her. Alice kept a dignified silence as she snatched up her bag and walked outside onto Aigburth Road just as the heavens opened.

She hadn't brought an umbrella, mainly because it was hanging in the hallway next to Hugo's lead and she hadn't wanted him to think they were going for a walk. It was almost laughable that she wanted to shelter her dog from disappointment, when her entire life seemed to be filled with it.

The rain beat against her skin, soaking her hair, cascading down her face and neck until her thin T-shirt was saturated. A car drove past, causing a tsunami of water to spray her, and by the time the traffic finally came to a halt she didn't even bother to run. There was no point. Her espadrilles squelched as she made the ten-minute walk home.

Once inside, she dropped her carrier bag and shrugged out of her jacket and trousers before running up the wooden stairs to the first-level bathroom. She longed for a long, hot soak but couldn't afford to waste time or hot water. She had to content herself with a towel.

She tied her hair up in the towel and slipped into a pair of tracksuit bottoms and one of Cassie's old T-shirts that she no longer liked. It had 'Boss Lady' on the front. But it wasn't like anyone could see her.

Now dry, she padded back downstairs to put on the kettle. Her phone rang from the depths of her sodden handbag. Still. At least it worked.

Lawrence's name flashed across it. That couldn't be good.

Unlike in the movies, where famous authors seemed to be on speed dial to their agents, Alice hardly ever received calls from him. In fact, half of her emails were from his assistant. Phone calls were only reserved for something really, really good. Or really bad. And considering how her illustrations were going, and the state of her life in general, Alice could guess which kind of call this was going to be.

'Hi, Lawrence,' she said in what she hoped was a breezy voice. 'How are you?'

'I can't complain,' he said in a brisk voice before making a ticking noise with his teeth. 'I've just been speaking with Louise. She said your final artwork was due yesterday and that she hadn't heard from you. What's going on?'

Alice rolled her neck, causing her makeshift turban to fall off so that her wet hair splayed out around her shoulders. She sighed. 'I was going to email her after lunch. I've almost finished it, but several of the watercolours... are not up to scratch. I need a bit more time for these last few paintings.'

Silence hung in the air, and it took all of Alice's willpower not to fill it.

'After what happened with the last book, they're not going to be happy. And if they choose to terminate your contract, you'll have to pay back the advance.'

Alice swallowed, trying not to think of the partial advance she'd received, and how it had been swallowed up by the mortgage and Cassie's school trip to France. Right now she wasn't even sure she could pay next month's phone bill.

'We could find another publisher. My books sell well. You know that.'

'Publishing's a small world, children's books even smaller. You'll get the reputation for being difficult to deal with.

Remember the last book: totally missed its publication slot and wasn't released until a year later.'

She winced. The fact she'd finished it at all had been a minor miracle. Especially since it was during the time Mark had announced he was leaving her. It was also before the true reality of her financial future had hit her. But now it was dancing in front of her, wearing sequins and a tiara. She really couldn't afford to mess this up.

'Please, Lawrence. Just ask. I-I can't...' Her voice fell away.

She didn't want to come across as being flaky but with everything else going on around her, she thought her head was about to explode.

'Is this about Mark?' Lawrence finally spoke.

She'd blurted out about all the issues going on in her personal life when they'd caught up at a writing conference. Alice hadn't intended to, but it was at a time when everything had got on top of her.

Like now.

Nothing so pathetic as a woman scorned.

'I thought he might change his mind and come back to me. But they're getting married soon. So what hope is there for me?' She sniffed and wiped away the tears. She hated getting emotional. But then again so did Lawrence, and he immediately made a gurgling noise, as if trying to figure out the best way to stop Alice from any more oversharing.

A silver lining to her pain.

'I'll call your editor and see what I can do,' he finally said. 'But promise that you'll have everything for them in a week. I'm putting my reputation on the line. You need to start treating this as your career, not just a hobby.'

Alice let out a shaky breath. 'Thank you so much. I won't let you down. *Alfred the Rabbit* is going to make you proud.'

Lawrence didn't bother to answer.

Alice finished the call and leaned against the wall. That had been way too close. Hugo suddenly appeared in the hallway, his fur sticking out and his left ear crumpled, as if he'd been sleeping on it. The little dog gave her a sleepy yawn before walking over to the wet clothes still sitting in a puddle on the floor.

She scooped them up and carried them into the concealed cupboard that housed the washing machine and dryer. She dumped them in and was just about to set the cycle when she realised she could no longer waste electricity on half-empty machines.

Sighing, she walked back upstairs to Cassie's room. There was clothing strewn everywhere, along with a pile of library books that Alice hoped weren't overdue. There was also a half-eaten packet of biscuits and a couple of glasses of flat soft drink.

'Christ, what a mess.' The washing basket was in the corner next to Cassie's dresser, and Alice cautiously stepped around the mess on the floor. She flipped open the basket. It had enough dirty clothes in to make a full load. There was also a crumpled towel on the dresser, so she dropped it in as well, then stiffened.

Propped up against the mirror was the wedding invitation. Like a scab that she couldn't stop picking, she'd already studied it several times while Cassie had been out. She put down the laundry basket and picked it up again now.

You're invited to the wedding of
Mark Hargraves and Norah Richmond.

It was written in a plain gold font and was the kind of understated invite that cost a fortune. The wedding itself was being held in Formby, in one of the ancient churches with the breakfast at Formby Hall. And, according to Cassie, there were going to be at least one hundred guests. Even bloody Scott was going.

Her insides clenched. Their own wedding had been rushed and in a registry office. No one was with them. Even their witnesses were random people they'd found on the street outside. It didn't help that Cassie had been a baby then, born before Mark had even proposed. But that was beside the point. It had been romantic and fun.

Or so she'd thought. Now it just seemed like a cheap version – a starter wedding for a starter wife. The unfairness began to work its way through her again. That Norah was enjoying what should've rightfully been Alice's.

She leaned forward and put the invitation back against the mirror, but her sleeve caught on a glass that was half-full of cola. It toppled forward and splashed out over the mirror and the surface of the dresser, spreading out like rivulets of mercury.

Shit. Shit. Shit. Brown stains soaked into the expensive card, leaving the beautiful golden font unreadable. She snatched a handful of tissues from the box on the side and started mopping up the mess. But it was ruined.

Her stomach knotted. Cassie was already mad over the whole gap year issue, and this would just make matters worse. She'd say that Alice had done it on purpose. But she hadn't. She hadn't even noticed the glass there. That didn't mean to say that she hadn't wanted to spoil the invite. Spoil the wedding, even. But of course she wouldn't.

Alice was an eldest child. And eldest children didn't do that. Not like Jasmine. Her younger sister might not have been loud and outspoken, but she'd had a reckless, impulsive streak that would suddenly appear. And when it came, anything was possible. Like burning the wedding dress or standing up in the church and announcing why Mark and Norah couldn't possibly get married.

But Alice could only think about doing things.

No wonder Mark had left.

She was hopeless. A wave of exhaustion rushed over her. It was so tiring to fight the rising tide. Mark and Norah were getting married, whether she liked it or not. She needed to accept that Mark was no longer hers. That following his fiancée around in the park like a crazy person wasn't going to make anything better. Nor was standing outside her old house, staring into the windows and dreaming about a life that was no longer hers.

It all had to stop. She needed to let go of her fantasy that Norah would somehow screw everything up and that Mark would come to his senses. The game was over.

Lawrence was right. It was time to stop treating her work like a hobby and start acting like it was a career. Because it might be the only thing she had left.

6

Norah smoothed down her jeans and checked her blonde hair was firmly tucked under the navy baseball cap she'd found in the back of the Volkswagen. It was her day off and her car was getting an MOT. Mark had an overnight meeting in the Lake District and had taken the Range Rover but still had his old car as a run-around.

She hadn't slept well, and each time she'd started to drift off, she'd remember the ruined photograph and turn to stare at the original copy, which was still sitting on the bedside table, secure in the frame. The fact it was still there had chilled her, because it meant someone had secretly come into the bedroom and made a copy of it. In the end she'd moved the photograph into the spare bedroom and double-checked the house alarm was set before finally falling into a fitful sleep.

Norah yawned, flicked on the indicator and turned in to the car park at Huyton Village.

Despite the name, it was less like a village and more like a pedestrianised high street, surrounded by a car park and full of pound shops, bakeries and empty storefronts. Norah checked the time on her phone. She was early. Her large leather bag was hanging over her shoulder and she resisted the urge to check the drugs were still in there.

The reply to her text message had come through last night.

11 o'clock @ Harold Wilson.

A quick Google search had shown her there was a statue of the former prime minister near the car park she'd come in through. Her stomach churned as she found it. A bronze statue of a man sitting down on a cement bench, as if waiting for a bus. Next to the statue, a small boy was playing something on a phone while his mother was nearby, vaping.

What if they didn't move?

Should she text the blackmailer?

Sweat beaded on her collarbone.

'Ms Richmond?' A familiar voice came from behind her, and she turned to see Ruth Jenkins. She was holding several carrier bags and her hair was limp. 'I thought that was you.'

'Ruth,' Norah said, trying to keep her voice calm. 'H-how are you?'

'Okay. Rose is at a birthday party.' Ruth nodded to an ice-cream shop on the corner. 'She's feeling much better, and it's nice for her to spend some time with her friends. I thought I'd nip out and get the shopping in.'

Norah swallowed. 'I forgot you lived around here.'

'Born and bred,' she said with a weary edge to her voice. 'What brings you to this neck of the woods?'

Norah licked her lips as she glanced around at the discount stores and bakeries. Was it that obvious that she didn't usually shop there? 'Oh, I just had a few things to pick up.'

A police siren rang out and Norah tightened her grip on the

bag. Had they been following her? Did they know? She spun around, half expecting a dozen police cars to be heading towards her, but there was nothing.

Her panic seemed to amuse Ruth, who quirked an eyebrow. 'The station's just up the road. Thought you'd be used to sirens from working in the hospital.'

'I guess they sound different,' Norah said, her heart still pounding rapidly in her chest. Ruth studied her before shrugging.

'Sure. Anyway, I'd better get going. We'll see you next week.'

'Will do. Say hello to Rose for me.' Norah checked the time. Ten minutes to go. The small child was still sitting at the statue, and she was just about to go over and consider asking them to move when two police officers walked over to the child.

One bent over and retrieved a stuffed animal from the brick pavement. The mother smiled at them, and the police moved on. Her heart pounded in her ears, almost deafening against the noise of the traffic and shoppers all around her.

That was twice in five minutes she'd thought she was going to be caught.

She shouldn't have come.

If she was caught by police, not only would she lose her job, but she could possibly go to jail. All because she didn't trust Mark with the truth. What way was that to start a marriage? She'd been a fool to risk everything like this. A wave of anger washed through her at how stupid she'd been. Mark loved her, and if he couldn't forgive her, then it meant they weren't right for each other.

And her job. All those years of hard work and she'd almost thrown it away.

All because some unknown person had threatened her. Her irritation gave way to relief. At least she hadn't gone through with it. It wasn't too late for her to leave and fix the mess she'd made.

Norah glanced around to see if anyone was watching her. But if they were, they were well concealed. She turned back towards the car park, walking as quickly as she could without drawing attention. Once inside the safety of the car, she took out her phone and sent a message.

I'm not playing.

Her hands were still shaking as she dropped her bag onto the passenger seat. She could use a drink to help calm her nerves and give her the courage to face Mark.

The seatbelt ding immediately started, and Norah let out a long groan and transferred the bag down to the floor. It always happened, since the car manufacturers obviously didn't make allowances for large bags full of things she might need at a moment's notice. The cruel irony was that it had never occurred to her she might need a bottle of gin in the bag. The ding finally stopped, and she put the car into reverse. She needed to get out of there in case her blackmailer had seen her leave.

She navigated her way out of the car park and back towards the familiar streets of Knotty Ash before she finally pulled over to the side of the road. Her stomach churned like she was going to be sick.

Suddenly remembered the small bottle of Rescue Remedy she carried.

She leaned forward and fumbled through the large bag on the floor until her fingers tightened on the small bottle. It was made from flower essences and while not all doctors agreed with it, Norah had found it useful. After putting a couple of drops on her tongue, she closed her eyes. She waited a couple of minutes before turning the engine back on. It was probably a good thing Mark was away because it would give her time to go over everything. Get it all straight in her head before she told him the truth.

* * *

Norah dragged her wet hair back into a ponytail and walked back into the bedroom, not even bothering with make-up. Her phone flashed with a missed call from Mark. Guilt caught in her throat. Last night her nerves had deserted her and she'd feigned an early night to avoid talking. It would be better to do it in person when he got back tonight.

There were a couple of messages from Felix, but nothing from the blackmailer. It didn't make sense. Had they changed their mind? It was entirely possible. After all, Norah had lost her nerve. What if they had as well?

What if this whole thing just disappeared?

It could be like a second chance. A sliver of hope flared in her chest. Could she get away without telling Mark anything?

No. She caught herself. He deserved to know the truth. Besides, it meant no one could ever threaten her again. But first she had to return the drugs.

And turn off her phone.

She finished getting dressed and hurried downstairs. There were several plates piled up on the counter and a jar of peanut butter was out, along with an empty bottle of oat milk. Cassie. Norah had vaguely heard her come in last night after her shift at the restaurant.

A quick glance at the clock told her there was no time to

tidy up, so she was forced to leave it, in the hopes Cassie would do it before Mark got home.

She'd collected her own car yesterday afternoon from the garage, and she climbed in. The commute passed in a blur and twenty-five minutes later she was walking through the corridor, back towards the dispensary.

It was a busy morning and several colleagues nodded and waved. Norah plastered on a smile and kept walking. Ironically, her heart was pounding just as hard now she was returning the drugs as when she'd taken them. She turned a corner and reached out for the door handle.

'Ms Richmond. There you are. We've been calling you all morning.' Jill Heather, the department matron, appeared, her face a tight mask. Norah's stomach dropped. Oh God. She knew.

'Flat battery,' she lied. 'I-is something wrong?' It took all of her training to act like she was calm.

'Rose Jenkins was admitted this morning with a high temperature and vomiting. She's stable now, but there's possible liver damage. We're running tests.'

Norah snapped to attention, the drugs in her bag forgotten. 'Is it a reaction to the Tasigna? I only just changed her over. What's her blood pressure?'

'Better than what it was.' Matron's face was grim. 'We suspect the culprit was a bottle of fruit punch that had levels of grapefruit in it. The mother didn't seem to be aware it was something she had to monitor and had let Rose go to a birthday party.'

Shit. The words hung in the air. They both knew how dangerous a seemingly harmless grapefruit could be when it was taken with certain medications. And Norah was always so careful to go through the list of things to avoid. Except, had she? Doubt pushed its way into her mind. That day in the office was when she'd seen the photograph the blackmailer had sent her.

And yesterday she could've reminded Ruth – but she'd been equally distracted. Hell. A rush of guilt went through her. Was this her fault? The idea of putting Rose's compromised immune system under more stress clawed at her throat.

'S-she's under a huge amount of stress,' Norah managed to croak. 'I'd like to go and check on her.'

'Yes, of course,' Matron said as they both turned and hurried to the third floor. Norah took a deep breath as she tried to calm her mind down. Just because she couldn't remember telling Ruth about the dangers of grapefruit, it didn't mean she hadn't. It was like driving a car and going on autopilot.

As they reached the ward, Norah sucked in a breath. No more distractions. Right now she just needed to focus on making sure that Rose recovered, because the alternative didn't bear thinking about.

* * *

'God. Would you look at those two morons.' Deb waved a can of cider in the air. Cassie gently pushed it away. The last thing she needed was to lose her licence. They'd taken the day off school to drive to Crosby and study the hundred Antony Gormley life-like naked statues that spread out along the beach and into the water. Each one was six-foot tall and made of cast iron. And although they were weathered from years of being so close to the Mersey estuary, their stillness somehow seemed very human.

Technically the day out was for an art history assignment. However, the real appeal had been the chance to get some good

TikTok videos in front of the iron figures. Her dad had gone to Windermere yesterday and wasn't back until later in the day, so Cassie had sent him a quick text assuring him the loan of the car was for school. He'd replied with a thumbs up. God. Parents could be so embarrassing.

Scott had been keen to come but it wasn't until she'd arrived to pick him up that his two cousins had clambered into the back of the car. The twins had been wasted before they'd even arrived at the beach and were now clumsily attempting to put a cigarette in between the iron lips of one of the statues. They were laughing hysterically like it was the first time anyone had ever thought of it. Scott was off to one side, ignoring his cousins as he spoke on the phone. Cassie paused to admire the afternoon light bouncing off his pale blonde hair. He was like a statue himself – the black jeans and hoodie making him appear alien against the beachside setting.

'So, which one should I sleep with?' Deb took another slug of cider and studied the twins.

'Neither.' Cassie took the can out of her friend's hands. 'We've already established they're stupid. Plus, you need to finish this assignment while everything's still fresh in your mind.'

Deb poked out her lower lip like a three-year-old. 'Since when do you care about homework?'

'This isn't homework. It's art.'

'Please. The statues are all casts of Gormley himself. It's the ultimate expression of narcissism,' Scott said from behind her, his arms wrapping around Cassie's waist so she was leaning into his chest.

Deb's eyes widened. 'Christ, you're a bloody genius. Mind if I use that on my assignment?'

'Knock yourself out.' Scott shrugged, and Cassie felt a tickle of pride race through her. Despite the fact he hated school and never bothered to study, he was literally the smartest person she knew. She could listen to him forever.

'Hey.' He leaned forward and kissed Cassie's neck. 'Having a good time?'

'I am now.' She dug her toes deeper into the sand. Despite the heat of the day, the lower layers were cold against her skin, but she didn't care. The sea breeze whipped her hair across her face, as Scott's fingers burned against her skin. It was exhilarating. And soon this would be her life. Just the two of them. 'Thanks for coming.'

'You kidding? I love this place. And I was joking about the narcissism stuff. I think Gormley's inviting us all to look at how we interact with the space around us,' he said, pressing another kiss into her neck. 'But I have to head back to town. I just got a call for a last-minute gig at Flamingo.'

She swivelled around. 'You did? That's so great.' He'd been trying to get his foot in the door for a couple of months now, with the hope it would lead to a residency. This was one step closer. 'I wish I didn't have this assignment otherwise I could've come.'

'I'll go,' Deb said, before retrieving the half-drunk can of cider and taking another swig.

'No can do. I need to make a bloody good impression, which means I can't have any distractions.' Scott shook his head.

'What about Tweedledee and Tweedledum over there?' Deb pouted.

'Definitely not them,' he said before turning to Cassie. 'You sure you don't mind if we split a bit early? I could always catch an Uber—'

'Not happening,' she said, and reluctantly untangled herself from his arms so she could stand up. His green eyes were almost blue, and he held her gaze, as if silently trying to convey his feelings to her. Her heart pounded but before she could say anything, the twins bounded over.

'Who wants to go to the pub?' Aaron slurred.

'No one,' Scott retorted, turning away from Cassie. 'We're heading back. Then you can do what you want.'

'Interesting,' Ned said with a leer, throwing an arm around Deb.

'Not that,' Scott said in warning and Cassie gave him a grateful look. Deb didn't have the best impulse control when it came to boys. She picked up the empty cans and crisp packets and they trudged along the sand as Cassie tried to hold on to the electric feel of freedom.

The traffic was slow, but Scott played beats from his phone as they snaked their way back along the A565. Aaron and Ned wanted to be dropped off at Bootle. It was a relief to have their hyper energy out of the car, and the rest of the trip was a lot more relaxed as they drove into Liverpool. She dropped Scott off at his house so he could sort out his gear.

'Sure you don't want me to drive you in?' she said but he shook his head.

'Nah. My old man will do it. Plus, then he can give me a hand carrying everything in while I get set up.'

'Okay. But text me when you have a break and let me know how it's going. They'll love you.'

'That's the plan.' He gave her a kiss and climbed out of the car. As soon as he was gone, Deb wriggled from the back into the front with all the grace of a baby elephant.

'I still think it's weird we can't go tonight,' Deb said, her bottom lip poking out.

'It's not weird.' Cassie didn't want to go into detail about how nervous Scott got before every gig. No one would ever guess that he battled with stage fright. 'I need to get this assignment done. If I flunk, my dad will cut my allowance and then I'll never bloody get out of this shithole.'

'Tell me about it,' Deb moaned as she scrolled through her phone. 'Hey, Lauren's at the pub. Can you drop me off?'

Cassie winced. She loved Deb but it was hard to get her to focus on anything that wasn't a party. 'What if I take you home first and you can get a shower and change. Then if you still want to go you can catch the bus.'

Deb was about to protest before holding up her arm and sniffing her pits. 'Fine.'

Twenty minutes later, Cassie finally pulled into her dad's house. It was only five in the afternoon and Norah's Fiesta was nowhere to be seen, but her dad's Range Rover was parked in its regular spot. He was obviously back.

She let herself inside. The door to his study was shut but the drift of classical music sounded out. Cassie was starving but she didn't want to risk being grilled about her day. And it wasn't like he even asked decent questions. Just the usual shit, which was barely worth answering.

'How was it?' her dad called out, as if needing to prove her point about asking stupid questions.

'Fine.'

'Did you clean the car?'

Cassie rolled her eyes. Her dad had never vacuumed the house but was obsessed with the cars. That was the other reason he hardly ever let her borrow it. She sighed. 'I promise I'll do it later. I need to get started on the assignment, plus I'm dying for a shower.' She dropped the car keys into the small wooden bowl in the hallway and hurried upstairs. Thankfully he didn't follow her, which was Alice's favourite trick. But just in case, she turned on one of the playlists Scott had made her.

Music pumping, she kicked off her shoes and opened her laptop. She wrote a couple of pages of notes and then checked her phone. Deb had posted a photo of herself, her jeans and T-shirt changed for a yellow dress that rode up her legs.

A wave of restlessness suddenly crept through her. Not for the pub, but for Scott's gig. Maybe she should go? She brought up his number on her phone; her finger hovered over it. But before she could decide, her bedroom door swung open, and her dad stood on the threshold.

'Seriously?' she said, dropping her phone. 'What about knocking?'

'My house, my rules,' he said in a voice she'd seldom heard before. His jaw was tight, and his dark eyes were like stone. In his hand was a plastic bag with five pharmacy boxes in it. From the way he was holding them, it was like they were anthrax. 'Care to explain this?'

'Explain what?'

His face tightened. 'The drugs that I just found in the car when I was cleaning out the sand. They were under the seat.'

Cassie stared at him. It was like he was speaking another language. 'I don't do drugs. You know that.'

Silence swept between them, sharp as a razor.

'And what about your friends? Who went out with you today?'

'Deb and Scott,' Cassie said, still trying to catch her breath at what was happening. 'And—'

She broke off. Shit. Aaron and Ned had been off their faces all day. Scott had told her they only smoked weed and took the occasional upper. But he'd also said that they had a knack for finding trouble.

'And who?' her dad said, his voice dangerously low.

'Scott's cousins,' she said in a whisper. 'I don't think they're into *that* kind of thing,' she said, pointing to the bag that was still in his hand.

'Which just proves why you're not ready to go travelling yet. Now, sit down. Because we need to have a serious talk.'

7

'What now?' Alice flinched as the doorbell went. It was almost seven at night and she'd hoped to get a couple more hours of work done.

She'd spent the last two days in the attic. It was amazing what fear of a looming financial crisis could do. But thanks to her previous procrastinating, she was still behind. Should she ignore it? Pretend to be out. It made the most sense.

Bang. Bang. Bang. The sound of the door now being knocked echoed around the room. Whoever it was had no intention of leaving quietly. Hugo let out a bark from down below, which was soon followed by the neighbour's dog.

It was like the gods were conspiring against her.

She reluctantly put down her paintbrush and navigated the narrow attic stairs. Hugo was dancing around at the bottom, as if eager to remind her there was someone at the door.

'Yes, thank you,' she told the dog before glancing in the mirror. Her hair was a mess and there was a smudge of paint on her nose. Still, it couldn't be helped. Making sure the safety chain was on, she cracked the door open.

Mark was standing there. His dark hair was longer than when she'd seen him last and it had turned silver at the tips. It would have been more satisfying if it didn't seem to enhance his tan, making him look younger. Of course it bloody well did. Though why nature persisted in rewarding the bastards and cheaters of the world, she'd never know.

'I hope I'm not interrupting,' he said, perhaps noticing that she hadn't taken the security chain off.

'You are, as it happens.' She hadn't intended to snap at him, but like everyone else, he didn't think. Then again, maybe it was good that she'd snapped at him. Up until recently she'd still been doing everything in her power to make him fall back in love with her. Hanging off his every word. Not saying how she really felt. All in the hope that he'd change his mind. And it had failed spectacularly. 'What do you want?'

'It's about Cassie.' He let out a sigh, and up close she could see worry lines etched around his eyes. Her annoyance fled and she shut the door to take off the safety chain, and then opened it up. Hugo immediately darted out and jumped up and down at Mark's feet.

A couple of people on the street looked over with interest as Mark bent down to calm the excited dog.

'What's wrong? Is she hurt? Why didn't you call me first?' She quickly scooped Hugo up and carried him inside, nodding for Mark to follow. The last thing she wanted was an audience. Hugo seemed to sense her panic and wriggled to be put down.

'Sorry. I didn't mean to scare you. She's not injured or sick. But there's been a situation.'

Alice swallowed and walked through to the tiny lounge. She'd taken the two-seater velvet sofa from her old office and paired it up with a single armchair that she'd found in a charity shop. He sat down on the sofa, leaving her the armchair. Hugo jumped up on Mark's lap and pushed his nose against his hand, waiting for a pat. It was such a familiar scene. Same man and dog. It was only the house and her that were different. And suddenly the room felt too small. Too full of his cologne and bigness. Maybe they should have talked out on the street after all?

'Okay. Tell me what's going on,' she said, irritation once again sliding into her voice.

'I let Cassie use the car and when she came back, I found this.' He rolled his neck and then pulled out a plastic bag. It had five white boxes in it. Drugs.

Drugs.

Alice lurched to one side as the world slipped away. Mark was quickly by her side, his hand on her knee. The raw concern in his eyes almost undoing her. He knew what it meant. They both did. The terrible fear that Cassie had somehow inherited the same predisposition to addiction that Alice's sister, Jasmine, had battled.

No. She couldn't go through it again. The agony of never knowing what each day would bring. What each phone call or news story might contain. Of her sister's beautiful face staring up at her from the coffin, still and lifeless.

The best of them.

Jasmine had been the sweet, sensitive angel who'd never stooped to being petty and calculated. To being pragmatic and settling. Instead, she continued to be herself, trying to survive in a world that was far too brutal for her.

And Cassie was so similar to Jasmine. From the set of her mouth and eyes through to the way she cried every time she found a broken bird egg underneath the oak tree in the garden. Each time it had jabbed at Alice, making her worry that somehow drugs would take away her beautiful glowing daughter, like they'd taken her sister.

'Just breathe,' Mark said in a gentle voice that managed to break through the whirling panic. Alice followed his advice and managed to compose herself. He went back to the sofa.

'H-have you spoken to her? What did she say?'

'She denied it all.' He put the bag on the coffee table. 'Her friends were with her, and she swears that it doesn't belong to her, Deb or Scott. But she's not sure about Scott's cousins. Apparently, they spent most of the day stoned.'

Fury roared through her.

'And Scott introduced them to our daughter? I knew he was no damn good.' Alice gripped at the velvet arm, her nails raking small channels into the pile as the emotions choked her throat. Why hadn't she just locked Cassie in the house? Why hadn't she forced Mark to make more of a stand? Why had any of this happened?

'I loved Jasmine too. But Cassie isn't her. Your sister was sweet and trusting and could never see the bad in anyone. It's what made her so special. But she was also shy and susceptible. Cassie isn't like that. Remember the time she punched Reuben Litchfield in the nose for trying to give one of her friends a cigarette?'

Again, Alice managed to push back to the tornado of emotions that were threatening to overwhelm her. Mark was right. Jasmine and Cassie might look the same, and have the same terrible radar for boys, but Cassie had an inner strength running through her.

Cassie had only been ten at the time but had had no qualms in punching a boy who was almost twice her size. Alice rolled her shoulders and gave Mark a grateful smile. It was different. It *had* to be different.

'Okay. Tell me everything.'

It didn't take him long to go over the conversation with Cassie and how she'd seemed genuinely shocked to see the drugs. He finished off, 'I believe that they're not hers. But—'

'But they didn't get there by magic,' Alice said, hating the way her heart calmed down in response to him. 'So, what do we do?'

'I don't know. We could go to the police, but what if it somehow blows back on Cassie? After all, it's my car and she was driving it. If they're looking for low-hanging fruit, she's it.'

Alice wanted to protest, but he was right.

Several months ago, a boy from a prestigious school had been caught dealing cocaine during the lunch break. Since then, the *Liverpool Echo* had published a spate of similar articles, showing an appetite for the narrative. Cassie would definitely fit the bill.

'So, how did you leave it?'

'She stormed out of the house, convinced that someone's set her up. At least she's got work tonight, which should help her cool down. But we both need to talk to her tomorrow. Together.'

'Okay.' Alice nodded, trying not to think about her looming deadline. 'And we need a plan. She's too old to ground, but there have to be consequences.'

'No more car privileges, for a start.' He ran a hand through his hair, his eyes suddenly filled with fatigue.

Alice couldn't blame him. He'd been the one to find the drugs and to confront Cassie. She couldn't imagine what that must have been like. 'Do you want a tea or coffee?'

'Coffee sounds good.'

She led him through to the kitchen and put on the kettle. While she took out the mugs from the cupboard and spooned some instant into each one, Mark sat down at the table and tapped his shoe on the floor. Like he was agitated. Except Mark didn't get agitated.

'Only instant, I'm afraid. I can't afford the good stuff now.' She carried the two drinks over to the table and gave him one.

Mark shrugged. 'This is fine, thanks.'

'Okay, tell me what's wrong. Normally you'd never drink cheap coffee,' she said, but instead of protesting, he rolled his shoulders and sighed.

'It's nothing.' He toyed with the cup, then looked up. 'I feel guilty. There's been so much going on with Norah and the wedding, and now Cassie has a job, I haven't really spoken to her much. What if I missed something?'

Alice shivered. They'd always parented together. Was that why it had happened? Because they were no longer a team? Annoyance crept up on her. The divorce hadn't been her idea, yet here she was again having to deal with the fallout. Then she looked at the genuine pain in his eyes.

Despite herself, Alice patted his hand. Mark had many faults, especially when it came to ruining Alice's life and hooking up with a younger woman. But when it came to being a father, he was exceptional.

Before Alice had even known she was pregnant, Mark had taken a job in Denmark, and they'd split up. She hadn't planned to ever tell him about Cassie, not wanting to make him feel guilty. But he'd found out via a friend's social media account and had instantly moved back to England to meet his daughter.

Cassie had been four months old, and despite Mark missing out on those early months, he'd instantly fallen in love with her. Fatherhood had come so naturally to him. A lot easier than she'd found it. And while together they'd been wonderful parents, she'd always known that Mark was the gifted one.

Which was why his deep worry concerned her.

'Hey. She's a teenage girl. They're wired to push us away,' Alice said, with the kind of wisdom that other people usually had. Not that she could ever apply it to herself, of course. But despite everything, she hated seeing Mark beat himself up. 'At least she talks to you from time to time. When she's here, she hardly comes out of her room, except for food.'

'I never thought we'd be that family. We're losing her – and it's happening right in front of our eyes,' he said, pain lacing his words. Alice put down her coffee and walked over to the cabinet above the fridge. She pulled out a bottle of Scotch.

It was one she'd taken from the house when she moved out. Which was stupid really because the only time she ever drank the stuff was when she was with Mark, curled up on the sofa.

'You want something a bit stronger? It might help us come up with a way to bring Cassie back to us instead of pushing her away.'

'God, yes.' His eyes lit up at the bottle. She was pretty sure it was one of the better ones he'd kept in the cellar. Then he reluctantly held up his hand. 'Christ. I can't. I've got the—' He cut himself off as colour travelled up his neck.

'Got what?'

He pressed his lips together, as if contemplating whether to answer. Then he sighed. 'I have to give a sperm specimen tomorrow.'

The room went silent, and Alice's mouth dropped open. It was a joke. It *had* to be a joke. But Mark's steady gaze was unflinching. He was serious. Hysterical laughter rose up in her chest and she tightened her grip on the bottle of Scotch to stop herself from exploding. First the news about Cassie, and now this? It was too much.

'Y-you and Norah are trying to get pregnant?'

He gave her a sheepish nod. 'I'm a shitbag for complaining. I know Norah wants kids, but I figured we'd do it the old-fashioned way. Not all needles, sperm samples and IVF. Especially since you got pregnant so quickly. Hell, we'd only been dating a few months. But I guess not.'

'So, you're saying you don't want another baby?' She scanned his face, and then stiffened. There they were. The tiny tics that she knew so well. The upturn of his mouth. The way he looked to the left when he was uncertain. So, Mark didn't want a baby. It was Norah's idea.

He bowed his head. 'It's complicated. I love kids, and God knows I love Norah. But I'm fifty-one and thought my baby years were behind me. Especially with the wedding and now this thing with Cassie. It seems like a lot.'

Because it was. It was a *whole* fucking lot, and Norah didn't seem to care that it was affecting Mark's relationship with his daughter. Not to mention Alice's own life.

Pain tore through her, sharp and bitter as it wrapped its way around her.

She'd been so blindsided by the divorce that she hadn't realised that there was more to lose. Further to fall. She should have considered that Mark and Norah might want a baby. After all, there were lots of older fathers around these days. And older mothers for that matter. But she'd always just assumed that Norah was one of those women who was deliberately childless.

Or had Alice just hoped it, because the alternative was dangerous?

And now it was happening.

The damn wall that Alice had tried to construct to stop her fury at Norah from spilling out into the world seemed to crumble, and before she could stop herself, she was on her feet.

'Jesus, Mark. You need to tell her how you feel. You have a teenage daughter; it's not unreasonable to say no to having a kid,' she snapped, unable to keep the edge out of her voice. Still, being furious was better than crying.

He stiffened and he took a step back. 'That's not any of your business.'

Except it was.

It bloody well was.

Alice walked over to the window, trying to ignore the way her heart was hammering in her chest.

The mounting fear she'd lived with for years. Her own personalised Damocles' sword. The truth about Cassie – that she wasn't Mark's biological daughter. Of course Alice had planned to tell him. She wasn't some awful manipulative woman who didn't care about Mark or his feelings. But seeing him hold Cassie in his arms for the first time had done something to her. The chemicals in her mind had realigned and shown her a glimpse of an alternative future. One she hadn't even dreamed was possible.

After all, the break-up had been sudden and abrupt, with the edge of finality that hadn't even allowed her to dream there might be a second chance. But it had somehow happened.

Mark had come back, taken one look at Cassie and fallen in love with them both. And when he'd proposed, it wasn't just to make them a family. It was to also give Alice and her tiny daughter the kind of life that she'd given up on achieving.

Financial security, support and love. And once there was a second baby, and possibly a third, then she'd tell Mark the truth. Perhaps when they were on a family holiday in Provence. The children would be asleep in the farmhouse they'd rented, limbs brown and tangled in white linen sheets, exhausted from a day of play. And Mark and Alice would be sitting in a rustic gazebo, night birds singing, as they shared a bottle of wine. He'd laugh when she told him, and then kiss her hard.

Cassie is mine, he'd say. And that would be that.

But it had never happened. After five years of trying to get pregnant, Alice had been stuck in a holding pattern of what to do. That was when Cassie's glands had swollen, and the doctor ordered a blood test. She was O, and a quick check on the internet had told Alice her worst fears. That Mark, who was AB, couldn't father a child with O-type blood.

Since then, her secret had hung like a shadow, waiting for its day in the light. Her dread on how it might play out had taken many forms. What if Cassie desperately needed a bone marrow transplant and Mark stepped up to be tested? What if Mark became fascinated with ancestry and bought one of those stupid DNA tests online for them all to do? The list had gone on and on, keeping her up at night with all the reasons why her carefully constructed narrative might unravel.

She'd never thought to add IVF with another woman to her list.

Especially when that other woman was a nurse. What if Norah somehow found out what blood type Cassie was and did the maths? It wasn't a stretch. Not that Alice knew if blood tests were even done in IVF. She would google it later. But regardless of the answer, it didn't change the fact that her carefully constructed lie was in danger of unravelling.

She was in danger of unravelling as the tiny pieces of glue that had been holding her all together pulled apart.

Alice leaned over, trying to ease the clawing sensation that was wrapping around her throat, as the conversation with her agent ran through her mind. She was barely holding it together as an illustrator, but financial ruin was nothing compared to this. She tried to imagine what Mark's reaction would be if he found out the truth. It would destroy everything they'd built over the last seventeen years.

He was the most important man in her life, and that entire history would be wiped out in the blink of an eye. Oh, God. And what about Cassie? Would Mark disinherit her if he knew she wasn't biologically his? Of course he would. And Norah would support him, since it would mean her child would receive the entire fortune.

The pressure on her throat increased.

The knowledge that her daughter would grow up with financial security was sometimes the only light that kept Alice sane during the dark nights. But now Cassie could lose everything. And the extra cheques he still sometimes sent Alice to help cover the mortgage and insurance would also disappear.

So, no. Norah Richmond wasn't going to have a baby. She'd taken enough from Alice, but she couldn't have this. Cassie was Mark's daughter and Alice would do whatever she had to, to make sure that didn't change.

8

Be careful what you wish for. Norah stared at her phone. After pretending she'd had a flat battery all day, her phone refused to turn on. Still, after the day she'd had, it was probably better not to check her emails or messages before driving home.

She started the car and pulled out into the traffic. The sun was bright in her eyes, and she fumbled for her sunglasses. Probably best to hide the huge bags under her eyes. It had been a long and exhausting day, and while Rose was stable but serious, Norah still didn't know if her own negligence had been responsible for what had happened. Added to that, in all the chaos, she hadn't been able to return the drugs. Or work out exactly what she was going to say to Mark when she told him the truth.

No wonder her head was pounding.

The traffic moved at a snail's pace, but she finally arrived back at the house. There was no sign of Mark's car. That was odd. She let herself into the house and called out his name, but there was no answer. His overnight bag was sitting on a stool in the hallway, which meant he'd come home, but had obviously gone out again.

She automatically reached for her phone, before remembering it was dead. Great. She walked into the kitchen, hoping for a note on the counter. Instead it was to discover that Cassie's mess had increased to include a half-eaten packet of digestives, two discarded saucepans and an empty packet of noodles. And no note from Mark.

Annoyance at not knowing where he was, and relief that their conversation would be delayed, at least for a short time, battled in her chest. She let out a frustrated sigh and tried to shake it off. She was just tired and hungry.

She opened the fridge for the wine, and a box of eggs that had been tentatively balanced on a bunch of bananas teetered back and forth before crashing down onto the floor.

'Shit.' Norah stared down at what had once been twelve free-range organic eggs but was now a mass of yolks and broken shells. She couldn't even retrieve a dishcloth without moving the pile of dirty dishes.

Her skin prickled with irritation. Was this Cassie's way of passive-aggressively staking her claim? Had Alice been whispering in her ear? Norah bristled as she walked to the laundry to get another cleaning cloth, before stopping in her tracks.

No. If she cleaned it up, then Cassie would just keep on doing it. Or, worse, she'd think that Norah was weak for letting her get away with it. Not to mention that her head was still throbbing from the intensity of the day. She needed to get out of there.

The local pub did an okay pizza, and Mark sometimes went there with Larry at the end of the road. Except she wasn't in the mood to make small talk if he was there with a friend. Or she could go and see Felix at his restaurant. After all, he had both wine and food. Matter decided, she left the house without writing a note of her own.

It was almost seven when she walked into The Blue Radish. Most of the tables were full and the low conversation bounced off the brick walls, giving the whole place an inviting ambience. Felix was perched on a stool at the end of the counter, working on his laptop.

'Hey.' His eyes widened. 'This is a nice surprise. You here for a drink?'

'And some food.' She leaned in and kissed his cheek.

'You should have texted me.'

'Would you believe my phone died, Mark's out somewhere, and I've had a shit of a day.'

Felix opened his mouth, as if to say something, but closed it again.

'You've come to the right place.' He shut the laptop and walked to the other side of the bar. He ignored the opened bottles at the front of the wine fridge and retrieved one from the back. 'You'll like this. It's a New Zealand Pinot Gris.'

'It's wet and cold. I love it already.'

'You're easily pleased.' He poured a generous measure and slid it across to her. Then he grabbed a bottle of ginger beer for himself. 'So, what do you want to eat? The usual?'

'Thank you.' She gave him a grateful nod. He poked his head into the kitchen to order the cauliflower and chickpea burger, then led her to a small table in the corner.

'So, what's going on?' Felix took a sip of his own drink. About ten years ago he'd had a tough break-up and had been drinking a bit too much. It had resulted in a DUI and a decision to stop. She'd always admired that about him. He certainly hadn't been an alcoholic by any stretch of the imagination, but he'd decided to cut it out. If only she had that kind of strength. Maybe tomorrow?

She took a sip of her wine and told him about Rose, not mentioning her own possible error.

'Christ.' He blew out a breath ten minutes later. 'I know you love what you do, but it's a brutal job.'

'It's also a rewarding—' she started to say but was cut off by the all-too-familiar scent of her own – very expensive – perfume. She looked up to see Cassie standing at the table, holding her burger. First the mess in the kitchen, and now stealing her perfume? Norah's mouth tightened before she caught sight of Cassie's face.

Her hair was pulled back and while her mouth was pushed in the semblance of a smile, her mascara was smudged, and the whites of her eyes looked like they'd been put through the wash with a red jumper. She'd been crying.

Norah's anger faded. 'What's wrong? Has something happened?'

'Like you don't know,' Cassie said, her lower lip starting to tremble.

'Know what?' Norah blinked.

'Her phone died,' Felix told Cassie, as if that somehow answered the question. 'And I figured it wasn't my place to say anything.'

'What's going on?' Norah looked from her brother to her soon-to-be stepdaughter.

'Dad's being a total prick,' Cassie said; her cheeks brightened but she kept her voice low. 'He found drugs in the car and is convinced that Scott and his cousins are crackheads. It's bullshit, but instead of believing me, he's around with Alice, who'll turn it into an even bigger drama.'

Drugs? Norah's throat went dry. 'W-what kind of drugs?'

'That's the whole fucking thing – I don't even know. Some boxes of pills. Fentanyl, I think. But it's nothing to do with me or any of my friends. Someone's setting me up, and when I—'

'Cass, table eight's up,' a girl called from behind the bar and Cassie wrinkled her nose, as if remembering she was at work. She gave Felix an apologetic grimace, but he waved her off with a smile. Once Cassie was gone, Norah turned to her brother.

'What the hell? You knew, and didn't tell me?' she said, trying to keep her voice calm. But her mind was whirling. She'd used Mark's car yesterday to drive to Huyton Village, but she hadn't left the drugs in the car. They were in her bag.

Well, they were meant to be.

She tried to recall if she'd seen them when she'd rummaged for her car keys. But she'd been so preoccupied with Rose that she couldn't remember. But that still didn't explain how they'd ended up on the floor of the car.

The Rescue Remedy. She let out a soft groan. She'd been looking for it on her way home, trying to stave off her panic attack. They must've fallen out. *Shit. Shit. Shit.*

'I'm Switzerland, remember. You didn't want me to inter-fere.' Felix leaned in to study her face. She'd always been terrible at playing poker – and he'd always been way too smart for his own good. His jaw dropped. 'Oh, shit. Norah, please fucking tell me that you don't have anything to do with this? I just assumed it was some kind of counterfeit pills that Scott had bought on the street.'

Norah tried to look away, but his unrelenting gaze held hers. She let out a soft whimper. 'Oh, God, Felix. I've messed up so badly. That day we had coffee after my dress fitting, someone sent me a text message. They know about—'

She broke off, the words catching in her throat. She couldn't say it. The thing that had haunted her for so long. The mistake that she'd paid for over and over again. A flash of something dark rippled across Felix's face and he reached out to grab her hand.

'Those fucking bastards. Why the hell didn't you tell me?'

She swallowed, the shame of her past battling with the relief of finally telling someone what was going on. 'I didn't want you to worry.'

'Worry that you were being blackmailed?' His eyebrows shot up and his mouth twisted into a flat line. She returned the grip on his hand. Her brother hardly ever lost his temper, but she knew how protective of her he was. And how guilty he felt about what had happened. 'Let me see the messages.'

'I can't. My phone's dead, remember?' Norah said, suddenly pleased. 'Besides, it doesn't matter. I've decided to tell Mark everything. I can't have this hanging over my head any longer.'

Felix dragged his hand back, his anger turning to something else. Concern. 'Norah, are you crazy? You seriously think you can tell him you're being blackmailed without telling him why?'

The horror in his voice broke something inside her. He'd stood by her side through everything, but his anger and despair about it only added to her own shame. Because he loved her more than anything, and still struggled to accept what had happened to her.

It was the whole reason she'd never told Mark.

'There's no other way. Surely you can see that. Especially after what's just happened.'

'That's my point. Norah, think about it. Some arsehole has blackmailed you into stealing drugs for them, and you've accidently left them in his car, making Mark think his kid is involved. It's already sent him straight around to his ex's house.

What will this do? And wasn't there an aunt or someone who died of a drug overdose?'

Oh, shit.

Jasmine. Alice's younger sister. She'd heard the story numerous times. Sweet girl who went down a dark path. Dead at twenty-one. Mark had known her and, of course, having lived with Alice for over seventeen years, had also witnessed the ongoing devastation Jasmine's death had on Alice.

No wonder he'd been so hard on his daughter.

Horror seeped through her, paralysing her entire body as Felix's words sank in. God. He was right. Even if Mark did understand about her past, would he understand about what she'd accidently done to his daughter? And what about Cassie herself? Their relationship was already tentative. This could tip it over the edge.

'So what do I do?'

Felix bowed his head, as if thinking. Then he looked up. 'First you had better hope that no one saw you take the car. I'm guessing Cassie didn't, since she would have mentioned it. But what about a neighbour?'

'I don't know,' she said, heart pounding so loudly it was giving her a headache. 'And what about the police? If Mark hands them in, they'll be able to trace them back to me.'

'Cassie said that he didn't want to do that. Worried it might end up in the paper. Thank God he's a raging snob.'

Norah stiffened. Mark wasn't a snob. But he was from a well-established rich family, and she doubted he'd want to subject Cassie or his family to anything negative. But it didn't solve all her problems. Because if she couldn't tell Mark the truth, then she still had to deal with the blackmailer.

And explain that she no longer had the drugs they wanted.

There was a crashing noise from behind the bar, and Felix swore.

'Shit. I'd better give them a hand. But this conversation isn't over. We need to deal with it together and next time the shithead contacts you, I need to know. Are we clear?'

'Yes.' Norah nodded. Her head still hurt and her body was aching, as if she'd run a marathon. Her bag was hanging over the chair and she dragged it onto her lap, searching for a headache tablet. It wasn't a good idea with wine, but she was going to do it anyway.

She stiffened as her fingers brushed across a crisp white envelope tucked down in a side pocket.

She lifted it out and flinched. The one-hundred-and-twenty-gram matte pearl envelope with an embossed monogram of M and N was achingly familiar. It was the design she'd chosen for the wedding. Her hands shook as she eased open the back flap. Inside was a single piece of paper with a message scrawled across the middle. The writing was almost identical to the first message.

The price has gone up. Ten boxes or your wedding's off.

Her headache had turned into a vice-like grip around her temples and Norah shut her eyes. It seemed like every choice she made was leading her down a path that she didn't even know existed. And who was behind it? She could have sworn the envelope hadn't been in her bag when she'd left the house. Did that mean her blackmailer was here, watching her now? Laughing at her despair?

She turned and looked from table to table. But she had no idea who she was searching for. Norman had said the first envelope had been given to him by a woman, but was she young or old? Or had she been delivering it on behalf of someone else?

The faces around her blurred together as wave after wave of panic ran through her.

Felix, who was over at the bar, glanced over, a concerned expression in his eyes.

Shit. Any relief from sharing the truth with him was gone. Because if she let him know they'd been back in touch, he'd want to get involved. And then she'd have him to worry about as well. She forced a reassuring smile onto her face, and it seemed to satisfy him.

What a mess. Felix was right. It was no longer possible to tell Mark. He might have understood her own bad decisions of the past, but would he forgive her for dragging his daughter into her current dilemma?

No.

Somehow she'd trapped herself into doing the one thing she hadn't wanted to do. And this time there was no way out. She couldn't tell Mark or go to the police. And she couldn't even risk Felix knowing in case he tried to do something stupid.

She stared at the note.

It wasn't a bluff. Whoever was behind this didn't just know her secret. They were letting her know that they could go through with their threat to ruin her life. The room began to swim, and she swallowed her wine, hoping against hope it would stop her from crying.

* * *

'Seriously?' Cassie tensed as the all-too-familiar squeak of the front door rang out. Hugo, who'd been happily curled up on the shabby chair in the open-plan lounge room and kitchen immediately opened an eye and barked, before trotting into the hallway to the front door.

There was only one person it could be.

The house had been empty when she'd walked in two hours earlier. Cassie loved it when her mum wasn't there because she could chill without being nagged about absolutely everything. Even if she did need to do some revision, which was the whole point of exam leave, it wasn't up to Alice to remind her. Cassie wasn't stupid. She knew that it was important for her to pass her exams. It was her passport out of there. At least her dad didn't go on at her all the time. He trusted her.

Correction. *Had* trusted her.

Frustration churned in her stomach. They'd been in an uneasy standoff since he'd found the drugs in the car. He and Alice had cornered her in his study last night when she got back from her shift, in what they said was a family catch-up, but stank of an intervention.

Ha. It was laughable. They were the ones who needed a bloody intervention. Not her. All she was guilty of was trying to sort out her future. Her parents should be pleased. Most of her friends either drank too much or were on a cocktail of anxiety and depression tablets, not to mention the self-harming, body dysmorphia and the rest of it. Yet, here Cassie was, well-adjusted, working part-time *and* keeping up with her schoolwork.

And now everything was ruined. Her plan to impress her dad with how hard she'd been working and how mature she was acting was totally up in flames. Which meant so was her gap year.

It was why she'd come back to Alice's house. Hoping for some peace and quiet. So much for that idea. She sighed as the door opened and Alice came in, dumping bags of shopping on the table.

'Hello, love. Why didn't you tell me you were going to be here?' her mum said, grabbing items from the bag and throwing them into the cupboards.

'I didn't realise that was a requirement of my parole.'

Alice had the good grace to wince. Which was another reason why she'd come around. Because for once it had been her mother who'd been the quiet one, while her dad had been the one to rattle off all the consequences of her so-called terrible crime. The main one being no use of his car.

'It's not like that.' Alice put the frozen peas down on the bench. 'We both believe the drugs didn't belong to you *and* that you haven't ever tried any. But we have every right to be worried. Especially after what happened to...' Her mother trailed off and Cassie resisted the urge to roll her eyes.

Jasmine. Not that she was trying to be disrespectful, but the fact her parents thought she was in the same league as her aunt was irritating. Especially since the drugs weren't even hers. Scott had asked his cousins point blank about it, but they'd both denied any knowledge. She hadn't fully believed them, but even if they had been theirs, she could never tell her parents, since they'd just try and tar Scott with the same brush. And then there was Deb.

Her friend had laughed at the idea, but Cassie knew Deb had been going out a lot more often. Staying up late and still managing to be bright-eyed the next morning.

'Whatever.' Cassie slid off the stool she'd been perched on and shut down her laptop. 'I'm going to my room.'

'Wait.' Alice was suddenly in front of her, blocking the way. Seriously? Cassie went to push past her, but Alice didn't budge.

'Before you go, I need to talk to you. Did you know about the IVF?'

Crap. She'd found out. Cassie had predicted that sparks would fly once her mum found out. That was why she'd kept quiet about it.

'Umm...'

Alice's eyes widened, obviously reading Cassie's response as affirmative. Hugo, suddenly interested in the conversation, started to bark.

'Why the hell didn't you tell me? It's ridiculous. Your father's way too old to have a baby. And Norah's no spring chicken. I can't believe this is happening.'

'It's nothing to do with you. Okay, the idea is gross, but it wasn't up to me to tell you. You're crazy enough these days as it is.' Crap. She hadn't meant to say that. Hugo barked again and Cassie scooped him up into her arms. He licked her face.

'Being concerned about what your father is doing can hardly be construed as being crazy.'

Cassie raised an eyebrow. 'Yeah, right. Does ruining the wedding invitation ring any bells?'

'That was an accident. Besides, this isn't just about me. Your father might decide his new family is more important than his old one. Or what if Norah has a baby and divorces him? I didn't try and claim half of the house, but who's to say she won't? Then your inheritance will be blown.'

'Seriously? They're not even married yet and you're already planning the divorce?'

'It's not unreasonable. She's younger than him... and I saw her meeting a guy in Sefton Park last Sunday.'

Cassie widened her eyes. 'And how exactly did you see that?'

'I was walking Hugo,' Alice retorted. 'Like always. And

Norah happened to be there. She met a man. Older than her and a bit rough-and-ready-looking. She kept checking that no one was watching them.'

'Except my stalker of a mother. You know that's illegal, right?'

'Walking the dog?'

'Following Norah,' Cassie corrected. Her mum was obsessed with playing the victim. How hard everything was now that she was slumming it in a tiny terrace house instead of living in a mansion. That life had somehow given her a bad hand of cards. But that was because Alice had never even tried to be responsible. She'd always been happy to play married families and was now pissed off that she had to fend for herself. Even worse, she was trying to make Cassie think the same way. She was trying to stop Cassie from standing on her own two feet. Okay, so yes, her plan was to get her dad to give her money. But that was different. And she certainly didn't want him to pop his clogs for it to happen.

'Don't be ridiculous,' Alice said.

'I'm not having this conversation with you.' She gave Hugo a kiss, letting his soft fur brush against her skin. Then she put him down and headed towards the hallway. 'I have to go to work.'

'Again? That's three times this week. The deal was that it wouldn't interfere with your schoolwork.'

Cassie only just resisted laughing out loud. Far from interfering with her schoolwork, The Blue Radish was the least stressful part of her life. Felix, Tamsin and the rest of the crew had been so great and had never even asked for an explanation about why she'd turned up crying after Mark had first discovered the drugs. They'd just given her cups of tea, tissues and enough space to pull herself together before starting her shift.

If only her only bloody family could be half as sensitive.

'Felix is short-staffed,' she said by way of an answer. Then she pocketed her phone and grabbed her jacket on the way out of the house. The sooner she went on her gap year, the better. Then she'd be away from all the crap that was going on.

Once she was outside, she checked the time. Shit. It was too early to go to work, so she'd see if Scott was at home.

You free?

His reply came a few seconds later.

Thought u were studying.

Tell my mum that.

Cassie added several devil emojis.

Where ru?

The fountain.

Cassie quickened her pace. The fountain in Sefton Park was just up the road at the end of Lark Lane. Scott was waiting for her five minutes later, leaning against the ornate gateposts that flanked the park. His blonde hair hung across his eyes, giving him an edgy look, and his hands were thrust into the pockets of his jacket.

As she reached him, he gave her a half smile – the kind that he saved only for her. To the rest of the world, he was all deadpan scowls and indifferent shrugs, but with her there was a secret language, used to show her that it was just the two of them.

'Your ma still giving you grief?' He pulled her to him and kissed her mouth. Cassie sighed and the heat of his skin pushed away her latest fight with Alice.

'Yeah. What a shocker. Bound to make the front page of the *Echo*.' Cassie finally untangled herself from his arms.

'Is she still banging on about the drugs?' A flash of guilt passed across his face. Even though his cousins hadn't admitted the pills were theirs, she knew he still felt terrible.

'No,' she assured him. 'She found out Dad and Norah are going to have IVF. Oh, and get this. She actually followed Norah and reckoned she was speaking to some guy at Sefton Park. It's almost like she wants me to tell my dad, and cause problems between them. She's worried I'll suddenly be cut out of the will. Like I give a shit about stuff like that.'

'I hear you. Though it seems a bit extreme. Do you really think he would?'

'No way.' Cassie shook her head. 'My dad's cool. Well, about stuff like that. But any chance of him giving me money for the trip is well and truly blown. Even though he says he believes me, he's got this whole *I'm so disappointed in you* look. I wish we were leaving tomorrow. I'm so over all of this shit.'

'Me, too,' Scott said, throwing an arm around her shoulders as they walked back towards the fountain. 'It's impossible to make anything happen here.'

A dark look crossed his face and Cassie winced. The trial gig that she'd dropped him off to on the way back from the Gormley sculptures the other day had been a complete fuck-up on the management's part, and the whole set had tanked because of their lousy speakers. Then they refused to pay him, saying that he was an amateur.

'I'm so sorry. I shouldn't have been going on about my own problems. How are you feeling?'

'Sick of sucking up to dickwads who don't know good music when it slaps them in the face. As soon as I get the money Aaron owes me, I'm out of here,' he snapped, the darkness settling in his eyes. Cassie pressed her cheek into the side of his neck. She was used to his mercurial moods and in a strange way loved that she was the only one who could reach him when he started to spiral.

But instead of returning the pressure, his arm dropped from her shoulder, and he walked ahead. The warmth of his touch faded away and Cassie wrapped her arms around her torso. Shit. What had just happened? And what did he mean by saying he was out of here?

He couldn't go without her. They'd planned it together. Them against the world. She hurried to catch up with him, trying to ignore the tears prickling in the corners of her eyes.

'Even if I haven't saved enough money up? I mean, we could wait another six months. Felix said that once I've finished school I can pretty much work full time at The Blue Radish. I'd have enough saved up in no time.'

'And I'll get dragged further into the bullshit. Your parents already seem to think I'm an underground criminal mastermind, and God knows what will happen now. Your dad will probably go to the police and tell them what he found.'

He gave her a pointed glare, as if somehow it was her fault because it had happened in her car. Her stomach lurched, like she was on a roller coaster, and she tightened her hands to stop the world from dropping out from under her.

'He wouldn't do that,' Cassie said, not daring to add how much convincing he'd needed to not call them. 'Please, don't be mad at me.'

He didn't smile. 'Why should I believe you? For all I know, he was the one who put them there. Or Saint Norah. After all, she works in a hospital. She's probably handing out smack all day long,' Scott said, but at least he'd finally stopped walking.

Cassie reached him and studied his face, looking for any sign that he was joking. There was none. 'Are you serious? You think Norah could've planted them there? But why?'

'How the fuck should I know how rich people think? Maybe it's their twisted way of breaking us up. And hey presto—' He let out a bitter laugh and Cassie could feel the blood draining from her face.

'No, don't say that.' She grabbed his hands and forced him to look at her.

'Why not?' he sighed, though some of the fight seemed to have left him, and he returned her gaze. 'It's obvious what they think of me. And it's not like we can prove anything.'

'We don't need to prove anything,' she insisted. 'I know you didn't do it. Nothing else matters.'

'Grow up, Cassie. Of course this shit matters. And we have no way to prove it. I mean, even if it's on the security footage, it's not like we could see it. Your dad's probably wiped it anyway.'

Cassie went perfectly still. Of course. The security cameras. Scott had been around when they were being installed and she'd mentioned that her dad kept all his passwords in the safe as a way to avoid being hacked. It was stupidly old school. Not to mention that her dad still used the same combination he'd used since Cassie was ten. Her birthday.

She could get access to the footage and see what was there. She knew it was wrong, but the idea of Scott keeping up this cool façade between them was too terrifying for words.

'W-what if I could get into the safe?'

He turned to her, his hooded eyes brooding. 'How could you get in?'

'I just can. W-would that help?'

He rubbed his chin, as if considering it. Then tilted his head. 'It would clear my name, but it won't change my mind about going. Every day I'm stuck here is another day people like your dad and Norah can mess with my head.' He licked his lips and ran a finger down her cheek. 'Of course, passwords probably aren't the only thing he keeps in there.'

The words hung between them, like a doorway. Cassie's breath caught in her throat as he stepped closer to her, his scent catching in her nose and muddling her senses.

'You want me to steal money?' she said, feeling off-kilter as he took her hands in his. He was back now. This version of Scott. The intense, tormented poet that only she could reach. The one who'd called her his rock, his island. His soulmate.

What he was asking her to do wasn't right.

But saying no to him would only end in one way. With him gone and her all alone.

Scott's grin faded. 'Not steal. You said it yourself. It doesn't matter how mad your dad is, or how many future kids he has, he's never going to disinherit you. Besides, if they really are about to have a baby, he probably won't even notice. It's not like you'll need much. Just enough to pay your share of expenses once we get ourselves set up. I've got my half covered, so this is just for you.'

He was so close to her now, her breath brushing across her skin like a promise. She felt dizzy. Alive. Loved. He was the only good thing in her life. And it was true. If this hadn't happened, her dad would've caved. The signs had already been there. It made sense. Plus, it meant they could get the hell out of there.

'I'll do it.'

9

Norah tapped her foot and tried not to look at the time on her phone. Her other one still wasn't working so she'd put her SIM into an older model that she'd kept in the drawer as a back-up. They'd been sitting in the muted beige reception area of the IVF clinic for what seemed like hours. The tinkling music had started to resemble water torture and the low murmurs of the two receptionists were shredding up the last of her nerves. Next to her, Mark shifted and continued to read the *New York Post* on his phone. Norah wished she could relax, but it was impossible to settle.

Was this how her patients felt?

This terrible feeling of wanting things to go back to the way they were before.

Except that was now impossible. The one mistake she'd made all those years ago kept escalating and escalating, and the more she tried to fix things, the worse she made it. Until now she had no choice. Do it, or risk losing her job and the man she loved.

And she still didn't know who was behind it all.

She'd already fielded several calls from her brother, wanting to see if they'd been back in contact, and each time she'd assured him they hadn't. It was a lie. They'd given her until tonight to get the drugs, and then they'd be in contact. And if she backed out again, Mark would be getting a whole screen dump of photos – including one of her at Huyton Village looking pale and on edge.

Felix would be furious if he knew, but managing his concerns and expectations had just given her an extra layer of stress. The exact opposite of what she needed to conceive.

Everything was such a mess. And then there was Mark.

The fact they were there at all was a minor miracle.

He'd been morose and withdrawn since finding drugs in the car, and hadn't seemed interested in discussing wedding details. None of it was helped by the phone calls to Alice.

A nurse with short grey hair walked over to them. Her blue eyes were bright, and her mouth was upturned into a smile. 'Norah and Mark, would you like to follow me?'

They were led down an equally beige hallway to a large office. A young doctor was sitting behind the desk. She stood and smiled as they entered.

'Good morning. Please take a seat,' she said. 'I'm Harriet Gunnel. I've got your referral letter from your GP, but why don't you tell me your history.'

Painstakingly, Norah went through her history, and her decision to not wait any longer. Doctor Gunnel nodded patiently, every now and then stopping to ask a question. Once Norah finished, the doctor turned to Mark.

'I'd love to know how you feel about this. Especially when you already have a teenage daughter.'

Norah stared, trying to hide her alarm. Was this a test? Was Doctor Gunnel going to study Mark as he answered, or was she looking at Norah? And what would happen if she wasn't happy with his answer? Would she put a big X through their file, and that would be the end of everything? Logically, Norah knew it was unlikely. But with all the roadblocks that had been appearing in her life, it seemed like another terrible possibility.

The Cassie situation wasn't helping. She knew he took his fathering responsibilities very seriously. It was one of the things she loved about him. But now he was questioning everything.

'I've always known how important it is to Norah. I'm committed to our upcoming marriage and our future together,' Mark said, but his face had gone a dull grey colour and his tone was flat. Norah's stomach dropped as Doctor Gunnel scribbled down something on her notepad.

'Is it what you want?' the doctor pushed. 'It can be an arduous process and needs full commitment from both parties. Especially as there are no guarantees that it's going to work. And it's not a cheap option. I have some couples who still can't conceive after several rounds of treatment.'

'The money isn't a problem,' he said, not really answering the question. The doctor studied him before seeming to accept that was all he was going to say on the topic.

'I see. Well, the next step is to carry out several more fertility tests. Norah, we've already given you an ultrasound, but we still need a blood test for ovulation and you both need a chlamydia test. And a sperm sample from you, Mark. I appreciate that you've already fathered a child, but our bodies change over time. Take this sample bottle and the nurse outside will take you to one of our designated rooms. After which, please hand the bottle to the nurse and wait in the waiting room while I examine Norah and take some bloods. The results will be available in a few days and then we can arrange a time for you to come back in.'

Norah, who'd been clenching her fingers, relaxed her grip and didn't know whether to laugh or cry. In terms of the clinic, money obviously talked. And while she should be relieved that the doctor wasn't going to roadblock them, the fact that Mark was still so distracted wasn't quite what she'd hoped for.

Mark didn't look at her as the nurse ushered him out of the room. Once Norah's own tests were finished, she went back out to the reception area. Mark wasn't there so she checked her work emails, flagging the ones that needed a reply, and deleting everything else. She'd just finished reviewing some other patient notes as Mark finally emerged.

'How was it?' She turned her phone off, desperately trying to read his expression. 'Did you...'

She let the words hang, too scared to ask if he'd gone through with it. What if he'd got in there and couldn't manage to get a sample? Or didn't want to.

He let out a sigh and dropped into the seat next to her. 'Yes. I handed it in at the desk.'

The tension in her shoulders that had been building up like a dam lessened, and Norah let out a tiny sob. Something washed over Mark's face. Was it guilt?

'Shit.' He reached for her hand and clasped it in his. The heat of his skin only made her cry harder. Everything was such a mess, and it was all because she wanted them to be together and have a baby. It had always been about this, and she'd been so close to losing it all.

'I'm sorry.' She took a shuddering breath and used her free hand to wipe away the tears. 'I didn't mean to do that. I've just had a lot going on, and I was worried you'd changed your mind.'

He lifted her hand to his mouth and pressed a soft kiss on it. 'I should be the one apologising. This whole thing with Cassie scared the shit out of me. I guess I wasn't sure if I had the energy to do it all again. But I should've had your back in there.'

Norah let herself be sucked back into the orbit of his warmth. 'You're a great father and Cassie's lucky to have you.'

'You're pretty great yourself,' he said, a playful smile returning to his lips. 'What do you say we head out for a nice lunch to celebrate, and then later on we could...'

Norah swallowed. She'd booked the whole day off, but that was before she'd received last night's message. 'Sorry, I need to go into the hospital this afternoon.'

'Everything okay?'

'Yes.' She nodded, not wanting to extend the lie more than she had to. 'But I'll take a rain check.'

'Sure,' he said as he carefully pulled her up to her feet and walked her back to the car. He gave her a lingering kiss before heading back to his own office.

The traffic through Old Swan crawled along and Norah was almost regretting not taking Mark up on his offer of lunch... and afternoon sex. She'd read about how gruelling IVF could be on relationships, and with all the added complications, things were already feeling strained.

Soon, she promised herself. Soon everything would be back to normal.

Finally the traffic started flowing again and she reached the car park. Her usual spot wasn't available, and she was forced to circle a couple of times before finding one. Her drug-stealing window was getting smaller by the minute.

Norah climbed out of the car and headed towards the large brick building. The usual array of people were scattered around the entrance. Some with tired expressions on their faces, others with phones clamped to their ears, while staff members came and went. Norah waved to a colleague as she stepped through the wide glass doors. The atrium – with its high dome and curved wood panels – could be overpowering, but today she hardly noticed. Which was why she almost missed the woman stepping in front of her.

She had straight hair that had probably been caramel once but now was a dull brown, with watery blue eyes and a tight expression on her thin lips.

'Alice?' Norah came to a halt, not quite able to hide her surprise. They'd met a couple of times in passing, but Mark had always been there to act as a buffer. So why was Alice here now? Was she visiting a patient, or supporting a friend who had a sick child? A stab of concern ran through her. There was something unnerving about the way Alice's eyes were focused on her. 'How are you?'

'We need to talk,' Alice said abruptly, obviously not interested in small talk. Norah's stomach dropped. She'd imagined this moment so many times. Alice confronting her and accusing her of stealing her husband. Sometimes she'd break down in tears, and sometimes she'd rage and rant, calling Norah every name in the book. But it had never materialised.

Until now.

Norah swallowed and glanced at her phone. Hell. She needed to try and get the fentanyl before there was a shift change, and before her own day became too busy.

'Could it wait? I have—'

'Don't worry. It won't take long,' Alice cut her off. Up close, Norah had the chance to finally study her. There was a resemblance with Cassie, but it was faded – as if the years had sucked it out of Alice's skin and hair – so that where Cassie glowed with life, her mother was more of a tired shadow. A stab of guilt went through her. That was unfair. Alice was a mother, and that came with its own set of physical requirements. 'Mark told me about the IVF.'

The words jolted Norah back into the present moment.

'He what?' She took a step back, her concern evaporating as a surge of anger ran through her. Talking to his ex-wife about Cassie was one thing, but how could he talk to her about this? Especially when he could barely talk to her about it. A sense of betrayal ran through her as Alice's blue eyes never left her face. And how did she even know that Norah had a shift?

She took a second step back.

'He was upset about Cassie, and he talked about his concerns of becoming a father so late in life,' Alice said, her words hammering into Norah's skull like nails. 'Do you have any idea what you're asking him to do? What you're asking him to give up?'

'T-that's none of your business.' Norah's heart pounded, ringing out in her ears like a siren. This wasn't right. She shouldn't have to be talking to Alice about this. About something so personal.

'It is when it affects Mark. And our daughter,' Alice said in a cool voice. Norah's hand automatically dropped to her flat stomach, hating the reminder that she still hadn't conceived. And to have it thrown in her face by the woman who *had* become pregnant with Mark's baby was too cruel.

'What? So you're allowed to have a child, but I'm not?

'Not with Mark,' Alice corrected as a flash of something crossed her face. Was it pain, or malice? Norah couldn't be sure. 'And if you want a baby so much, you should've thought about it more before you stole my husband.'

And there it was. The truth of the matter. The thing that Norah had always known, but Mark had promised her didn't exist. That Alice – while upset about the divorce – had accepted it. Clearly that wasn't the case. And it meant that it was pointless having this conversation.

'And you should have thought twice before coming here,' Norah said, her words fuelled by her guilt. 'What Mark and I do is none of your business. Please don't come to my workplace again.'

Alice pressed her lips together into a flat line, but whatever had been powering her righteous anger was gone now, and suddenly she looked like the woman Mark had always described. Mundane, predictable and not one to rock the boat. And Norah had been foolish enough to believe him.

'Just remember what I said,' Alice said, then walked back through the atrium, leaving Norah alone. She let out a shaky breath and rubbed her brow. Her anger at Mark was mixed with the disconcerting discovery that there was more to his ex-wife than he'd ever let on. Now Norah needed to figure out just how far Alice would go to ensure that Norah didn't have a baby.

* * *

'Seriously? Are you blowing me off again?' Deb complained from the other end of the phone. Cassie flipped it off speaker and held it up to her ear as she walked out into the garden where Hugo was running around, delighted to be back in his own home.

'I told you, I have to study.'

It was a lie, but she did have plenty to do. Like open the safe. Her dad and Norah were at an IVF appointment, which was why she'd walked over from her mum's house. She hadn't planned to bring Hugo, but Alice had handed her the lead and then disappeared back into the attic room, leaving behind an excited dog.

Still, she'd been neglecting Hugo lately, and he'd been so happy to be back in his old garden, digging up the grass by a crab apple tree. Blossoms fell down on him like pink snow, which kept making him look up and bark.

'Everyone's going to be there,' Deb complained.

'Not everyone,' Cassie said logically as she walked back into the house, leaving Hugo to his digging. 'I've got to go, but don't do anything dumb.'

'Rude,' Deb said with a snort before ending the call, but Cassie doubted her friend was really offended. Especially since Deb managed to hook up with the wrong people or lose her phone or shoes on a regular basis. Not to mention that it was eleven thirty on a Tuesday morning. Hardly a great time to skive off to the pub.

Cassie usually would've tried harder to talk her friend out of it, but right now she could barely think. Scott had wanted to come, but she'd refused. She'd needed to concentrate, and to keep a clear head, and when he was with her, it was like she'd lost the power to think. It didn't help that he kept saying it was no big deal. Except that wasn't true. It was a big deal. And yet here she was. So, what did that make her?

Someone who was desperate.

She tucked her phone into the back pocket of her jeans and walked into the study. The motion detectors were turned off but there were still several cameras, including the one tucked away behind the cover of a book. She'd considered putting a cover over it, but decided it was just as easy to get the access code to the footage and delete herself from the feed while she was looking for the footage of the cars and the driveway.

A huge bookshelf ran the length of the wall, with a big oak desk at the far end of the room. The safe was concealed in what looked like a mid-century dresser. Cassie reached it and dropped down to her knees. Her hands shook as she jabbed in the combination and twisted the handle.

There was a soft click and it opened up.

She let out a breath and sat back on her heels. It had worked. She was in.

With the help of her phone torch, she peered inside. A stack of papers was bunched up to one side, as well as everyone's passports, including hers. Well, she'd be taking that for a start. And there it was. The small handmade notebook for passwords.

Her heart was slamming into her chest with nerves as she flicked through until she found the security codes. They were all there. She took a photo with her phone and carefully put it back where it had been. At the back was the same black metal box she'd loved playing with as a child.

It had been filled with several gold antique rings, a couple of brooches and a heavy diamond and pearl necklace that had been in his family for several generations. She picked up the necklace, suddenly remembering all the tea parties she'd had, with her teddy bears regally adorned with the jewellery. Sometimes Mark would even join her, there on the study floor, drinking from the tiny cups, the rings all crammed onto his fingers.

Shit. She quickly put the necklace back down and pushed the memories away.

Her dad would forgive her. He'd understand. After all, look what he'd done for love. He'd come home one day and told Alice that he wanted a divorce, and a week later Cassie had been dragged out to a restaurant to meet Norah.

It had been brutal. For her, and for Alice – who'd walked around like an extra in a zombie movie. Her face pale and her eyes unfixed and vacant. It was also when things had started to go pear-shaped between Alice and Cassie. Cassie had just assumed she was being a bitch, but now she wondered if it was because Alice was still in shock.

And why the hell was she thinking about this now?

She carefully lifted out the rest of the jewellery, looking for the soft leather wallet that her dad had used to keep an emergency cash fund.

It wasn't there. Shit. Shit. Shit.

She turned back to the stack of papers. There was a will, a marriage licence, stuff about the house and a bundle about his business. But nothing else.

Cassie rocked back on her heels, not sure how she should be feeling. Part of her was upset in case Scott thought she was lying, or that she hadn't really tried. But the other part of her was relieved. If there was nothing there, there was nothing she could take.

And then Scott would leave her.

She took a deep breath and looked again, but there was still no money, so she reluctantly put everything back where she'd found it and closed the safe.

She walked back into the hallway and called Scott. He didn't pick up. Cassie pressed her lips together. It was okay. Scott loved her. He showed her every day. And it wasn't her fault that there was no money there.

He would understand. He had to.

She sent him a text message.

There's nothing here but papers.

A little tick appeared next to it, along with three tiny dots to show that he was replying. At the same time there was a loud crashing sound from the lounge.

Cassie's whole body stiffened, and she jumped to her feet as Hugo came racing in, his entire body trembling.

'Hey, it's okay.' She scooped him up in her arms, but his panic only increased her own. She pressed his furry face up to her cheek and walked into the lounge. There was no one there, but on the floor was a puddle of water and long-stemmed roses lying in disarray – all surrounded by hundreds of pieces of crystal shards. Her heart seemed to stop. It had once been a vase that had been in the family almost as long as the jewellery Cassie had just been holding.

She never should have brought him along. Or left him alone. Hugo, who was still shivering, seemed to sense her panic and let out a soft moan.

'It's not your fault,' she assured him as the tyres from her dad's car crunched against the tiny stones on the driveway. Hell. He'd mentioned going out to lunch, but that clearly hadn't happened.

Talk about terrible timing. She hadn't even had a chance to delete the security footage yet. But that would have to wait. At least she'd closed the safe and covered her tracks. She quickly glanced at her phone to read Scott's message, but there wasn't one. The three little dots were gone, and for whatever reason he hadn't bothered to answer.

Panic churned in her guts. What did that mean? Was he angry with her? No. She couldn't read too much into it. She just needed to see him face to face. Then he'd know it wasn't her fault and that she'd tried. Plus, the best way to start their new life together would be for her to make it on her own. That's what her dad always said. And once she explained it to Scott, he'd definitely understand.

But first she had to face her dad and try to pretend that she hadn't been trying to steal from him.

* * *

Alice carefully stepped over the bluebells that were scattered around the base of the beech tree. The crab apple tree was ablaze with blossoms, though the branches were long and spindly, while the common lime had grown and the green leaves were pressing up against the living-room window like it was being held at gunpoint. The gardener never did prune them hard enough, but Mark obviously hadn't noticed. Still, it wasn't her garden any more. She hurried across the open expanse of soft grass until she reached the potting shed. The door creaked open, and she stepped into the familiar sanctuary.

The work bench was covered with discarded seedling pots, pieces of string and a collection of trowels. Ignoring them, she stepped over to the grimy window. It was covered in a fine layer of dust and had taken on a foggy appearance. But it still had a full view into the kitchen.

Because apparently this was her life now.

Skulking around in the shadows of her old house, staring in at the life that was no longer hers. Resentment at the unfairness of it all swelled in her chest. Did Norah have any idea just what ripples her actions had? Not only had she stolen away Alice's future and Cassie's security, but she'd also taken away Alice's dignity – reducing her to this.

Someone who didn't even have the right to go in through the front door.

It was humiliating and cruel.

But after their conversation, Norah had left Alice with no choice.

Her resentment had turned to anger, bitter and cold. It was as if Norah knew just how to kick Alice while she was down. It wasn't enough to steal Mark away and prance around with her perfect hair and holier-than-thou attitude, but now she'd really gone for the jugular. The one place that Alice couldn't ignore.

Cassie.

Alice didn't dare think about what would happen if Cassie found out the truth about her heritage. Their relationship would be fractured forever, not to mention Cassie's future. She might lose her inheritance, and even if Mark didn't discover the truth from the IVF tests, it would always be there waiting. Hanging over Alice and her daughter like a cartoon piano waiting to crush them.

It wasn't something she could risk happening. And since Norah wouldn't listen to reason, she needed to show Mark that his future wife wasn't the person he thought she was. That his perfect shiny replacement had secrets of her own. Because everyone had secrets, and it was up to Alice to find out what Norah's were, before her own terrible secret was revealed.

She tried not to think of the half-finished illustration still sitting on her desk. Still, that was a problem for future Alice. Right along with stalking charges. She bit back hysterical laughter as she realised that out of the two activities, it was the stalking she'd become an expert at. Not that it was really stalking. More like gentle observation.

She peered out of the smudgy window into the kitchen. It was empty, but all three cars were in the drive. After ten minutes, her leg started to cramp from leaning forward so she opened one of the drawers, pleased to see her neatly folded clean rags were still there. She spread one out on the bench and sat on it. It was a little bit more comfortable, and she continued to look. Her patience was rewarded twenty minutes later when Norah walked into the kitchen, closely followed by Mark.

Instinctively she leaned forward, even though she couldn't

hear anything. Mark folded his arms, and Norah turned her back to him – stiff and tense. Alice blinked. Were they fighting? Panic filled her. Was it about her? Had Norah told him about Alice turning up at the hospital? But if she had, then *why* were they fighting? Wouldn't Mark be mad at Alice? And—

Her eyes widened as Norah suddenly spun back towards Mark, now clutching a crystal figurine of a swan that Alice knew all too well. It had belonged to Mark's grandmother, and it weighed a bloody ton.

Norah said something else to him and then threw the swan towards him. Her aim was terrible, and it fell to the floor two feet away from him. The muffled crash reached the shed and Alice jumped back in surprise.

Well, shit. It was clearly more than just a little tiff.

Mark's mouth dropped open, but instead of saying anything, he simply held up his hands in defeat and disappeared back into the main part of the house. It was the way he usually responded to arguments, and for once Alice was glad, because it was clear by Norah's behaviour that she was frustrated with him. Which in turn would just make Mark more reserved and detached.

Alice sucked in her breath. So if they weren't fighting about her, what were they fighting about? Was it about the wedding, the IVF, or both? God, she hoped so. Norah had managed to disrupt all of their lives, and the sooner Mark realised that the better.

Her speculation was cut off by her phone beeping with a text message. She winced and fumbled for it. Next time she did something like this, she'd need to put it on silent first. She looked at the screen.

Mark.

Hey, sorry to be that kind of ex, but would you mind if I came around? I really need to talk.

She straightened in surprise and managed to hook the sleeve of her favourite blue cardigan on a nail jutting out of the bench. Instinctively she pulled it away but that just made it worse, and she stared at the large hole she'd created. Alice swore. She loved the cardigan, but it was already bedraggled from Hugo's rough treatment of it, and now this. It was probably time to throw it away.

Her phone pinged again.

Please, Alice. I wouldn't ask if it wasn't important.

Hope flared in her chest. Why was he reaching out to her? Was it because of what she'd said to him about IVF? Or because he wanted to talk to her about the fight he'd just had with Norah? Either way it could only be a good thing. Because it meant she was still the person he trusted.

And in time he'd remember just how great they'd been together. How much better it was for Cassie as well. There had been no trouble then. No Scott, no drugs, no talk of gap years. She'd been the perfect daughter, and, if given the chance, this time around Alice would be the perfect wife. She'd do the things Norah did. The trips to get her hair touched up... even the bloody yoga. She'd do whatever it took.

Because if Mark came back to her then she could forget about this terrible new life of hers, with bills and deadlines and the endless worry over what her future looked like. And there'd be no more talk of babies or IVF. Everyone would win. Well, everyone but Norah. But the bitch needed to learn first-hand what it felt like to have your life ripped apart as you watched the man you loved leave you for someone else.

Alice glanced back towards the house. All she had to do was wait until he drove off, then she could slip out of the garden and back to her car, which was parked around the corner.

Her fingers trembled as she replied.

Give me half an hour. I'm always here for you.

10

Norah scraped the bottom of the pan with the wooden spoon. Damn. How could she manage to burn mince when she'd been stirring it the whole time? She was cooking a bolognaise sauce, but even that was proving a problem for her. She should've just gone to Lido's Pantry like she usually did and bought one of their homemade meals. It pretty much summed up her day.

She'd had a huge fight with Mark in the morning and instead of coming home to make up, he'd sent her a text to say he had a work dinner to attend. It was unfair. If he was here, they could talk about it, and sort it out. But now she was left with far too many emotions and nowhere to put them. It left her untethered and off balance.

What she really needed was to hit the yoga mat and try and work it out of her system, but she was too wound up to even try. The worst thing was that the fight had been over nothing. Well, not nothing. He'd discovered that the day before Cassie had been at the house with Hugo and the dog had knocked over and broken a family heirloom.

But instead of intending to punish her, Mark had just said it was an accident. And something in her had snapped. She'd grown up in a household that would earn you a beating if you walked in the path of the television, yet Cassie could just come and go as she pleased, making a mess in the process. Which was when she'd picked up a crystal swan and thrown it on the floor – saying that if it worked for Cassie, it might work for her.

Shame flooded her.

She hardly ever lost her temper, especially around Mark. But the building stress was becoming harder to manage, and the swan had been in her hand before she even knew what was happening. It wasn't her finest hour, but the release of the shattered glass somehow helped calm down her own frayed nerves, which were still raw from her encounter with Alice – and the fact Mark had told his ex-wife about their efforts to get pregnant. Not to mention her trip to the supply room yesterday.

She'd gone back there at the end of her shift, waiting until her colleagues were in a health and safety meeting. There had been no mention of the missing drugs and while that should have calmed it down, it had just increased the surging adrenaline that had been going through her body. But it didn't stop her. Because she was past that point now, and so she'd ignored her clamouring heart and slipped ten boxes of fentanyl into her bag.

The rest of the evening had been spent waiting for the dreaded text message from the blackmailer. But it hadn't come. Nor had there been anything today. None of which was helping her nerves. All in all, it had been a shit of a week.

Cassie walked in from upstairs, wrinkling her nose. 'Whatever you're cooking, it's burning.'

'Yes, I know,' Norah snapped as she dumped the whole saucepan into the sink. Cassie lifted a brow in surprise and Norah winced. Shit. She really needed to pull herself together.

She plastered on a smile that she wasn't feeling. 'Thank goodness for frozen pizza. Want some?'

'Pass. I'm working tonight.' She slung a backpack over her shoulder and left, not bothering to say goodbye. Once she was gone, Norah's shoulders slumped forward. So that had gone well.

Her relationship with Cassie was getting worse by the day. Not exactly the way she'd intended to start her new life as Cassie's stepmother. Or her own journey into having a baby of her own. Norah swallowed. Did she even deserve to have a baby if this was the way she acted?

No. She shut the thought down. Norah had always known she was meant to be a mother, and she'd love her baby like no one else ever had.

As for Cassie, she needed to grow up. It was almost laughable how hard done by Cassie thought she was, with two loving parents who seemed almost obsessed with her, and the perfect childhood growing up in Mark's glorious house. It was so far away from the council estate she and Felix had grown up in with the drunk mother and absent father. And while Norah wouldn't wish that on anyone, she'd like Cassie to at least acknowledge her privilege.

She scraped the ruined bolognaise into the bin and fished out a frozen pizza. Once it was in the oven and the timer was set, she turned on her laptop, which was sitting on the kitchen counter, and went through her emails. They were mainly wedding-related, and she answered them one by one.

Tap. Tap. Tap.

Norah's brows knitted together. It had come from the back door. Except that didn't make sense. To get round there meant leaning over the garden gate to open it and then walking down the side of the house. She looked at the window where one of the trees was pressing up against the glass. Was that what had caused the noise? It really needed to be cut back again.

Tap. Tap. Tap.

The tree branch didn't move and Norah swung around as the back door creaked open. Someone was coming in. Her heart pounded and her entire body began to tingle. She'd been so hypervigilant lately that the slightest noise seemed to set her off. But this wasn't a random noise. This was someone trying to get into the house. Shit.

When Mark had first discovered footprints in the garden beds and upgraded the security system, she'd thought he'd been overreacting, but now she wished she'd paid more attention to making sure it was always set.

She reached for a wooden rolling pin that was on the bench and grabbed her phone with the other hand.

Her throat was tight, and the familiar paralysis had overtaken her legs, leaving her glued to the spot as a skinny teenager with pale blonde hair strolled into the kitchen.

Scott?

Norah didn't lower the rolling pin as the roaring adrenaline thundered through her. What the hell was he doing here? And why was he smirking like that?

'Hello, Norah,' he purred.

'Why are you using the back door?'

'I didn't want to be seen at the front door,' he said, as if she was five years old and had asked a stupid question. Without asking, he lowered himself onto one of the barstools and pulled a face at the smell of burnt mince. The casual way he splayed his legs caused her to tighten her grip on her phone. 'Ouch. Dinner smells like a disaster. Lucky that Mark's out tonight. I've heard Alice is a great cook. Must be hard to live up to.'

'Excuse me?' Norah swallowed, trying to get her bearings. But between her shattered nerves and exhaustion, she was feeling wildly off-kilter. Up until this point she'd only had a couple of conversations in passing with him, before Cassie had dragged him away. Which had been fine by Norah. But there was something about his smirking eyes and smug smile that she didn't like.

'What? You don't like home truths? I thought we were past that stage of our relationship, Norah,' he said, casually pulling out his phone and swiping the screen. He then held it up and took a photo of her before jabbing the screen a couple more times.

A moment later, her own phone pinged. She jumped in surprise before reluctantly staring at the screen. It was a message from the blackmailer.

Surprise.

But it wasn't the message that stopped her dead, it was the photo of a woman with dishevelled hair and a face drained of colour as she held up a rolling pin and stared at something off-screen. It was her.

Her stomach churned. Oh God. She was going to be sick.

Her blackmailer was Scott. A fucking arrogant eighteen-year-old kid who thought it was okay to saunter into her kitchen and try and screw up her life. Another wave of nausea raced through her as the pieces all fell together like a sick and twisted jigsaw puzzle.

Scott could've easily slipped into their bedroom to get access to the photograph of her and Mark. And the wedding invitations and envelopes had been in the top drawer of the writing desk. But why hadn't she suspected him? Because there was nothing in the house that connected her to the past. So how had he known?

'Who told you about me?'

'You did, you stupid cow.' He arched an eyebrow, though it was barely visible under his long hair. 'Last year you walked into The Eagle and had a conversation with Roy Walsh – who, in case you haven't figured out, is a world-class prick. But the real surprise was when I saw you collecting Cassie from school. Took me a few days to place why I recognised you. What a surprise it was... or should I say gift horse? So I figured I'd hook up with her and see where it led me. Fast forward to now.'

She closed her eyes. Poor Cassie. What a brutal way to learn about the disappointment of first love. And what a terrible way for Norah to learn that the world continued to make arseholes.

'I don't deserve this.'

Scott let out a bark of laughter. 'Poor you. Look how tough you're doing in your lovely new life. And I'm not a bastard. I just think it's fair if you share a bit of your good fortune.'

'You don't understand. I can't do this. I'll get fired.'

'That will be the last of your worries if you mess me around again. And don't think for a minute about trying to frame me again.'

'What are you talking about?'

'The drugs in the car? Trying to get Saint Mark to ban Cassie from seeing me again? A power move, I'll give you that.'

'Why go to so much trouble? Why not just confront me directly?' Norah said, not bothering to correct him. Let him think what he wanted. She needed to think about her next move.

'I like to test the waters first.' He shrugged. 'And I must say I'm disappointed, Norah. I thought we'd reached an understanding, but clearly not.'

'Have you told Cassie about this?' she asked, trying to buy time. Was there still a way she could get out of it? She could tell Mark the truth, now that it was Scott behind it. After all, Mark hated Scott and it would finally be a way to ensure Cassie no longer dated him.

Except it wouldn't work.

She'd already stolen from the hospital. Twice. *And* she'd managed to leave the drugs in the car while Cassie had been driving. Which meant her job and relationship were still at risk. And judging by the expression on Scott's face, the smug little shitbag knew it.

'No.' He shook his head. 'And if I had, then you'd already know about it. And so would Mark. Now let's get this over with.'

His green eyes were devoid of emotion as he stared at her. A restless energy rippled off him, as if a predator was trapped inside, just waiting to be released. She'd never liked him, but up until this moment she hadn't feared him. But looking at him now, the sinewy muscles and the wild gleam in his eyes made her realise just how much she'd underestimated him.

'They're in my bag.' Norah swallowed and walked over to the side table where she'd dumped everything earlier. She rummaged in there before producing the ten boxes. Then she had an idea. What if she got a photograph from the security footage of her handing them over to him? Then she could blackmail him back. He smirked, as if reading her mind, and made a tutting noise.

'Just stay there.' He joined her, pausing only to glance up at the tiny camera hidden behind a painting. Cassie had obviously told him exactly where they were. He bundled them into his backpack, then gave her a wink. 'Thanks.'

'These drugs are extremely dangerous. Not just for us if

we're caught. But for whoever you're planning on selling them to.'

'Little bit late to start being Miss Prim and Proper. Our arrangement will stop when I say so, and not before. I want thirty more by next week.'

Thirty?

Her chest tightened and her pulse pounded in her ears. She dropped down into the nearby chair. This had to stop. She'd already risked too much. There was no way she could take more without being caught.

'If anyone finds me out, then you'll be in just as much trouble,' she said.

'Then don't get caught. Oh, and Norah, I'm looking forward to attending the wedding. If it takes place. Because if I tell Mark the truth about his blushing bride, then it'll all be over. No wedding, no fancy honeymoon, no baby. Remember that.' He turned and left the way he'd come.

His words hammered home the terrible truth. She was no longer a free woman. How could he do this to her? And it wasn't even personal. He was just a stupid teenager who'd seen her at the wrong place and the wrong time, and somehow thought he'd won the lottery. But the game he was playing was bad for them both. She had to find a way to convince him that it was all a mistake.

'Scott. Wait. This has to stop.'

'I decide when it's over and not you.'

All she could hear was him laughing as he slammed the door behind him.

* * *

'Am I still your favourite patient?' Rose asked as Norah put down her chart. She turned to the little girl and smiled. Even though Rose was stable again, the prognosis wasn't great.

'My favourite *person*,' Norah corrected, though this time the lump in her throat made it hard to speak.

'Does that mean I can go home soon?'

'Let's see how you do tonight first.'

'Okay,' Rose said and returned her attention to the puzzle on the tray over the bed. Ruth, who'd been sitting by the bed, stood up and gestured for Norah to talk with her out of earshot. Her face was strained, and she seemed to have aged in the last few days. Another stab of guilt raced through Norah, hating that she might have caused it.

'I've just had a phone call from Billy,' Ruth said once they were outside the room. 'That's Rose's real father. He's been abroad but came back last night.'

'I see.' Norah swallowed. From what she'd gathered, Billy's version of being 'abroad' was actually prison.

'He's got it into his head that you should've done more to stop Rose drinking the juice. Said that doctors should be liable. I tried to tell him that you're not a doctor, but—' She broke off and laced her fingers through each other in an agitated manner. 'He wants to speak with you this afternoon.'

Norah flinched. The tests had been inconclusive about what had caused the reaction, and Ruth had insisted on blaming herself for not remembering about the grapefruit. But it didn't help appease Norah's own guilt.

'I know it can be hard when there are setbacks.' She tried to keep her voice professional. 'But there's not always a magic solution. I'm sorry.'

Ruth sniffed. 'That's what I told him, but he's... well... he is very insistent.'

'I'm not here this afternoon,' Norah said. She and Mark had their follow-up appointment at the clinic, and she'd decided to take a half day to tie up the last-minute wedding details. Now she was pleased she had. The last thing she wanted was to confront someone like Billy Jenkins on her own. It wasn't the first time she'd had to face down an angry parent, and while their words and accusations could sometimes sting, she'd never taken it personally before. It was just a reflection of the enormous stress and grief they were under.

But right now, with so much going on in her own life, she wasn't sure she could handle an irate father who probably had his own issues of guilt that he was looking to offload.

Her brow pounded again. She'd worked so hard to be a good person. To be loving and kind to as many people as she could. But what if she had been responsible for Rose's readmission into hospital? And what if the drugs Scott had taken from her caused someone to die? Or if Mark kicked her out, disgusted at the truth about her?

Then who was she?

Ruth coughed, jolting Norah back to the conversation. God, what had she been thinking? Now wasn't the time to have an existential crisis.

'It would be best if he made an official appointment to discuss Rose's care with the entire team. There is a charter of conduct that he needs to abide by.'

A flash of worry crossed Ruth's face, but she nodded. 'I'll tell him. A lot of the time he's all hot air. And I know how much you care about our Rose. You'd never do anything to hurt her.'

She hoped it was true.

'We're all trying our best,' Norah promised, and spent another ten minutes talking to Ruth before walking back to her office. It wasn't until the door was closed that she allowed herself to collapse into the chair. Her breathing was shallow, and her skin was clammy.

She had no idea if it was guilt, nerves or exhaustion, but she had to find a way out of it. This couldn't be her life for much longer. The price was too high.

She quickly logged the incident as a potential danger and copied in the rest of the department in case he turned up without any notice.

By the time she was finished, a headache was forming. There was an open can of Coke on her desk, and she used it to swallow down two painkillers.

The throb in her temples lessened and she went through her phone messages. The first one was from Carol, Mark's assistant. They'd had a couple of calls and text messages when Norah had been organising a surprise party for Mark's birthday but hadn't spoken in ages.

Norah listened to it.

'Hi!' Carol's voice sounded overly bright, like she was singing a song. 'So, Mark asked me to call you. A problem's come up in Manchester that was unavoidable. He's already there and has back-to-back meetings, so he won't be able to make the appointment today. He's so sorry and will call you later.'

He wasn't coming?

No. It wasn't possible. He had to be there. They were getting the results of his fertility test and would be discussing the next steps. It wasn't an appointment that could be shuffled around. She brought up his number but the call went straight to voicemail.

Damn it.

She sent him a text and then called Carol to find out what the hell was going on. It was a frustrating conversation and

Carol couldn't illuminate at all. He hadn't been in the office at all today, just sent her an email with a list of things to do, including the call.

Norah blinked. So why could he email Carol, but not her?

Pain tore through her. He'd always been so dependable. Always right by her side. And she'd let herself become used to it. Expected it, even. And now he wasn't here, it felt like a betrayal.

Her phone buzzed and she grabbed it, expecting to see Mark's number flash up on the screen. It was Felix.

'Don't sound so pleased to hear from me,' he said.

'Sorry. It's been a shit of a morning,' she said and instantly regretted it as he sucked in a breath from the other end of the line.

'Why? What's happened? Has that arsehole been back in touch?'

Norah swallowed. Her brother wasn't violent, but she hated to think what he might do if he found out that Scott was behind it all. Felix had taken a great liking to Cassie, which would add even more fuel to the fire.

'No, nothing like that,' she assured him. 'How are you?'

'Better than you, it seems. I wanted to wish you luck today.'

Norah filled him in on everything, including Mark's new closeness with Alice. 'I'm sure I'm overreacting,' she said, not sure who she was trying to convince. 'I mean, he's such a great dad, and he's still freaked about Cassie.'

'Yeah, well, maybe he should worry more about being a great fiancé,' Felix said in a sharp voice, before sucking in air. 'Shit. Sorry, I didn't mean that. But Cassie's a big girl who can take care of herself. You're the one who needs his support right now.'

Tears pricked the corners of her eyes, and she wiped them away. 'I'm okay. I promise.'

'I'll be the judge of that,' Felix said, but it was in his usual voice. 'And since Mark can't make it, let me take you out for lunch after your appointment. Deal?'

'Thanks, big brother. You really are the best.'

'That's not what you said when I gave you a ride on my bike and crashed into a tree,' he said and Norah reluctantly smiled.

'Apart from that,' she agreed. 'And I'll take you up on the lunch.'

She put her phone into her bag and stood up. Mark's betrayal still jabbed at her heart, but Felix's calmness had helped settle down her frayed nerves. She was fine. It would all be fine. Because the alternative didn't bear thinking about.

* * *

Alice pushed open the door to Mark's office. She just needed to act normal. If she could remember what normal was any more. It had been a while. And how did one tell their ex-husband the truth about their daughter? It hadn't been an easy decision, but it was the only way. Better now, rather than waiting until he received any IVF results.

At least that way she'd have a chance to present her side of the story.

She'd almost been tempted to tell him yesterday when he'd come around. But it had been easy to see how on edge he was. He hadn't mentioned the argument he'd had with Norah, instead just talking about how concerned he was about Cassie, especially after discovering she'd brought Hugo into the lounge and managed to break a vase. Alice had felt a little guilty about that, since she was the one who'd asked Cassie to take the dog with her, but she kept it to herself. Instead, she'd made sure to give him all the support and encouragement he needed.

And really, it had been easy – especially after she'd seen how Norah had behaved.

His assistant, Carol, was sitting at her desk. Alice flashed her a bright smile. See, that was normal. It must have worked because Carol beamed back at her.

'Alice, I haven't seen you in ages. How are you? Busy, I suppose, with your books. When's the next one out? I want to buy it for my niece. She's mad for them.'

'About a year away,' she said, crossing her fingers. It was best not to think about the pages she still needed to illustrate before tomorrow. Or what might happen financially if she didn't. But, if her chat with Mark went well, she'd be more motivated to pull an all-nighter.

'I'm sure it will be worth waiting for. Your books always are. Anyway, how can I help you?'

'I was hoping for a quick chat with Mark. I wouldn't normally bother him at work, but... well, it's sort of an emergency.'

Carol wrinkled her nose. 'He's in Manchester for a couple of meetings. It was urgent and he wasn't pleased about it, let me tell you. He was...' She paused a moment. 'Umm...'

'What is it?'

'He'd booked himself out of the office later this morning to go for a medical appointment at twelve. I had to phone Norah at work for him because he didn't have time. She seemed very upset. But don't say I told you any of this.' She blushed, as if belatedly realising her error.

'My lips are sealed.' Alice held a finger up to her mouth, grateful she'd stayed on such good terms with the other woman.

Bidding Carol a quick goodbye Alice hurried back to the car. If the medical appointment was for the IVF results, then she had a brief respite. Unless Norah decided to go on her own. Her relief turned sour as visions of Norah sitting in the doctor's office as the news was delivered sprang into her mind.

What if the results revealed his blood type and Norah somehow figured out about Cassie? Or, worse, that Mark really was infertile? God, wouldn't Norah just bloody well love that. Alice could only imagine how much she'd play it up. She'd be in Mark's ear the whole time reminding him that Alice had betrayed him and that he needed to cut all ties with her.

Worse, what would happen with Cassie? What if Norah convinced Mark to disinherit their daughter? It would break Cassie's heart and destroy Alice's own relationship with her daughter.

She tried calling Mark but it went straight through to his voice mail. She hung up. Shit. It wasn't something she could say in a one-minute message. But if Norah went to the appointment before Alice had a chance to talk to him, she'd lose her only chance of confessing to him.

She *had* to find out what the results were before Norah told Mark. But how?

Could Alice reason with Norah about it? Probably not. Then again, she hadn't told Mark about Alice's visit to the hospital. Would this be the same?

Mark had mentioned the clinic was on Rodney Street. An internet search soon gave her the address. It wasn't too far from his office, and she drove to a nearby car park and walked the rest of the way.

The street was filled with impressive red-bricked Georgian buildings that were often used for film sets. But Alice ignored the stunning architecture as she walked down the cobbled street. Most of the terraces had been split into apartments and offices, including numerous medical consultants. She finally reached the building in question and then realised her mistake.

In true Georgian style, the buildings were identical with front doors almost on the footpath, meaning there wasn't anywhere to hide. Short of holding a newspaper in front of her face like a bad movie cliché, she'd just have to keep moving.

She checked her phone. It was ten past twelve. Which meant if Norah had gone to the appointment, she'd still be in there. Alice walked up the block and back again. She'd kill for a cigarette. It had been several years since she'd given up, mainly because Mark and Cassie had kept nagging her. At the time she'd been glad, apart from the additional seven pounds in weight she'd put on, and failed to shift.

And it wasn't like it had worked, since Mark had left her anyway. Maybe she'd buy a packet when this was all over.

'Alice?'

Shit. Cigarettes forgotten, she turned to face a good-looking man, with a square jaw and all his own hair. Alice frowned before remembering the café website that Cassie had shown her. It was Norah's brother, Felix.

No. No. No. How could this be happening?

Alice had only met him once about a year ago, when she'd picked up Cassie from the house, not long after Norah had moved in there. Alice was surprised he'd remembered her, because she certainly would never have recognised him.

Which was a pity, because if she'd seen him sooner, she definitely would've found a place to hide. Anything to avoid facing him now. She could barely convince herself she wasn't stalking Norah; she wasn't sure how she could convince Felix.

'What are you doing here?' His voice was sharp as his eyes swept over her, as if looking for clues.

Definitely not waiting for your sister to come out of the IVF clinic across the road.

'Um... I'm visiting a friend in Falkner Square and couldn't get a parking spot.' She gave a vague wave of her hand, hoping like hell he couldn't see how much she was shaking. 'You?'

'I'm meeting Norah for lunch. She's had some... challenging news,' he said.

Challenging news?

Alice's stomach dropped. The whole way over she'd been trying to convince herself that she was worrying over nothing. That Mark would be fertile and that her terrible secret would remain exactly where she needed it to be – buried deep in the recesses of her mind.

But his taut jaw could mean only one thing.

Norah knew.

'Oh. I hope she's okay.' Alice forced her voice to stay light. 'Anyway, I'd better be on my way.' She half-walked, half-ran down Rodney Street as adrenaline flooded her body. She had to get away before he saw her fall apart. She needed to clear her head. To think. To stay calm. But it was impossible because the one message kept roaring in her skull, over and over again.

Do whatever it takes to keep your daughter's future safe.

11

Cassie jabbed a finger at the screen of Alice's crappy phone. It had been Cassie's phone a million years ago and Alice had found it in a drawer after her own phone had died and had continued to use it. Cassie was pretty sure that Alice had been trying to teach her a lesson in not throwing things away when they still worked. But if that was the mountain Alice wanted to die on – using an outdated phone with too much lag and not enough memory for updates – then she could knock herself out.

So it sucked that Cassie's own phone was flat and the charger cable was broken. So irritating. Downstairs, Alice was shuffling around in the kitchen. Her mother was almost gleeful. Like she'd been let in on some big secret. It was irritating. She pressed the screen again and brought up another video. She'd been working through the surveillance footage that the cameras at her dad's house automatically uploaded.

Between getting yet more lectures about the broken vase, and the implied subtext that the chances of her dad supporting her during the gap year had moved into negative figures, she'd only just had a chance to log in. She scrolled through the various cameras until she came to the one in his study. She brought up the footage from Tuesday and located the study camera, which clearly showed her opening the safe. Delete.

Are you sure? The words flashed up on the screen. Hell, yes, she was sure. Cassie pressed the button, and the video disappeared.

Not that it really mattered. Even if her dad had seen the footage, she hadn't taken anything. She then went back to Monday to see if there was a camera in the driveway, showing the cars.

But there wasn't. Disappointment caught in her throat, and she was about to log out of the account when Hugo's furry face appeared in one of the camera feeds. It was from the day she'd gone around there.

Everyone knew that misery loved dog videos, so she hit play and watched as the little dog trotted into the lounge. Her mood instantly lifted as he sniffed the sofa. His ears were up, and his nose was twitching – obviously excited to see more of his old home.

The movements were a bit jumpy thanks to the video, but he still looked adorable as he wandered around the room, tail wagging. Then a bird flew in through the open door, and Hugo let out a shocked bark and charged towards it, knocking the vase off in the process. He then jumped in surprise and ran behind the coffee table, his ears still clearly visible.

Poor little guy. Cassie's heart exploded with affection at his antics. Maybe she should stick it up on TikTok and make money that way? It wouldn't be the dumbest thing people had ever posted.

She pressed in Scott's digits and called him. Alice would freak if she knew Cassie had used her phone to call him, but it wasn't like his name would show next to the number. It was just a random call.

'Hey,' she said when he finally answered the call. 'So, I've had this crazy idea. What if we start a channel with Hugo doing stuff? I've just found this cutest—'

'Jesus. Are you fucking serious?' Scott cut her off. 'That's your solution?'

Her body tensed up as if she'd been slapped. She loved Scott but sometimes it was like trying to navigate a minefield, and she was never certain what things would cause him to explode. What she did know was that the quickest way to calm him down was to backtrack.

'It's just an idea. I need to do something, but I swear I'll get the money. I'm coming with you.'

'Whatever,' he grunted, and there was a thumping noise in the background. As if he'd returned to his music deck.

'Are you mad with me?' she pressed, hating that he seemed so far away. She wanted to reach out and touch him. 'Can we meet up? I could come to yours.'

'I'm busy.'

Oh. She swallowed. 'At least tell me what's going on.'

'For fuck's sake, Cassie. Give it a rest. I can't deal with this right now.'

Tears jabbed at the corners of her eyes.

'Deal with what? Are you finishing with me?' She hated how needy the words sounded. How little they made her. Suddenly she felt exhausted. Meeting Scott had been the greatest thing that had ever happened to her, but it was also the most challenging. The laughter and the kissing and the sex were wonderful. But this flip side was... full of things that made her feel totally out of her depth.

And there was no one she could talk to about it. Deb was

incapable of keeping a secret and would tell Scott about it the minute she was drunk. Her dad was too tied up with Norah and the wedding. That left Alice. Suddenly Cassie longed to be six years old again. Back when it was okay to climb into the bed with her mum and ask her all the questions she had, while being cloaked in a feeling of warmth and security.

The silence dragged out between them before Scott finally let out a long breath.

'No, of course I'm not. We're good. It's just... look, it's nothing to do with you and me. Okay? I gotta go,' he said. Then without another word, he ended the call.

A lump formed in her throat. She knew he was disappointed about the money. Maybe he sensed that she'd been secretly relieved? But it still stung that he'd dismissed her idea like that. Was it worth sending him the video? If he saw it, he'd understand. She brought up the video of Hugo again and flopped back on her bed, so she was staring up at the phone.

Definitely hilarious.

She was about to send it to him and then stopped. If he was in a mood, it would be better to wait until later. She logged back into the security footage to see if there was anything else worth downloading.

She flicked back through the older videos, but they were just her dad and Norah doing boring crap – her dad singing, Norah doing yoga, and then suddenly Cassie's own face appeared in the shot.

Curious, she tapped on it. It was the day Norah had been cooking in the kitchen. The smell had been gross, and Norah's face was hilarious. Like she'd been busted. As if Cassie and her dad didn't already know what a crap cook she was.

She dragged it back and took a screenshot when Norah's face was all wrinkled up. Perfect. She was so keeping a shot of that. There was no sound, but all the same Cassie watched Norah try to engage her in the most pointless conversation. It was two days after her dad had found the drugs, which explained her own scowl.

Just like now. Her mood darkened and she was just about to log out again when the video flicked to Norah randomly picking up a rolling pin. Okay, that was weird. Cassie sat up on her bed. In the shot Norah walked around the kitchen bench and then lowered the pin when Scott appeared at the door.

What the actual fuck?

Cassie's whole body stiffened, her attention now fully on the screen. What was happening? Her mind whirled, trying to recollect if Scott had been there with her. But no. She'd wanted to get him around to hang out, but he'd been stuck with Aaron and Ned, who'd been off their faces, and he hadn't wanted to leave them in case they did something stupid.

Had he changed his mind and arrived too late to see her?

But why hadn't he told her?

Or why hadn't Norah mentioned it?

She stared at the screen as the pair of them continued to talk. Scott was smiling, but it wasn't friendly, and Norah's fingers were clenched. What were they saying? Then Norah walked out of the shot, towards the lounge.

Scott followed her and then the kitchen was empty. They both appeared several minutes later. Scott was properly smiling now. Like he did when he'd had a great night on the decks. But Norah's face was white, and her lips were twisted into a tight grimace. Scott disappeared out of the back door, and as soon as he'd left Norah rushed to lock it.

Cassie watched it a second time and then went searching for the camera feed from the lounge, but it only showed an empty room. Shit. She went through it all again several more times but there were no shots to explain the encounter.

Except the obvious. Something had happened between them – and they'd lied about it. And it was the lying that hurt. The pair of them had walked around with the same Scott and Norah faces, but on the inside they were different. The video proved that. There was a secret part of them that Cassie knew nothing about.

And she bet her dad didn't either.

A sense of urgency raced through her. Old Cassie would have worried about pressing Scott for an answer – too afraid she'd hit a nerve and he'd explode. But new Cassie needed to know the truth. For her sake and her dad's.

She called him, but this time he didn't pick up. She tried again, and then sent a text, but still there was no reply. Where the hell was he? Irritation for all the times he disappeared without explanation choked her, as she realised she was always the one waiting for his calls, not the other way around.

She wanted to call Norah too but had no idea what her number was. All the same she scrolled through Alice's address book and was surprised to see Norah's name and number in there. Before she could think about it, she made the call.

Adrenaline surged through her in a Wagner-like crescendo as she gripped the phone, but the call went to Norah's message box. Shit. Her entire body was still jangling with too much energy and nowhere to channel it.

Downstairs, Alice was still humming. Cassie was torn. Should she go and show her mother the video? See if together they could work out what it meant? Part of her longed to confide in Alice. But she stopped herself. Her mother hated both Scott and Norah, and would automatically think the worst. Not to mention that she'd totally take over, as if Cassie wasn't capable of thinking or acting on her own.

No. Alice couldn't help her. She needed to get the answers on her own. But first she had to find Scott. He often went out to various pubs and clubs with the twins to check out different DJs. But she had no idea which ones were hot right now. It was one of the mysteries she'd never mastered, of how a club that had been filled with people one week was suddenly empty and lame the next.

Thankfully, while Cassie didn't keep up with the underground whispers of where to go on a Thursday night, her best friend had a gold medal in it.

Reaching for a jacket, she called Deb. Her friend answered on the second ring. In the background, music was being played and there was a buzz of conversation.

'It's our girl!' Deb squealed, already sounding half-tanked.

'Have you seen Scott?'

'Christ, no. You should know your boyfriend never goes out before ten.'

Cassie bit down on her lip. The idea of staying in the house was unbearable. She needed to do something. To find answers. 'And where do you think he'll go?'

'Here, of course. The Stanley Arms,' Deb said as if offended to be asked such a stupid question. 'You should come down. It's Mike's birthday.'

Cassie had no idea who Mike is. But that didn't matter. One way or another she was going to get this whole mess sorted out tonight. And having a drink first would give her the courage she needed.

'Deal. I'll see you in half an hour.'

* * *

Norah picked up her glass of wine and took a large swallow. It was almost six o'clock and she needed something to help stop her mind from racing. There was no sign of Mark or Cassie, but she was getting used to that.

On cue, her phone rang, and Mark's name flashed up on the screen.

She couldn't speak to him. Not yet. Not until she had time to think it all through. The ringing finally stopped and went through to voice message.

'It's me. Sorry, this is taking longer than I thought. Not sure when I'll be back. How did it go with the doctor? Love you.'

She placed her glass on the table and leaned forward, wrapping her hands around her head. Why was it all happening to her? She hadn't done anything wrong.

Apart from stealing another woman's husband.

It always came back to that. Was this her punishment? That Mark couldn't give her the one thing she wanted. A baby.

Because he was infertile.

Except he couldn't be. He had Cassie.

She'd asked Doctor Gunnel what had happened to render him unable to father children, hoping they could reverse it. But the doctor said that he'd always been that way. That's when Norah had stopped listening. Instead, she'd nodded and pretended to listen before escaping the office, too late forgetting she'd planned to meet Felix for lunch.

She hadn't told him the truth. Mainly because she didn't want to say it out loud, not until she'd had time to think. And so she'd just pretended that it had all gone well, and kept talking about what a great father Mark would be. Then she'd made her excuses as soon as she could so she could be alone.

Infertile.

The word tore at her insides with razor-sharp accuracy. A

kind of rage that she didn't know existed swept through her, and her mind began weaving stories together, looking for a target to blame.

Was it Mark himself? Did he know he couldn't father children? He certainly acted like Cassie was his. And yet he'd almost been reluctant to go through with the fertility test itself. Not to mention his absence today. The idea that he could be so cruel as to lie about the one thing she wanted more than anything coiled in her stomach, feeding off the rage and anger she felt.

But what if he didn't know? A tiny voice called her rampaging thoughts back. What if he was just as much a victim as she was? The doctor had talked Norah through the options of using donor sperm, and how it had helped many couples. She'd been prepared to go that route once. Before she'd met Mark – back when the tick of her biological clock had been her constant companion. But since meeting him, her dreams of motherhood were all connected to a tiny human with dark hair and eyes.

And what about Cassie? Unless she'd been an immaculate conception, Mark wasn't her father. And thanks to the fact Norah had pushed for him to go through this process, she was the one who had to tell him.

It would break him.

He loved Cassie and was fiercely protective of her. How would he take the news that she wasn't his? Shit. How would Cassie take the news? What if they both blamed her for it? After all, she was the messenger. The woman who'd come in and accidently destroyed the status quo of their lives.

Norah's temples pounded as the anger and disappointment suddenly flared up again as it occurred to her who the real culprit was.

Alice.

She must know the truth. She must've kept it hidden from Mark for all this time. The guilt and shame that Norah had carried with her for her part in the destruction of Mark and Alice's marriage lifted from her shoulders. After all, what kind of woman was Alice to hide the truth from her husband? And to then make Norah feel like the villain in the whole scenario. It was so calculated. So cruel.

And what would Alice do once her secret was revealed?

Norah shuddered. No doubt she'd lie about it. Or deny any knowledge. And Mark and Cassie would probably forgive her. Another blast of anger went through Norah at the unfairness of it all.

Alice shouldn't be allowed to get away with it, but that's exactly what would happen if it was left to Mark. He'd simply forgive her, like he always did.

Well, not this time.

She emptied her glass and reached for the bottle. Damn. It was empty. Unsteadily, she stood and retrieved a second bottle from the wine fridge. She didn't even bother to look at the label. It was cold and white. That was all she required.

She filled her glass as her phone pinged with a message. It was from one of the oncology nurses.

Billy Jenkins has just been removed for abusive behaviour.

Norah winced. At least she'd filed him as a potential problem, but hoped he hadn't been too threatening. It was unfortunately part of the job, and while there was a lot of support to protect staff, it wasn't always enough. She rolled her neck as another message came up on her phone.

This time it was Scott.

Arseholes really were like buses. None for ages, and then they all came at once.

Norah let out a drunken laugh at her own joke. She was numb now and problems like Billy Jenkins and Scott no longer had the power to scare her. They could do what they wanted. It was no skin off her nose.

She studied the text message.

There's been a problem. I need the next lot by tomorrow.

Christ. What did he think she was? A vending machine? Hysterical laughter bubbled up in her throat. Suddenly it seemed insignificant. Laughable really that she'd gone to all this trouble to hide her past, only to discover that Mark had secrets of his own. She took another gulp of wine, spilling a bit down her shirt.

No can do.

She hit send, not really caring. In fact, in the list of her problems, Scott was now only hitting page two.

His reply pinged back at her.

Not good enough. Tomorrow or else you'll be sorry.

Sorry?

What the hell did a kid like Scott know about making someone sorry? Irritation prickled her skin. The arrogance of youth to think that their clumsy attempts and threats could work. It was nothing compared to the complex barbs of pain that her relationships with Mark, Cassie and Alice Hargreaves had caused her. Now *there* was a masterclass in how to deliver a thousand tiny cuts, until there was nothing left.

Belatedly, Norah wished she hadn't gone to so much trouble to keep her own secrets. Because if she'd been honest about her mistakes, then maybe other people would have been honest with her. But she hadn't, and now here she was.

That's what sorry looked like.

She turned off her phone and tossed it onto the coffee table. Scott could do what the hell he wanted. They all could. She didn't give a shit. Tonight, she was going to drown her sorrows and tomorrow she'd figure out how to make everything right.

There was a faint scratching sound coming from the kitchen. It must be that overgrown tree by the window. It still hadn't been cut. She'd better call the man tomorrow.

The tree scraped again. Or was it the back door?

Fear prickled up her spine as a figure suddenly emerged from the kitchen. The flash of a knife blade caught in the light. Norah blinked as adrenaline surged through her. She needed to stand up. To move. To scream. But she was frozen to the spot, unable to move as the figure reached her.

No—

She tried to protest but it was lost as something sharp and icy cut through her skin. The wine glass fell from her hands and pain ricocheted along her body, along with numbing shock. And then nothing.

12

'Ryan, you come with me – a suspicious death has been called in at North Road,' Belinda Day said. It had already been a shit of a day, trying to get warrants for a drug raid. And now a potential murder. At least she'd managed to get home in the afternoon to take Hetty for a quick walk. The fact this was how her mind processed information made her wonder if she'd been in the job too long.

'Yes, ma'am.' The detective sergeant jumped to his feet. Ryan was one of her best, and unlike some who complained about murder and violent crimes impacting their social lives, Ryan was always ready to pitch in. They both put on their stab vests. Something they'd done ever since an officer had been killed while door-knocking for witnesses over in Kensington last month.

'The pathologist is on their way and so is SOCO; we need to get there before them.'

Belinda climbed into the driver's side of the car and Ryan joined her. Admiral Street Police Station was an ugly red brick building, wedged between Princes Park and Toxteth, with

Dingle and the Mersey flanking it from below. It also meant they never had to throw a stone very far to find trouble.

She started up the engine. It was ten at night and the street lights illuminated the rows of tiny terrace houses that stepped straight out onto the footpath. She drove past Aigburth and on to Grassendale Park, which was like another world. Tree-lined streets and huge detached houses – some of them not even broken up into apartments – filled the streets.

The one in question had a red-brick wall and heavy gates that were open. A security light was on, flooding the driveway and clearly displaying three cars parked up in front of the house. There was also a security camera, which might just make life a bit easier.

Belinda pulled up at the same time as two uniformed officers from her station. She knew them both.

'Fran, I want the scene cordoned off and no one is allowed to enter until the pathologist and SOCO have been here. We're going in.'

'Yes, ma'am.' Fran nodded as Belinda and Ryan walked up the bricked path that led up to a wide front door. It was open and sitting on the bottom step was a man. He was well dressed with dark hair, which was tousled from running his hands through it one too many times. At the sight of them, he stood up and tried for a smile. It didn't work. There were circles under his eyes, and a general sense of bewilderment that Belinda had seen many times before. The shock hadn't properly set in yet.

'Thank God you're here. It's Norah. My fiancée. S-she's through there in the sitting room.' He turned and began to walk towards it.

'What's your name, sir?' Belinda asked in a firm voice, designed to stop him. He turned back to her and blinked.

'Right. Sorry. Mark Hargraves, I live here with Norah. I'm the one who called.'

'I'm Detective Inspector Day and this is Detective Sergeant Walton. Please wait here, Mr Hargraves.' Belinda turned and gestured for Fran to come inside. The constable had just finished taping off the driveway to stop any vehicles from coming or going. Once she'd made the introductions, Belinda pulled on a pair of disposable gloves and headed into a large open-plan sitting room, with Ryan behind her.

A woman in her mid-to-late thirties was lying on the floor. Her shirt was drenched in blood from the numerous knife wounds in her chest. Her eyes were open and staring vacantly at the ceiling, while her blonde hair was splayed out around her. Even in such a shocking state, it was clear to see she was beautiful.

Belinda sucked in a breath, fighting the urge to recoil. It never got easier. No wonder the man had been in a state of shock.

'She's definitely dead.' Ryan's face was white, but she knew from experience that, like her, he wouldn't throw up or faint. Instead, he walked around the room, his focus intense.

'Any sign of a weapon?'

'Nothing that I can see, ma'am,' he finally answered after an initial search.

'Me neither. Go and check the rest of the house to make sure it's clear, and I'll get a statement.'

Ryan nodded and went towards the kitchen while she returned to the hallway, passing a pile of wedding magazines and fabric samples. Christ. He'd said 'fiancée'. Did that mean they'd been planning a wedding? Mr Hargraves was once again sitting on the bottom of the stairs, eyes shut. Fran looked over, a worried expression on her face.

'The pathologist's arrived, ma'am,' the constable said. 'Should I bring her through?'

'Yes, please,' Belinda said and then turned to the man. 'Mr Hargraves, I'm so sorry for your loss. I know this is a very difficult time, but we need to leave the house and let forensics do their work. We'd also like to question you regarding what happened here tonight.'

'I don't know anything. I arrived home and found Norah lying on the floor like that...' The words trailed off and tears formed in his eyes. He brushed them away with his hand as Fran returned with the pathologist and her team. It was Jerry. A small Irish woman with a no-nonsense approach.

Belinda had a quiet word with her as Ryan descended the stairs. He gave a quick shake of his head to indicate he hadn't found anything important. Once Jerry and the team had gone into the sitting room, Belinda waved Ryan over.

'Call for back-up and a car so that you can take Mr Hargraves back to the station. I'll follow soon.'

'Yes, ma'am.'

Several neighbours had arrived by the time the police car drew up, all looking cautiously from across the road as Ryan helped Mark Hargraves into the back seat, as if he was a child. Two uniformed officers were there to keep anyone from stepping in, and once Belinda was happy everything was under control, she left the crime scene.

Mark Hargraves was waiting for them in the interview room; his face showed signs of shock, with grim lines covering his brow. Belinda swallowed and she and Ryan sat down opposite him.

'Once again, we're very sorry for your loss, Mr Hargraves. This interview will be recorded.' She nodded at Ryan, who pressed the red button. 'Interview between DI Day, DS Walton, and...' She nodded at him. As if in a trance, he stared blankly at her before realising it was his cue.

'Mark Hargraves.'

'We'd like you to run through everything that happened this evening up to when you telephoned the police. Will you be up to doing this?'

'Yes. Yes, of course. I want to find out what happened. I can't believe she's not here. She's—' He paused, ran his fingers through his hair and sat upright. 'Sorry.'

'It's okay, we understand this is going to be very hard for you. Please could you tell us what time you arrived home this evening.'

'I was working late. I'd let Norah know to expect me after eight, but I think it was almost nine. I went to the front door, as usual, but the chain was on. We don't use it as much now we have a security system, but I guess she put it on.'

'So, what did you do when you found the chain on?' Belinda asked, trying to move him along.

'I went through the side gate and to the back door, which was open.'

'Was there any sign of forced entry?' Ryan asked.

'I don't think so. Nothing that stood out. I went into the kitchen and called Norah's name. But there was no reply. Then I walked into the sitting room. At first I couldn't work out why she'd be lying on the floor. Then I saw the blood. So much blood—'

He broke off, as if reliving the moment again. Then a jagged flash of pain rippled across his face and his entire body began to tremble. Belinda let out a soft sigh. The shock of stepping into a murder scene worked in different ways, and this wasn't the first time she'd seen someone move from a mechanical delivery through to suddenly falling apart.

'It's okay. Do you know what time it was?' she said in a softer voice. They'd already asked him that, but it was a good way to help take his mind away from the memories of what he'd found in the living room. Once upon a time Belinda had thought it cruel to interview someone so quickly after a crime, but they needed to get down the first recollections before the truth got obscured and twisted under the weight of too many thoughts and feelings.

Mark blinked, and, as she'd hoped, the despair left his eyes. 'Um. Around nine o'clock.'

'Good,' Belinda said in an encouraging voice before asking a few more closed questions to help get him more relaxed. Once his breathing settled, she gave him an encouraging smile. 'After you found the body, what did you do then?'

'Sorry, it's all a blur. It didn't seem real, so I went over and kissed her, thinking it was some kind of joke. But her skin was cold, and—' His voice cracked. 'I felt for a pulse. But there was nothing, and her eyes... I could tell she must be dead. So I phoned the police and waited in the hall. I couldn't bear to see her in that state.'

'Did you notice anything out of place in the room?' Ryan asked.

'No. At least I don't think so.'

'And does anyone else live in the house with you?'

At this, he looked up, mouth wide. 'Christ. Cassie. I didn't think to look upstairs. Oh, God. What if—'

'It's okay. I checked the house and there was no one else there,' Ryan assured him and some of the panic left Mark's face.

'Who's Cassie?' Belinda asked.

'M-my daughter. She's seventeen years old. My ex-wife and I have joint custody, but lately Cassie's been turning up whenever she feels like it, so I'm never quite sure if she's going to be there or not. What if she goes to the house?'

'Then one of the PCs will bring her here. What was the relationship like between your daughter and your fiancée?'

He gave her a sharp look. 'They were very close. Cassie loved Norah. We all did.'

'Okay.' Belinda decided to move the questions in a different direction so that they could get a full picture of the timeline. 'You said that you were late home. Where had you been?'

'In Manchester. I had a series of meetings. They'd been postponed and rescheduled at the last minute.'

'Can anyone vouch for you?'

'Yes, Charlie Wilson is a consultant, and was with me at all of the meetings.'

'And Norah knew about the meetings?'

A flash of guilt stole over his face. Interesting. What was it about the meetings that made him react like that?

'I had my assistant call her. We had an appointment at the clinic. We were both meant to attend, and I knew she'd be disappointed,' he said as he rubbed his wrists, making her think he was close to losing himself in anguish again.

'Clinic?' Belinda raised an eyebrow.

He paused before answering, his eyes not meeting hers. 'We're trying IVF and were due to get the results of my sperm sample today. Norah wanted a baby.'

'Didn't you?'

'It's complicated. I already have a teenage daughter from my previous marriage. But Norah really wanted a child, so I agreed.'

'Even though you didn't want one,' Belinda said, gently pushing.

'It wasn't like that. And why does it matter, now? She's gone and...' A sob erupted from him.

Belinda passed over the box of tissues that had been sitting on the table and made a mental note to ask if the clinic results had been found at the house.

'Had Norah been worried about anything or anyone?'

'Not at all. She was looking forward to the wedding. She was a bit stressed but that's only natural with so much to organise and she'd insisted on doing everything herself.'

'When was the wedding meant to take place?' she asked, trying to keep her voice as neutral as possible.

'The twentieth of May,' he said before his face crumpled again.

'So, she'd been stressed recently, but you put it all down to the wedding,' Belinda reiterated.

'And work, of course. She's a nurse practitioner at Alder Hey. In oncology. It's not an easy job, as you can probably guess. Kids and cancer – pretty heart-wrenching.'

Belinda inwardly winced. The media were going to eat this up. A beautiful nurse about to be married, only to be brutally murdered in her own home.

'We'll need to get contact numbers for her workplace, your colleague in Manchester, the name of the IVF clinic, your daughter, and Norah's immediate family.'

'O-of course. Her parents are dead, and she only has one brother. Felix is a few years older than her and is here in Liverpool. They're very close. Is it okay if I call him first? He's going to be devastated.'

She nodded. 'Please do. And if you could call your daughter as well. Is there somewhere you can stay? You won't be able to

go back to the house, because it's a crime scene.' It was unnecessary and Mark's eyes filled with horror at the idea.

'I can check into a hotel somewhere. I'll need to talk to
Cassie first, and let Alice know.'

'Alice?' Ryan raised an eyebrow. 'Is that your ex-wife?'

'Yes, we co-parent and have a good relationship,' he said,
fatigue filling his voice. Belinda knew that any more questions
were going to have to wait. She nodded for Ryan to finish the
recording and the pair of them left the interview room so that
Mark could have some privacy with the calls.

'What do you think, ma'am? Did he do it? It's usually the
husband or boyfriend.'

'Too early to say. Though he's certainly in the frame,'
Belinda said. It was always hard to judge a person based on
how they reacted to a traumatic event, but the way he'd looked
away when he mentioned the business meeting definitely had
her policing instincts tingling. Especially since he seemed to be
having second thoughts about going through IVF treatment
with his younger fiancée.

They waited fifteen minutes and returned to the interview
room. Mark was hunched over the table, rocking backwards
and forward. He glanced up when they entered.

'I can't get hold of Cassie so I'm going to stay at Alice's place.
That way we can tell her together. Will someone take me home
to pick up my car?'

'Forensics will need to check it over. I'll ask one of the officers to take you directly to Alice's house. But first we need to get
your fingerprints so we can eliminate them from what we find
in your house. Oh, and we'll need access to the security
cameras I saw on the property.'

Mark nodded, but it was doubtful he heard her.

'Here's my card. I know this is a lot right now, but if you

think of anything else, or have questions, call me. Also, please don't leave town without first checking with me.'

'I'm not going anywhere,' he said in a weary voice. He was the very picture of a devastated man in shock at the death of his fiancée, but Belinda had learned long ago that how people thought and acted were two very different things.

For now Mark Hargraves was definitely at the top of her suspect list.

* * *

'Hugo, no,' Alice said as the little dog bolted to the door. She should have locked him in the kitchen until after Mark had arrived. But she'd been too stunned as a police car had driven up outside her house and Mark had stepped out of it. His phone call half an hour earlier had been surreal. Unbelievable. And she'd almost thought it was a terrible dream. But as the police car slid back into the night, her hope had been shattered.

Norah was dead. Murdered.

She'd immediately called Cassie, but her daughter wasn't picking up. It wasn't uncommon, especially when she was out with Deb. Normally Alice would have gone into panic mode and called Andrea, Deb's mother. But right now, she was almost grateful that Cassie wasn't here. It would let Mark have a chance to digest everything before having to tell their daughter.

She picked Hugo up in her arms and opened the door. Mark's face was leached of colour and his eyes were unfocused. He looked terrible, but as she reached out to hug him, he held up a hand to stop her. Alice caught herself. Mark was a stoic and hated not being in control of his emotions. If she touched him, he might retreat, making his grief more difficult. Or he might lose control and resent her for it.

The dog wriggled at the sight of him, and Alice lowered Hugo to the ground so he could sniff Mark's leg.

Her throat tightened and tears stung her eyes. 'I'm so sorry. Come in.'

He seemed happy for her to guide him through to the small sitting room, where he automatically sat down in the armchair. Hugo jumped up on his lap.

She'd made a pot of tea and it was sitting in between them. Without asking, she poured a cup and held up a bottle of whisky. It would help with the shock. He managed to nod, and she splashed in a generous amount before making one for herself.

'Have you heard from Cassie?' she asked after handing him the drink. 'I've left numerous messages.'

He shook his head. 'No. But I did call Felix. He's in shock, so I'm not sure how much he processed. The police were going to talk to him later, so I won't go around to see him until tomorrow.'

'Speaking of the police, do they have any idea what happened?'

'I don't think so. The pathologist was just arriving at the house when we went down to the station for questioning.'

Alice frowned. 'What do you mean? Why couldn't they just talk to you at the house?'

'They needed a timeline, and to rule me out of the investigation. I still can't believe this has happened. I don't understand how someone could do this to Norah. She was such a kind and gentle person.'

Alice had to stop herself from coughing.

Norah might have looked like that on the surface but underneath she seemed to have been just as fucked-up as the rest of them. Or at least capable of keeping secrets hidden.

Alice still had no idea who Norah had been fighting with in Sefton Park. Or what it was about. But the man definitely hadn't been part of Norah and Mark's usual circle of friends. And Alice should know, since his friends had once been her friends too.

Then there was the fight between Norah and Mark in the kitchen. Mark had underplayed it, but Alice had seen the crystal swan that Norah had hurled at him. If it had hit him, there would've been some serious damage.

Was it someone from Norah's past who'd killed her?

Or was it Mark himself? After all, he'd been having second thoughts about the baby. No. She cut off that thought. Alice had known Mark for almost twenty years, and he was the least likely killer she'd ever met. Even she had more potential to kill someone—

She stiffened as it suddenly hit. Oh, shit. What if the police thought she'd done it? After all, she was the ex-wife who hadn't exactly hidden her animosity. Not to mention how many times she'd followed Norah. The latest one being today, when she'd bumped into Felix.

It would look even worse if Mark found out he was infertile.

Had Norah told him the results?

'W-when did you last hear from her?'

A flash of guilt crossed his face. 'At breakfast. We were meant to go to the clinic together, but something came up. I... I wimped out of telling her and asked Carol to do it. Apparently, Norah wasn't happy about it.'

Alice wasn't going to admit that she knew all about his absence. 'I'm sure she would have understood. S-so you didn't speak to her at all today?'

He shook his head. 'I called at around eight; there was no answer. Oh God. What if she was already dead when I phoned?

I should've done something, I—' He leaned forward, resting his head in his hands.

'Don't do that to yourself. You had no way of knowing.'

'But I should have,' he insisted. 'We were meant to be getting married. Aren't you meant to know these things? What am I going to do? How am I going to live without her?'

Like a bursting dam, he let out a sob as the emotion overtook him.

His despair was like a knife to the heart, leaving her feeling like a fool.

All this time she'd harboured the secret fantasy that he would come back to her. That if he saw Norah for who she truly was, he'd realise just how great his first marriage had been.

But it wasn't true.

Norah's death hadn't changed anything. Did that mean it had all been for nothing?

He continued to sob and Alice automatically leaned over the chair to wrap her arms around him. It was how she used to comfort Cassie when she was young. It came as easy to her as breathing. Because she'd always given too much, and never received enough back. It was something she was used to.

'It will be okay. Just cry. It will make you feel better. I'm here for you. I can help with any arrangements. Anything you need. You know that.' She stroked his hair, and he relaxed in her arms.

'Thank you. And thanks for letting me stay. I know it's a lot to ask.'

'We're still family,' she said as the front door slammed. Cassie. Alice jumped up. 'I'll go and bring her in. Are you feeling up to it?'

Mark took a shuddering breath. 'She needs to hear it from me.'

Alice squeezed his arm and walked into the hall just as Cassie lurched in. Her hair, which was usually poker-straight, was hanging limply around her face, while her mascara had fallen under her eyes. None of it was helped by the fact she was carrying one of her shoes and reeked of beer.

What the hell?

'You're drunk?' Alice said before she could stop herself.

'Don't start lecturing.' Cassie stumbled to the right and leaned against the wall. 'It's not like you don't sit here every night tossing back the vino.'

Alice flinched. 'That's not the point. I need you to sober up. Your dad's in the lounge. S-something's happened...' She trailed off, suddenly feeling exhausted from the knowledge she'd have to witness his pain all over again. Knowing that it would crawl along her skin and clog up her throat until she was hollow and lifeless. Nothing. Because she'd never been good enough for him. And, finally, she had proof.

'What? Don't tell me the wedding's off.' Cassie giggled.

'No. It's something else,' Alice said with a forced smile, ignoring her instincts to run away and cry. She needed to be strong for Cassie and be there for Mark, in case he somehow did have a change of heart. 'Come in. I'll make you some coffee. There's something we need to tell you...'

13

Cassie opened her eyes and immediately regretted it. Shafts of sunlight stung her retinas and she immediately put her hands up to shield them. Why were her curtains open? She cautiously sat up, head pounding. There was a vile taste in her mouth and her stomach churned.

A glass of water was next to her bed, and she gratefully swallowed it. She leaned back against her pillow and waited until the nausea passed. Most of the night was a blur. Deb had handed her shot after shot and Cassie could barely remember what pub they'd been in, let alone how she'd got home. All she could remember was that Scott had been a no-show, and that when she'd arrived home, her mum was there by the door, waiting to start moaning at her again. Except—

Oh God. Norah.

Ice ran down her spine as it came back to her. Norah was dead. She'd been murdered. Her dad had hardly been able to speak so Alice had done most of the talking. Not that there had been much to say. Her dad had found Norah in the sitting room covered in blood.

'Who would do something like that?' he'd said, momentarily coming out of his stupor. 'Everybody loved her.'

That was when Cassie had started crying and Alice had herded her up to bed and put a damp towel on her forehead.

But now, as the bright light streamed in, Cassie couldn't avoid the terrible thought going through her mind. What had Scott and Norah been talking about the night he went over there?

Her stomach churned. It was bad enough that Norah was dead. But the idea Scott might somehow be involved was too terrible for words. She'd called and messaged him several times during the night, but he hadn't replied to any of them.

There had to be an explanation.

She picked up her phone.

There were over fifty notifications from various friends wanting to know if she was okay. One of them had linked to the *Liverpool Echo*, which had run a story of a murdered woman. It hadn't mentioned any names or addresses but did say Grassendale Park. She didn't reply to any of them. Instead, she scrolled down to see if Scott had tried to contact her.

He hadn't.

Her stomach plummeted as she went onto his social media accounts. None of them had been updated since yesterday morning. It didn't mean anything. He could've gone out and lost his phone. He could've been dragged into some stupid adventure with Aaron and Ned. There were a million reasons, and none of them ended up in murder.

Bile rose up her throat and Cassie scrambled to her feet and charged into the bathroom before being violently sick. Her throat burned and her limbs were weak as she staggered back to her bedroom. There was a logical explanation for it all. She knew there was. After all, just because they'd had a fight, it didn't make him a killer.

And the fact he'd been arguing with Norah the night before her murder? A small voice whispered in her ear. *Stop it*, Cassie retorted before swinging a mental sledgehammer at the voice.

Scott wasn't a killer, and that's all there was to it. She tried his number, but it went straight to voicemail. Her finger hovered over the call icon but before she could hit it again, there was a gentle tap on the door.

'Cassie, are you awake?'

'Yeah.'

The door opened and her mum walked in. She was pale and looked tired. 'How are you feeling?'

'Like crap.' She put down her phone and let the reality settle back in around her. Someone she knew was dead. Norah. Tears prickled her eyes. 'I just saw the article. It's really true, isn't it?'

Her mum sat on the edge of the bed. 'I'm so sorry. Your dad stayed here last night. He's in shock. It's such an awful thing to happen.'

'I still can't believe it. W-what do the police say? Do they know who did it?'

'Not yet. They called your dad this morning with more questions and said they'll be in touch with him today. He's shattered.' Her mum moved closer and pulled Cassie in for a hug. And suddenly the world unwound, and she was little again. Back when things were simple, and everything was fixed with a kiss and a biscuit. Cassie's chest heaved and she pressed herself into a curled-up ball in Alice's lap. The familiar scent and the gentle fingers that stroked her back just made Cassie cry harder.

Everything was so fucked-up. Yesterday Norah had been a real life, actual person, and today she wasn't. All the clothes in her cupboard were now useless. Just like the make-up in the bathroom, and the chocolate biscuits that she kept hidden in the laundry behind the spare pegs.

The tears streamed down Cassie's face. It had been sad when her grandfather had died. But he'd been old, so in a way it seemed okay. But Norah wasn't old. Yet, for whatever reason, that didn't matter. She was dead, and someone had killed her.

Someone who might be Cassie's boy—

No. She sat up and dried her tears. She wouldn't say his name. Because it couldn't be true. She just needed to find him, and then he'd tell her where he'd been, and what he'd done.

'I can't face school today. What if people know? I can't bear the idea of them looking at me. Or asking questions.'

'Of course not. It's a lot to take in. Your dad's gone around to see Felix but should be back soon.'

'Oh God. Poor Felix.' Cassie's hand flew to her mouth. It wasn't until she'd started working for him that she'd discovered just how close he was to Norah. It was hard to imagine how upset he must be.

'I know. It's terrible to lose a sibling,' her mum said, her own eyes glazing over, obviously thinking about Jasmine. Then she coughed, as if trying to snap herself out of it. 'Would you like some breakfast?'

Cassie recoiled at the thought of food. 'Not right now. I think I need to go for a walk and clear my head,' she said, not daring to mention Scott's name.

'Just don't go too far. I know your dad will want to see you.' Alice got to her feet and left the room.

Cassie stared after her. Alice hadn't even told her off for

getting drunk. If only she could always be so understanding, then maybe Cassie's life wouldn't be so difficult.

She got herself up, had a quick shower. The hot water helped clear her head and she dragged on the first pair of jeans she could find, along with a T-shirt. For once she didn't care about her wet hair, stopping only to cram it under a cap. She ordered an Uber from her phone and arranged for it to collect her around the corner.

Fifteen minutes later, it pulled up outside Scott's house. She'd tried calling him several more times on the drive over, with no answer. Her own phone continued to blow up, but she set it to silent.

Scott's house was a three-bedroom semi-detached house with flowerpots leading the way up the front path. She knocked on the door, but there was no reply. Where was he? She sat down on the front doorstep and rested her head in her hands.

She needed to think but her brain felt like it was filled with fog. Why had she got so drunk last night?

'Cassie?' Scott's mum appeared from around the side of the house, holding a basket of weeds. There were brown smudges on her cheeks and in one hand was a small trowel. 'What are you doing here?'

'Hello, Mrs Williams, I came round to speak to Scott.' She'd always liked Scott's mum, who was a lot nicer than his stuck-up dad, whose expectations of Scott were so unfair. At the mention of her son's name, Mrs Williams's eyes filled with worry.

'He hasn't been here since yesterday morning. He borrowed Frank's car without asking and the pair of them had a huge fight. The problem is that they're both so similar,' she said, dabbing at her eyes with a tissue. 'Every time it happens, Scott disappears for a few days, but he always comes home. Now that you two are together, I hoped he was with you.'

Oh. Cassie hadn't realised how much she'd been counting on finding him at home, with a completely logical explanation about where he'd been, and what his fight with Norah had been about.

But if he hadn't been home since yesterday morning, then where the hell was he? And more importantly... what had he done?

'I haven't heard from him since yesterday,' she said as the video image of Scott smirking as he walked out of the kitchen, leaving Norah looking sick with worry, played in her mind.

He wasn't involved. He *couldn't be.*

Mrs Williams seemed to pick up on her worry. 'Has something happened?'

Cassie swallowed. She doubted it would be much longer before everyone knew Norah's name. 'M-my dad's fiancée was murdered last night.'

For a moment there was silence between them before Mrs Williams let out a little wail. 'You poor thing. Come inside and I'll make us a cup of tea.'

It was more of a command and Cassie let herself be led into the house and settled into one of the chairs in the sitting room while Scott's mum bustled around the kitchen. She came out several minutes later, balancing a large tray, two cups and a plate of digestives. As she poured, Cassie told her everything she knew. It wasn't much.

'So terrible. Scott always said how lovely Norah was. And to think the wedding was only two weeks away.'

Cassie toyed with the teacup and tried to imagine Scott saying that Norah was lovely. She failed. Even before she'd seen the video footage, Scott had always had a mocking tone when Norah's name had been brought up. Saint Norah. That's what he called her. Cassie stiffened and pushed away the tea.

He'd accused Norah of leaving the drugs in the car to break them up. Was that what the argument had been about? Had Scott gone around and confronted Norah? But if so, why hadn't he told her?

'I just wish I knew where he was,' Cassie said.

'He'll be bunking down with someone. Probably with Aaron and Ned.' Scott's mother folded her arms, eyes darkening. It was obvious she didn't like the pair either. 'Though there's no point asking them since they will just lie through their teeth.'

'So, what should we do?' Cassie asked.

'The same thing I always have to do,' she said, voice tired. 'Wait until he returns.'

It was three o'clock when Belinda walked into the incident room. The walls were bright green, which she could only presume was meant to exude an air of calmness. She just hoped that the powers that be hadn't paid some fancy consultant too much money for the recommendation. Her team was based in the far corner, but they all looked up as she reached the whiteboard.

'I've just spoken with the pathologist. Cause of death was fatal stabbing through the chest, breaking the ribs. There is bruising from the entry point where the hilt of the knife was rammed against the body. There are multiple other stab wounds that were inflicted after the victim had died. In other words, it was a frenzied attack. Our time frame is between seven and nine p.m.' Belinda wrote it up on the incident board along with Norah's name, age and address. 'Forensics couldn't find the murder weapon, so I want that at the top of the list.'

'It could be in a nearby garden,' Ryan mused before glancing up at the map on the wall. 'Or the Mersey. The house is less than five minutes from the promenade. The murderer could have just tossed it into the water.'

'Then we need to find out when it's low tide, as well as begin a search of the nearby gardens and streets. I want that weapon,' Belinda said. 'The DCI wants to do a press conference tomorrow morning, and release names, which means we need something to go on. Tell me what we've got. Starting with Mark Hargraves.'

'Yes, ma'am.' Cheryl Reeves held up a wad of paper. She'd originally been an accountant before joining the force at age forty-five as a PC. 'He grew up in Crosby, where the family own a lot of land, and went to Merchant Taylors' before reading economics at Oxford. He inherited the house from an aunt and as well as the family money, he's privately wealthy from floating his company. Net worth seems to be about twenty million pounds.'

'In other words, he's bloody rich.' Belinda rubbed her head. Her fears about this becoming a high-profile case were now confirmed. 'What else do we have?'

'I've just come back from Alder Hey. There was an incident the day Norah was killed. The estranged father of one of her patients had come in and caused a scene. Billy Jenkins has been in and out of prison for burglary, drugs and battery. Norah wasn't there at the time, but he was mouthing off, saying that the victim was incompetent because his daughter, who has cancer, had a reaction to a certain drug.'

'Interesting. Did he make any direct threats against Norah?'

Ryan flipped through his notes and shook his head. 'No. He kicked a wheelchair and accused the NHS of covering things up, but there wasn't anything personal. According to the matron, there was no validity to the claims, and Norah had logged it as a possible threat the previous day based on what the ex-wife had told her.'

'Have you spoken to Billy?'

'I've sent some uniformed officers out to track him down. Now we have a time of death, I'll instruct them to get an alibi. I also asked if the victim had been acting strangely, but the matron said it was difficult to tell because working with young cancer patients was never a walk in the park. Her words, not mine.'

Belinda wasn't surprised. In her experience, most people were too caught up in their own dramas to really pay attention to the people around them. Still, she drew a line out on the incident board and jotted it in. Then she turned to Amy, who'd only joined the team last year but had a meticulous eye for detail. 'How are you going with her mobile phone?'

'As you know, the messages had all been cleared,' she said before grinning. 'But whoever did it forgot to delete them from the cloud. I'm just going through them now. And... it looks like our victim was being blackmailed.'

Belinda's eyebrows shot up. This kind of breakthrough wasn't something they usually found on day one of the investigation. 'Do we have a name?'

Amy shook her head. 'Not yet. They were all from a burner phone so I can't trace the number myself. There are twenty-three in all, starting two weeks ago. They were demanding fentanyl. There are several photographs as well. One of Norah at a park, and another of her standing in the kitchen. And get this. They have given her a time and place to meet. It was just over a week ago at a statue in Huyton Village. I'm looking into CCTV surveillance now and as soon as I confirm it, I'll put in the request for it to be traced.'

'Excellent.' Belinda nodded. 'And we need to go back to Alder Hey and see if any drugs are missing. Also, I want to know as soon as we have footage. If we can link her to meeting anyone, that will narrow things down. And speaking of footage, what about the home security system?'

'Still working on it, ma'am.' Tim Ramsey looked up from his computer. 'Considering Mark Hargraves is so keen to help us, he didn't seem happy about handing over the access details to the account. But I've got it now and am going through it. It goes back for three months. Unfortunately, all the footage from yesterday has been wiped.'

Belinda swore. Of course it had.

Still, there might be plenty of other things in there, though getting them could be a long slog. 'Okay, so we've got a possible blackmailer and a disgruntled father from the hospital – one who has a police record. Not to mention an ex-wife in danger of losing out on millions of pounds if the wedding goes ahead. I want us moving quickly on all lines of enquiry, because this is the kind of case that will start to cause us headaches if we don't get answers soon.'

She turned back to Ryan. 'Any updates on the brother? What was his name again?'

'Felix,' Ryan told her and shook his head. 'He lives down at the docks, but when I went this morning, he wasn't up to speaking about it. Doesn't help that the bloody *Echo* had it splashed across the front page. Poor bastard. I've arranged for him to come in first thing tomorrow.'

'Good. I'll sit in on it. If this is blackmail, he might have some insight. And we're going to need Mark Hargraves to come in again,' Belinda said as Tim let out a long whistle. She turned to him. 'Something you want to share with us?'

Tim gave an embarrassed cough. 'Sorry, ma'am. I didn't

mean to interrupt, but I've just found something on the home security footage. I think you're going to want to see it...'

14

The front door slammed.

'Cassie, is that you?' Alice called from the kitchen. She should never have let her daughter go out. Anything could have happened. What if the killer decided to target Cassie as well? The thought sent a surge of panic racing through her.

She swallowed it down and walked into the hallway. Hugo followed her.

'Yeah.' Cassie bent down and picked up the little dog, before pressing her cheek into Hugo's soft fur.

'Where did you go?'

'Nowhere,' Cassie said, not looking up. It was a lie, but Alice didn't try to push it. Not with everything else that was going on.

'Are you hungry? Some food could help. We could talk about what's happened.'

'Mum,' Cassie snapped. Hugo let out a small bark and wriggled back out of her arms. 'I'm going up to my room.'

'Sorry.' Alice held up both hands as Cassie trudged up the stairs. 'Text if you want anything.'

There was no answer and she sighed. Cassie hadn't even

asked if Mark had come back. Alice returned to the kitchen and continued with her lacklustre attempt at cleaning. Something she only attempted when her writing was going badly.

Or someone had been murdered.

She picked up the cloth and returned her attention to the stove top. The police had finished going through the house, so Mark had gone to collect some clothes and check into a hotel. She'd tried to convince him to stay another night or two at her place, but he'd been adamant. Norah's name hadn't been mentioned in the papers yet, but it was only a matter of time, and he didn't want to bring any unnecessary attention to her and Cassie.

She would have been touched if he hadn't sounded so bleak. And if it hadn't been so obvious that he wanted to be alone. To properly grieve.

Buzzzzz.

The doorbell cut through her thoughts. She removed the rubber gloves she'd been wearing, took a quick look in the window at her reflection and patted down her hair, before answering the door.

Standing outside was a tall woman with short hair. Next to her was a man in a neat shirt, and trousers. Alice frowned and searched their hands for a bible. The last thing she wanted was to be preached at by missionaries.

'Alice Hargraves?' the woman said, her voice sounding familiar, and suddenly Alice made the connection. Of course. They'd met in the park the other day. As if on cue, Hugo poked his nose out, and, recognising a friendly face, gave a little bark.

'Yes.' Alice frowned. What was she doing here? They hadn't exchanged numbers, let alone home addresses.

'I'm DI Belinda Day and this is my colleague DS Walton.

We want to ask you and your daughter a few questions about the death of Norah Richmond. Please may we come inside?'

The police? The woman from the park was a detective?

Alice's grip tightened on the door. Part of her had known this would happen, but now they were here, it was still a shock. And what if they found out that she'd been following Norah? How would that make her look? Would Felix tell them she'd been outside the clinic? God, she hoped not.

'Of course, why don't you come into the kitchen, and I'll make us all a drink, and then I'll get Cassie.'

'Thanks for the offer but we'd rather get straight on with the interview. We have a lot of people to talk to.' Gone was the friendly dog-owner she'd met in the park. The DI clearly had no problems setting boundaries and making sure her orders were followed. At any other time, Alice might've been impressed.

'Yes, I understand. The lounge is through there.' She pointed to the door on the left. Not that it was hard to find in such a small house. 'I'll get Cassie.'

Alice hurried upstairs, knocked on her daughter's door and went straight in, without waiting for an answer. Cassie was sitting on her bed, laptop in front of her. At the sight of Alice, she snapped it shut.

'Jesus. What are you doing? You can't just—'

'The police are here. They want to ask us both a few questions.'

Colour crept up Cassie's neck. 'T-the police? But we've got nothing to do with what happened to Norah.'

'I'm sure they'll be asking questions of everyone who knew her. To get a picture of her life. Don't worry, it will be fine.' Alice forced her voice to sound calm. It seemed to work, and Cassie stood up.

Downstairs, she quickly made the introductions and the two officers sat on the sofa while Cassie took the armchair, leaving Alice to drag in one of the kitchen chairs.

'Thank you both for your time. We appreciate how difficult this must be,' DI Day said before turning to Alice. 'How did you get on with Norah?'

She swallowed. Of course they were going to ask that question first. After all, Norah was the younger, glamorous replacement while Alice was just the old, bitter ex-wife. And she'd spoken about it when they'd first met at Sefton Park. What had she said? Hopefully it wasn't too incriminating.

'Obviously we were never going to be best friends. My marriage fell apart because of her. But Mark and I always swore to put Cassie first, so I made an effort. Not that we saw each other very often.'

'When was the last time you saw her?'

Alice swallowed hard, trying to work out how to answer. She couldn't say at Alder Hey Children's Hospital, or when she'd been spying through the kitchen window when they'd been fighting. No. She pushed that particular thought from her mind. Mark wasn't capable of hurting anyone. Then she realised they were still waiting for an answer.

'Um... sometimes she'd be in the car when Mark picked Cassie up. But the last time we spoke was probably two months ago when I bumped into her at the supermarket.'

'Did you notice anything? How was she acting?'

'Like anyone trying to buy food on the way home from work.' Alice shrugged, not wanting to mention she'd been too busy jealously looking at Norah's hair and flawless complexion to notice her mood.

'And yesterday between the hours of seven and nine, where were you?'

'I was here. I illustrate picture books, and I'm on a deadline so I was up in the attic working.'

'Can anyone vouch for you?'

'No. I was alone,' Alice admitted. It sounded so damning, and a tiny spark of anger filled her. She wasn't single by choice, and yet here was another way she was being punished, just because her husband no longer found her desirable. Belinda Day's shrewd eyes narrowed, as if somehow reading Alice's mind. Shit. 'I guess the dog doesn't count.'

'I'm afraid not,' the DI answered in a dry voice. 'Now, Cassie, we'd like to ask you a few questions. How did you get on with Norah?'

Cassie's eyes were wide, and Alice clamped down on her lip. She hated this. Hated that her precious daughter had to be involved in something this nefarious. Belinda seemed to notice, and she gave Cassie an encouraging smile.

'You're not in any trouble.'

'She was okay, I guess. I mean it was a bit obvious she was trying to suck up to me.'

'Did you notice her being different recently? Did she seem preoccupied at all?'

Cassie sucked in a breath. 'No. Not really. Well, she was busy with the wedding, but she seemed the same.'

'Where were you last night between seven and nine o'clock?'

Cassie's face went red, and she looked to Alice, as if unsure what to do. But there was no point lying since the police were bound to find out. She gave Cassie an encouraging nod.

'I went out to the pub with my friend, Deb. W-we drank a bit much, and... well, I don't remember much.'

'I see. And was there a reason you were out *under-age* drinking on a Thursday night? Did something happen to upset you? Did you have a fight with someone? Your boyfriend, perhaps? Or Norah?'

'What the hell?' Alice snapped before she could stop herself.

'Is there a problem?' The DI raised a brow, but Alice was past caring. She'd thought this was meant to be a simple interview to get more background. Instead, they were trying to bait Cassie into saying something. Over her dead body.

'You tell me. Should we have a lawyer present?'

'Not unless you feel you need one,' DI Day countered in a cool voice as she pulled out her phone. She jabbed at the screen a couple of times until she found what she wanted, and then held it out to Cassie. 'Perhaps you'd both like to look at this, and then we can continue.'

Alice refused to look at it; instead, she studied Cassie's face. Despite the splotches of colour, her daughter's eyes were wide and startled. It was an expression she'd seen enough times over the years when Cassie had experienced night terrors. 'It's okay, I'm here.'

Cassie took a shuddering breath and some of the fear left her eyes. 'It's alright. It was just a surprise.'

DI Day's mouth pressed together. She almost looked contrite. 'I'm sorry. That wasn't my intention. But I would like you to look at this. It's from your father's security cameras.'

Alice had forgotten all about the cameras. She'd been so careful to avoid them when she'd been there the other day but hadn't thought they'd be recording other things. Perhaps even the murder. Shit. She spun back to the DI.

'Is this anything graphic?'

'Absolutely not. Please. Just look at the video.'

Alice finally nodded to the DI, who hit play. It was a grainy video of Norah standing in the kitchen. It looked like she was cooking. Cassie appeared in the clip and they exchanged a few words, but there was no audio. The clip played on, and Alice was about to protest that it didn't prove anything, when suddenly a familiar figure walked into the frame.

Scott.

She'd always known he was trouble.

'Cassie?' Alice turned to her daughter.

'Do you know who the person speaking to Norah is?' DI said.

Cassie nodded. 'He's my boyfriend, Scott Williams.'

'Was he in the habit of speaking to your father's fiancée alone?'

'No,' Cassie said quickly before her voice broke. 'I don't know.'

'And where is he now?'

Cassie's face crumpled. 'I went to see him this morning, but he hadn't been home. His mum didn't want to call the police.'

'Probably because her son's a criminal,' Alice snapped, folding her arms to try and help herself calm down. She'd always known Scott was trouble, but Mark kept telling her that it would run its course. And now look where it had ended up. Her jaw tightened in fury. It still wasn't clear how Scott was involved, but the fact the police had felt it necessary to show the clip to Cassie meant that he *was*.

And that was enough to make sure he never saw her daughter again.

'Mum. He's not. You just don't know him like I do.'

'Do you have his mobile number and address?' DI Day cut in before Alice could say anything else. Cassie rattled off his number without looking at her phone, and then gave them the address. DS Walton jotted it all down. 'Has Scott ever used a different phone number?'

'No. Why would he?' she asked but didn't get an answer.

'And how did you feel just now when you saw your father's fiancée talking to your boyfriend?'

At this, Cassie's face drained of colour – a sight that sent another flicker of fury through Alice's spine. Though this time it was directed at the police. Were they seriously suggesting that Cassie was somehow involved?

'That's enough.' She stood up, hands clenched at either side of her.

'Of course.' DI Day didn't seem at all put out by Alice's reaction, and she inwardly winced. Had she just somehow made everything worse? But how was that possible? Norah was dead, and the police seemed determined to scrutinise everyone, including her daughter.

She had a terrible feeling that it wasn't going to end well for any of them. Especially if they found out the truth.

15

'It's clear that Alice Hargraves isn't a fan of the daughter's boyfriend,' Ryan said. 'But it's hard to get a take on what she really thought about Norah Richmond.'

'She isn't the first ex-wife to hide her feelings behind a polite smile.' Belinda pulled out of the tiny side street where Alice lived and headed back down Lark Lane. 'I actually met her a couple of weeks ago at the park walking the dog. We got to talking and she was definitely bitter about the divorce.'

'Enough to kill?'

Belinda shrugged. 'People have killed for less. And what about the daughter? She seemed pretty upset about the footage.'

When Tim had discovered it, he'd also found a time and date stamp of when it had been viewed in the cloud. And while it was all from the same account, the tech guys had confirmed the phone that accessed it. An older-model Samsung. It didn't belong to Mark or his daughter, and, according to Scott's mother, Scott owned an iPhone.

Mark Hargraves had agreed to come in and see them. He'd

been clearly shocked at the footage, and even more shocked when they told him that someone else had already viewed it. According to him, no one else had access. He'd also identified Scott Williams, but they'd wanted to see Cassie's reaction to it.

'Question is, was Cassie upset about the boyfriend, or the father's fiancée?' Ryan pondered.

'Hard to say. But it doesn't look great, especially if she claims to have been drunk. We'll need to find out exactly where she was.' Belinda drove around Sefton Park towards Scott Williams's house. They still had no idea what he and Norah had discussed, or if it was connected to whoever was blackmailing Norah. Which was why they were heading there now. They didn't have a search warrant but hoped that the parents would allow them to look through his room. And to get an update on his whereabouts.

It was a smart semi-detached house though not quite in league with Mark Hargraves's mansion. They walked up the short path and rang the bell. A woman in her forties opened the door. The dark smudges under her eyes suggested she hadn't been sleeping much.

'I'm DI Day and this is DS Walton,' Belinda said, holding out her warrant card. 'Are you Mrs Williams?'

The woman shut her eyes, as if bracing herself. 'Is this about Scott? D-do you have news?'

Belinda paused as she connected the drained face and worried tone to Mrs Williams's question. 'Were you expecting news?'

The other woman rubbed a hand across her eyes. 'I don't know. He hasn't been home... and when you said you were police, I'd hoped...' She trailed off, her voice suggesting it wasn't the first time she'd opened the door to find a detective wanting to discuss her son.

'I'm sorry, we don't have news of his whereabouts, but we need to talk to him about a conversation he had with Norah Richmond.'

'Cassie came around earlier and told me about what happened. That poor, poor woman,' she said, then paused. 'You don't think that Scott's involved in this, do you?'

'We'd like to come inside to ask you a few questions,' DI Ryan said, not answering the question. Mrs Williams sagged against the doorframe and something passed across her face, as if the stories she'd been telling herself about her son were starting to crumble.

She sighed and ushered them inside. They refused a hot drink and both sat down on a long grey sofa.

'When was the last time you saw Scott?'

'Thursday morning at eight. He ate breakfast and then went to school,' Mrs Williams answered. Belinda made a note of the time. He'd visited Norah the previous night, and according to Cassie had answered his phone on Thursday afternoon at around four p.m.

'Is this the first time he's stayed away for several nights without getting in contact?'

'Um... he's a bit of a free spirit and likes to do his own thing. My husband thinks he's out of hand.'

'What does he mean by *out of hand*?' Belinda asked.

'Just acting like a teenager. Goes out with his friends and doesn't speak to us much. He works as a DJ, which means he's often out late. And sometimes he stays on Smithdown Road with his two cousins, Aaron and Ned. But even when he stays away for a few days, he always comes home in the end.'

'Have you spoken to them about Scott's whereabouts?' Ryan asked. Mrs Williams twisted her fingers together, as if trying to stave off her worry. But the despair in her eyes was evident.

'I've tried, but it's hard to believe a word they say.'

'Would it be possible for us to see Scott's room. Just in case there's anything that might assist us.'

'I don't know. Um... Don't you need a search warrant?'

'Not if you say it's okay. This isn't an official search where everything is inspected in detail. Just a quick look around. It might help us work out where he's gone.'

'Well, in that case... Yes.'

'Where is his bedroom? We'll go there on our own.'

'Upstairs and the first room on the left.'

Belinda thanked her and they both climbed the stairs. Scott's bedroom was neat but had the underlying smell of sweat and damp that seemed to cling to teenage boys. A single bed was below the window and the doors of a built-in wardrobe were covered with A4-sized posters of various DJing gigs. On the far wall was a large desk with two record players, a laptop and a couple of speakers. To one side were several crates of records.

'You take the desk and I'll do the wardrobe.' Belinda pulled on some disposable gloves. Hardly anything was hanging on the rail, most of it dropped in a heap on the floor. She started going through the clothes, one item at a time. She held up a jacket and felt in one of the pockets. She pulled out a small box.

She brought it back into the light and swore. It was fentanyl. She turned it over. There was a serial number on it, which meant it was traceable. And it tied him to the text messages that Norah had received.

'This might be our connection.' She pulled out an evidence bag from her pocket and dropped it in there. 'Have you got anything?'

'No, ma'am,' Ryan said as he finished sifting through the

records and stood back up. 'Though considering what you've just found, we could be justified in taking the laptop as well.'

Belinda agreed. 'Okay, let's bag it up and go back to the station. We have work to do.'

* * *

'Ma'am, Felix Richmond has just come in. I've put him in the second interview room,' Tim said as soon as they returned to the station. Belinda nodded to Ryan to let him know she'd take this one. It wasn't something she always did, but this case felt like it had all the makings of a shitshow, so she was keen to wrap it up quickly.

'Thanks. While I'm in there, can you track this.' She handed Tim the fentanyl and turned to Ryan. 'And can you send around a uniform to talk to Scott Williams's two cousins. Also, run a check on them and see if they have any priors.'

'Yes, ma'am.' Ryan and Tim both hurried back to their desks and Belinda made her way to the interview room. There was no table in the middle. Just low chairs in each corner and a coffee table, so that it was easier to read body language. And in the case of Felix Richmond, it was obvious he was still in shock.

His legs were crossed, and his arms were hanging down by his sides, as if he'd forgotten what he was meant to do with them. There was a general air of confusion hovering over him. Despite that, he was clearly a good-looking man, with dark hair and a square chin. He looked to be in his mid-thirties, apart from the tell-tale wrinkles around his eyes, which were more in line with his real age of forty-two.

'Thank you for coming in, Mr Richmond. I'm DI Belinda Day. I'm so sorry for your loss, and I appreciate how challenging it must be for you right now.'

He opened his mouth before shutting it again and gently rocking back and forward. He tried again. 'Sorry. I keep thinking I'm okay, but then I try and speak, and it hits me all over again.'

'I take it you and Norah were close?'

'Very. She was almost five years younger than me, but our childhood was... difficult. Both our parents were alcoholics and there was a lot of fighting. They're both dead so it's always been my job to make sure she's okay—' He broke off, as if suddenly realising what he'd just said. 'Christ. I guess it didn't work this time.'

'What do you mean by *this time*?' Belinda pressed, noticing the way he'd phrased the sentence. He winced, as if regretting letting something slip. 'Has someone threatened your sister before?'

'No,' he said, but didn't meet her gaze. It wasn't uncommon for grieving families to be reluctant to talk about things that had happened in the past, especially when they put a victim in a bad light. But as a detective, it was frustrating since it often meant they weren't getting all the information they needed. But it was too early to press the point right now.

'Can you think of anyone who might want to harm her?'

'No.' He gave a vehement shake of his head. 'Everybody loved her.'

'Not everybody,' Belinda gently reminded him. 'Did she mention an incident at the hospital?'

He gave a grim nod. 'Yes. Though it was hard to make her take things like that seriously. She always said that some families start the grieving process early. Especially when the diagnosis is terminal. Is that a lead?'

'We're looking into all avenues. Is there anyone else that might have a grudge?' she asked. Again he was silent, but this time Belinda decided to push. 'We found evidence that your sister was being blackmailed.'

He didn't answer straight away, which confirmed it. He already knew. It explained why he'd hesitated earlier. He ran a hand through his hair. 'A few days ago Norah told me that someone was blackmailing her to steal drugs from the hospital. She didn't know who it was and swore that they hadn't been back in contact with her. Oh, Jesus—'

He broke off and lowered his head into his hands. His body was visibly shaking.

There was a box of tissues on the coffee table and Belinda nudged it towards him. He shook his head, as if mentally pulling himself together.

'Can you tell me what leverage they had on her?'

This time Felix looked away, his voice almost mechanical. 'There was a video of her, and—' He paused, the pain clear in his eyes. 'Years ago she'd gone out with a scum of a guy. After she finally saw the light and dumped him, he uploaded a video of them having sex onto a revenge porn website. Norah had no recollection of it even being filmed and it appears the guy had drugged her. It was terrible. She tried everything to get them to take it down, but in the end only money worked. So that's what we did. Can you imagine that we had to pay those arseholes five grand not to stream it? We thought that was the last of it. I guess not.'

Bile rose in Belinda's throat. Oh, hell. She knew those kinds of sites and just how terrible they were. She clenched her fists and forced herself to stay calm. She couldn't help anyone when she wasn't focused.

'Why didn't you tell her to come to the police?'

'Because then Mark would find out and Norah... we both... were worried he might not take the news well.' At this, Felix gripped the table, knuckles white. 'My sister was a good person. She'd already paid a high price for what happened, and the idea of her risking her future over it... well, at the time it seemed important. This is my fault. I should've insisted she go to the police.'

He slumped back in his chair, deflated.

Belinda had learned long ago not to pay attention to what people should have done. 'When was the last time you saw her?' she asked, keeping her voice stern. It seemed to break him out of his despair.

'Yesterday at about one o'clock. She had an appointment at the IVF clinic on Rodney Street. I was meeting her for lunch afterwards.'

'And how did she seem?'

'Definitely on edge. Mark was out of town and she was upset about going to the clinic on her own They hardly ever fought but she was worried he was getting cold feet about having a baby. She was born to be a mother and the IVF meant the world to her. But I don't believe he would have hurt her. He clearly loved her and he's a great dad. Well, I should say that Cassie's a great daughter. She works for me at the restaurant. Anyway, we met for lunch after her appointment. She had a big envelope with the results in it but didn't want to talk about them. She said it wasn't fair to discuss it until she'd spoken to Mark. But she was smiling and seemed happy. She kept talking about what a great father Mark was going to be. I... thought it must have been good news.'

Belinda nodded. Most of it confirmed what they'd already discovered, so she might as well wrap it up and see how the team was doing following up on Scott Williams.

'Anything else you can think of?'

No... actually... it might be nothing. But I did see Mark's ex-wife there.'

'Alice Hargraves?' Belinda raised an eyebrow. Had the woman known about the appointment? Or was it a coincidence that she was there? Either way, it needed pursuing.

'Yes. I'd only met her once but she has a passing resemblance to Cassie. I was surprised to see her on Rodney Street, right outside the IVF clinic.'

That made two of them. Belinda sucked in a breath as a picture of the ex-wife and the new fiancée began to form. 'Did you speak to her?'

His face darkened, suggesting he wasn't a fan. Though it was hardly surprising considering his sister had been about to marry Alice's ex-husband. 'It was hard to avoid her. I said hello and asked her what she was doing that end of town. She said something about a friend living nearby.'

'I see.' Belinda made a note of it, and jotted down the time. Alice had some explaining to do. Which reminded her: Felix had said Norah had an envelope from the clinic with her, but as far as she knew, nothing like that had been found at the crime scene. She'd have to get Amy to chase it up. 'Thank you for your time. And if you think of anything else, please call me.'

'I will do. And, DI Day, please catch the bastard that did this to my sister. Because they deserve to pay for what they've done.'

Belinda waited until a uniformed constable had taken Felix back out to the reception area before heading to the incident room. Amy and Tim were both at their computers and Ryan was on his mobile phone, standing at the window. It wasn't much of a view. The Mersey was only a few blocks away but instead all they got to look at was the line of jobseekers lining up for the social office next door.

'According to the brother, Norah Richmond had been a

victim of revenge porn. She eventually paid to have it removed, but there's a possibility that it's turned up again and was being used against her,' Belinda said, not able to hide her anger now that she was out of the interview room.

Everyone was silent, before Cheryl swore under her breath. 'Sometimes I hate people. I'll follow it up and see what I can find.'

Belinda gave her a grateful nod and turned to Amy. 'Where are we up to?'

'Ma'am, we've checked the CCTV footage at Huyton Village on the day the blackmailer arranged to meet her. We ran the plates of all the cars, and I've just heard that one of them was registered to Mark Hargraves.'

'Good work. So, we know that Norah was being black-mailed and that she most likely drove Mark's car to Huyton Village. And according to the text conversation, she didn't go through with the meeting. Which is possibly why Scott Williams visited her, and they appeared to argue. We also found fentanyl in Scott's bedroom. Do we have a trace on the drugs?'

Tim pocketed his phone and turned around. 'I was just speaking to Alder Hey. The fentanyl belongs to them, and there are fourteen other boxes missing. It looks like we've got a link.'

Belinda rubbed the bridge of her nose. So Scott Williams was blackmailing Norah Richmond into stealing drugs for him – possibly using the threat of the revenge porn. The two questions they didn't have answers for yet was what Scott was doing with the drugs, and was it enough to kill for?

* * *

'Would you like more tea?'

God, no. Cassie would burst if she drank another cup. But she knew Felix was only offering because it would give him something to do. 'Sure.'

'Not for me,' her dad said from his seat on the leather sofa. They'd all spent the morning at the station while the police held a press conference. It had been horrible seeing Norah's photograph up on the screen in the nearby room where they were sitting. It also meant that now Norah had been named, everyone who'd ever known them had started calling.

After leaving the station, Felix had suggested that they hide out at his dockside apartment and avoid any reporters. Cassie had grown up looking up at the iconic red-brick Albert Dock, longing to know what it was like inside, but now she regretted it. The apartment itself was gorgeous, with exposed walls and pitted wooden floors, but the minimalist furniture only made the photograph of Felix and Norah up on the bookshelf stand out even more.

The pair of them were on a boat somewhere, laughing like they had all the time in the world. Shit.

Mark hadn't wanted to go, but Cassie had dragged him along. More so she could get him out of his hotel room. But it was a mistake, and between the long awkward silences the only conversation was about Norah. Out of habit, she looked at her phone. They'd all agreed to put them on silent and she winced at the numerous missed calls and messages. There were some from Deb.

Call me.

Call me.

Call me.

And others from girls she'd hardly even spoken to. But there was nothing from Scott.

She jumped up and began to pace as Felix returned with a pot of tea and two china mugs, like the ones for sale in the upmarket shop near the restaurant. He poured out two mugs and then sighed.

'We need to talk about the funeral. Officer Richards told me that if we want the body cremated, we'll need to get special permission from the coroner,' Felix said in a dull voice.

'Cremated? Absolutely not. We have a family plot. She'll go there. And it's way too soon. What if they need the body for more evidence?'

Felix's fingers tightened around his mug. 'I think they've sliced her up enough, don't you? And she was always adamant that she didn't want to be buried.'

Cassie had been there yesterday when a policewoman had explained that until the coroner had released the body, they couldn't even have a funeral. But it was still strange to see Felix and her dad fight like this – made worse by the fact that if Norah was still alive, she would've been able to smooth it over.

'Christ. Sorry, Felix. I'm being an arsehole.' Her dad let out a long sigh, as if reaching the same conclusion about Norah. He rolled his neck. It scared her how old he suddenly looked. 'I still don't understand how this was all happening right under my nose, and I didn't see a thing. That bloody Scott Williams must have forced Norah to steal the drugs.'

His words jabbed at her skin like needles.

The police had found drugs in Scott's bedroom that had

been taken from Alder Hey and after her dad had told them about the drugs he'd found in the car, the police concluded that Norah had been attempting to pass them on to Scott. It was the same thought that she'd had, but it hadn't lasted long.

If Scott really was behind it, no way would he have come up with such a stupid way to do an exchange. And why would he have tried to convince Cassie that Norah had planted the drugs in the car to break them up?

Unless he was trying to teach Norah a lesson.

Her throat tightened as something in her shattered. The one last hope she'd been clinging on to was gone. Whatever had really happened, one thing was clear – Scott had been using Cassie to get to Norah, and he'd lied about everything.

He'd never loved her.

Not the way she'd loved him. Her chest tightened and tears prickled in her eyes. All she wanted to do was curl up in a ball and cry. Suddenly she longed to be at home. Not in her father's mansion, but in Alice's house with the creaky floorboards and the cramped living room. She longed for Hugo to be in her lap while Alice made her cups of sweet, milky tea and told her everything would be okay.

But that couldn't happen. Alice was having a field day over the fact she'd been right about Scott all along.

'We don't know that he did. What if Norah was the one who dragged Scott into all of this?' she said, though the fight had gone out of her.

'Cassie,' Felix said in a soft voice, his eyes filled with sorrow. Like he was about to tell her that Santa Claus didn't exist. 'I know it's hard to hear, but Norah's never done drugs in her life and would never be involved in supplying them to other people.'

'How do you know for sure?'

'Because both of our parents were alcoholics. Norah knew just how ugly addiction could be.'

All the air seemed to disappear from the room, and her frustration evaporated. 'I-I didn't know that.' Cassie swallowed, turning to her dad. But he was just sitting there staring at his hands. It obviously wasn't news to him. 'Sorry.'

'Don't be. It's not something we liked talking about. But I know that even if she did steal the drugs, she must've had a very good reason for doing so.'

'But what was it?' Mark said, almost angry now. 'What did Scott have over her?'

'I don't know,' Cassie said, hating the way her dad was looking at her. Like she'd somehow been involved. It hadn't helped that the police had found out there was a chunk of security footage missing from his study, but they could clearly see her in the hallway ten minutes later. She'd been forced to admit that she'd opened the safe to look for money. 'But no matter what it was, it doesn't mean he killed her.'

'Then who did?' Felix sounded utterly exhausted.

I don't know, Cassie wanted to shout at him. Yes, she was mad at Scott. Furious. But that didn't mean he was evil. He wouldn't hurt someone. Not even if he was upset. And if he really was blackmailing Norah, then didn't that mean she wasn't quite as nice as everyone thought? She certainly must have had a secret or two.

So why weren't the police looking into that? Finding out who else she hung out with that her dad didn't know about. And—

Sefton Park.

Cassie jumped up. 'The other day Alice told me that she saw Norah at Sefton Park, and she was talking to some guy. It looked like she didn't want anyone else to see her.'

'What the hell?' Her dad turned to her. 'Why didn't you tell me sooner?'

'I forgot all about it. Alice told me before – well… a few days ago. And I thought she was just being a bitch. She wasn't happy about you and Norah doing IVF.'

Felix's expression darkened and his eyes narrowed. 'What do you mean Alice wasn't happy about the IVF? Are you sure?'

Cassie blinked at the ferocity of his words. 'Um, yes. She was ranting about it the other day… why?' she suddenly asked, too late realising what he was getting at. 'You don't think my mum would've—'

'Of course he doesn't.' Mark seemed to break out of his trance as he looked from Felix to Cassie.

'I saw Alice outside the IVF clinic on Thursday,' Felix said by way of an answer, his dark eyes hard like stone. She'd never heard him mad before. 'The same day that my sister was killed. And now you're telling me that Alice also followed her in the park?'

No. That's not what she meant. Her mother hadn't followed Norah to the park, she'd just seen her there. Hadn't she?

Cassie's thoughts darted like minnows as she tried to process what Felix was saying. But a band of pain tightened around her skull, making it impossible to think. Alice was a pain in the butt at times, but she wasn't a stalker, and she certainly couldn't kill anyone. But neither could Scott. It was all such a mess and there was no way it could be fixed.

She let out a choked sob and Mark put an arm around her shoulders. He stayed there until she finally stopped crying and then pressed a kiss to her forehead.

'We need to tell the police, Cassie. If Alice knows something, she needs to tell them. Excuse me for a moment.'

Once he was gone, Felix bowed his head, and when he

looked up, the darkness was gone but his shoulders were visibly shaking. 'Cass... I didn't mean to upset you... or imply that Alice did anything. I just can't bear not knowing what happened to Norah. That someone out there killed her.' He swallowed, his Adam's apple bobbing in and out, as he tried to regain control of his emotions. 'This man in the park. Did your mum describe him at all?'

Cassie shook her head, trying to push away her rising guilt at even mentioning it. 'Not to me, but we've been arguing a lot lately. She might be able to describe him to the police. I... I really don't think she would do something like that. Not to anyone. I still can't believe this is happening.'

'I know. I keep hoping that it's some bad dream, but then I remember the photographs of her body and know it's not a dream. Some bastard had their own sick reasons, and now my sister's dead.' Felix's knuckles were white as he clenched his hands. Raw pain and grief were etched into the hollows of his cheeks and the grim line of his mouth, leaving him exposed and vulnerable.

It broke through her jumbled thoughts like a knife.

Instead of her father's zombie-like trance and Alice's insistence on the fact everything would be okay, Felix was treating her like an adult who was capable of handling complex emotions. Suddenly Cassie felt a hundred years old as his honesty stripped away all of the fairy tales she'd been telling herself. Someone had killed Norah and until they were caught, everyone was paying the price.

16

On a good day, Sefton Park was like stepping back into the Victorian era, with families walking around the winding paths, while children played on the sloping grass leading down to the water. But today was not a good day. Discarded crisp packets and drink bottles were dotted everywhere, and the sky was the colour of slate as the wind increased. Belinda drained her coffee and put her reusable cup into the pocket of her jacket before calling Hetty.

Hearing her name, the little dog looked up from where she'd been sniffing a tree, brown eyes wide and pleading. Belinda sighed. It was hard to explain to a dog that murder investigations meant neither of them would get what they wanted. For Hetty it was lots of walks and a couch companion every night. And for Belinda it was eight hours' sleep and the chance to go on a date with Diana from forensics.

After the press conference, her team had stayed up most of the night fielding the many calls that came in. There were always leads to follow up, and no matter how far-fetched they were, someone needed to go through all of them. Which explained why she was so tired.

And there was still no sign of the murder weapon.

'Come on,' she called again and Hetty finally trotted over. Belinda snapped on her lead and walked down to the spot that Alice Hargraves had described. Unfortunately, there were no CCTV cameras around and since it happened two weeks ago, the chances of finding any witnesses were low.

Belinda studied the photo of Norah that the blackmailer had sent. It was in a park but there were no identifying features to prove it was Sefton Park, and the surroundings didn't match the area Alice had directed her to.

Did it mean Alice was lying?

It was entirely possible. She'd come into the station yesterday to be questioned about her assertation she'd seen Norah arguing with a man in Sefton Park. At first she'd been happy to cooperate, but when Ryan had started probing into Felix's claim she'd been outside the IVF clinic on the day of Norah's murder, she'd clammed up.

It wasn't hard to guess why.

Alice could easily explain away how she'd managed to see Norah at Sefton Park, which was minutes from her house, and where she frequently walked her dog. But being caught outside the IVF clinic on the day Norah had been murdered, well... that was something else entirely. And Amy, who'd been going through all of the surveillance footage at Mark's house, had stumbled across Alice climbing over the fence and walking towards a garden shed. All of which meant her claims to have seen Norah arguing with someone could easily be a way of deflecting from the truth. That Alice Hargraves had been stalking Norah Richmond.

The evidence was certainly stacking up against her.

But was that enough for murder? Belinda thought of the woman she'd met in the park two weeks ago. Yes, she'd been bitter and upset about her break-up, but she'd also been self-deprecating and warm. And who hadn't lost their minds a bit over a betrayal?

Then there was Mark Hargraves. Belinda still hadn't made up her mind about him. He was playing the part of grieving fiancé, but his decision to not go to the IVF clinic that day with Norah smacked of someone getting cold feet. Was it because of the drugs in the car? Or had he somehow discovered the sex tape in Norah's past?

And Cassie herself. She might only be seventeen, but Belinda had learned not to let age rule anything out. The fury in the girl's eyes as she'd watched the footage of Norah and Scott together hadn't been lost on Belinda. And there was her alibi. Despite saying she'd been drunk at the pub, so far the team hadn't managed to get any reliable witnesses or CCTV footage to prove that was the case.

And where was Scott Williams? She'd sent Amy and Tim to talk to his friends and neighbours, to try and establish a time-line. He was still at the top of her suspect list, and his disap-pearance possibly meant he'd gone into hiding. But until they located him, it was hard to move forward.

What a shitshow.

Belinda shielded her eyes from the sun as she walked back to her flat in Aigburth.

She fed the dog and grabbed a quick shower before arriving at the station half an hour later. Ryan immediately stood up and beckoned her over. His eyes were wide, and his mouth was set into a pensive shape. *It was bad news.*

'What?' She crossed the floor, barely acknowledging the

rest of the team as she looked over his shoulder to the computer screen. Cheryl, Tim and Amy followed her over.

'Still no sign of Scott Williams, ma'am, but we spoke to his cousins, Aaron and Ned Phillips. The pair of them have a list of crimes going back to an ASBO for terrorising a neighbour.' Cheryl rolled her eyes. 'And they weren't forthcoming about Scott. However, after a long and tedious interview, they did reveal that Scott had been DJing on Thursday night at The Crofter's Arms, just past Anfield.'

'The manager has just sent over the CCTV footage. There are numerous updates on social media from various people in the pub, and plenty of witnesses,' Ryan said, bringing up four screens of shots. 'He was there from six thirty to well after one a.m. There's no way he could have got across town and killed Norah.'

Shit. Scott Williams had been their most likely suspect and with him out of the picture – and missing – they were back to square one. The DCI wouldn't be happy.

'Some slightly better news. Tony Gibbs and his team raided a house on Grafton Street last night, and half of the stolen fentanyl was recovered. The dealer confirmed that he'd bought it from Scott. So we can still charge the little shitbag for that,' Ryan said, voice grim.

'Good,' Belinda said, though it was little consolation. She walked over to the whiteboard and picked up a marker. She was half tempted to wipe everything off and start again, but sometimes it was the spaces between the evidence that helped reveal who was responsible. 'Cheryl, any update on the revenge porn?'

'Sorry, ma'am. I've got alerts set up and Bugs owes me a favour so he's working on it today.'

'Keep me posted.' Belinda nodded before turning to the rest of the team. 'Let's go over what we know about Norah's last day.'

'Yes, ma'am. On Thursday she had an appointment at a fertility clinic on Rodney Street. I contacted them and spoke with Doctor Gunnel. She told me that Norah and her fiancé had done the initial fertility tests, and Norah went to collect the results on Thursday. However, they weren't found in the house after a search. Which is why we went back to the clinic.'

'And?' Belinda gave an impatient nod.

'The doctor was reluctant at first, but I reminded her that under Section 29 of the Data Protection Act she could disclose information because it would assist in a murder investigation. She informed me that Norah should have had no trouble conceiving but that Mark Hargraves was... infertile.' Cheryl let the last word hang in the air.

Belinda whistled. She might have lost her prime suspect, but it seemed like someone else was standing in the wings.

Namely Alice Hargraves. Because suddenly her appearance at the Rodney Street clinic seemed a lot more sinister.

'The daughter isn't his. Does he know? He wasn't at the appointment and Felix said that Norah wouldn't tell him the results because she was waiting to talk to Mark first.'

'Except she didn't get the chance. He came home and found her dead.' Ryan picked up the thread. 'Throw into that he's found out about Norah's past, and he's got two very good reasons for being angry. And then there's Alice Hargraves, who might be wanting to protect her secret, not to mention making sure her daughter isn't disinherited from a substantial amount of money. *And* if Norah is out of the picture, who knows, perhaps she thinks they'll even get back together?'

Belinda nodded. It made sense. But it didn't rule out the other players. 'We also have Cassie. She's already pissed off at Norah and then discovers she might not have an inheritance, or a father.'

'That's assuming that Cassie knows her dad is infertile, and we don't know that she does.'

'True, but that doesn't negate the fact that she's really annoyed with Norah. And what about Mark? Maybe he killed the messenger in a fit of rage?' The last one seemed less likely, but she always found that when it came to piecing together the evidence it didn't hurt to go through as many options as possible before ruling them out.

'Who do you want to tackle first, ma'am?' Amy's eyes were wide with the adrenaline that came from finding a missing piece of the puzzle. Belinda couldn't blame her. And while she knew better than to put her eggs in one basket, it was definitely a way forward. An old boss had once taught her that they didn't need to have all the answers, they just needed to have bloody good questions, and that the more they pushed people, the more the truth started to reveal itself.

It was time to start pushing.

Belinda looked around at her team. 'I think we should start with Mark. Let's get him in and see how he reacts to the news he isn't Cassie's father.'

The next two hours were taken up with catching up on paperwork and updating the DCI before cramming in a sandwich and cup of tea. Belinda was just wiping away the crumbs when Ryan appeared at her desk.

'Ma'am, Mark Hargraves has arrived. He's in interview room three,' he said. The room in question was the least pleasant, and therefore often used when they wanted to unsettle people.

'Thanks, Ryan. You can join me. And heads up, let's not mention the revenge porn until we know more about it,' she said as they walked down the corridor and into the room. Mark Hargraves's clothes were crumpled, and red rings lined his eyes.

He looked like crap. She quickly went through the formalities involved before starting the interview.

'We want to talk about the appointment Norah went to at the IVF clinic. The one you missed.'

A flash of irritation crossed his face. 'Why are you focusing on that? What about the man Alice saw talking to Norah? And about Scott Williams? Has he been found? They're who you need to concentrate on.'

'We have several lines of investigation going.' Belinda gave him a pleasant smile. She was used to civilians with zero experience telling her how to conduct an investigation. She blamed Netflix. 'Now, about the appointment. Did Norah tell you the results from your fertility test?'

The fight seemed to leave him as quickly as it had come. 'No. I presume she was waiting for me to get home. Is this relevant?'

Next to her, Ryan tensed ever so slightly but Belinda kept the relaxed smile on her face. 'From our discussions with the doctor, we understand that Norah didn't present any problems regarding her ability to conceive. It seems the problem was you. Did you know you're infertile?'

He stared at her, eyes properly focused for the first time. 'That's not possible.'

'The doctor assured us it's true.'

'Well, they're wrong. I have a daughter. Cassie is...' His voice fell away, as if understanding finally hit. 'A-are you sure?'

She leaned forward to meet his gaze. 'Has Alice ever mentioned anything to suggest there might have been... someone else?'

'Absolutely not.'

'So, you never suspected anything?' Belinda asked again. She knew from experience that it was always best to tackle a question from a few different angles, to make sure that what-ever a person was telling you was the truth.

'No. Not a thing.' He closed his eyes and leaned back in the chair. 'I can't fucking believe this. Shit.'

Belinda and Ryan exchanged a glance before she coughed. 'Mr Hargraves, were you aware that on the day Norah was killed, her brother was waiting outside the clinic so they could go to lunch, and he saw Alice there?'

Mark sighed. 'Felix mentioned it yesterday after the press conference.'

'And how did she know about the appointment?' Belinda said.

'How should I know—' He broke off and swore. 'I did mention we were trying. It was after all the stuff with Cassie when I found the drugs in the car. I went around to talk through our options. I was doubting my parenting abilities, and I told her about the IVF.'

'Did you mention the name of the clinic to her?'

'No. I don't think so. I'm not sure. But why would she go to the clinic, anyway?'

'Your guess is as good as mine. Could it be because she was worried about the test results? About the fact Cassie isn't your biological daughter?' Belinda said.

Mark's face drained of colour. She couldn't blame him. Right now the evidence was all pointing in one direction. And that was at Alice Hargraves.

* * *

Alice stared at the phone. It was her agent. She almost laughed at how comical it was. Now that she didn't care two hoots about the book or the contract, Lawrence was going out of his way to be accommodating. She'd emailed him and her editor about the news yesterday and both of them had been more than happy for her to take her time with the final few illustrations. It wouldn't last forever, of course, but since there was zero chance of her concentrating until this was all cleared up, she was happy to make the most of it.

The phone rang again but she continued to ignore it. It had been non-stop since the press conference. At first she'd been touched that old friends and acquaintances cared. But she'd become a lot more cynical now. Most of them just wanted some insider gossip.

'You could just put that on silent.' Cassie appeared in the kitchen and gave Alice a long-suffering sigh – obviously mortally offended at the fact her mother didn't know how to change a ringtone.

'It's fine.' She stuffed it into the back pocket of her jeans. 'Are you hungry?'

'No. I'll grab something at work later.'

'Work?' Alice blinked, only just noticing that Cassie was wearing her favourite denim overalls, Doc Martens and a T-shirt. Typically, it was what she wore while she was waitressing. 'I don't think that's a good idea. It's not long since it all happened. What if there are photographers there?'

'Then I'll show them what I think,' Cassie retorted, raising a middle finger. 'Besides, it's not fair to Felix if I don't go in. Three staff have quit because they don't like all the people who come in just to get a gawk at him. But if he stays away then how will he pay the rent, or staff wages? Besides, if I'm working I can't worry so much...'

Her daughter let the words trail off, and Alice sighed.

They'd heard this morning that Scott Williams was no longer a suspect because of CCTV footage and numerous witnesses placing him across town. But he was still missing, and Cassie was becoming more concerned. And while Alice would've been happy to never see Scott again, she hated that her daughter had so much to deal with.

'Whatever you think will help. Do you want to borrow the car?'

'Seriously?' Cassie raised an eyebrow. 'You don't mind?'

Alice fished out the keys from her bag and passed them over. The truth was that if Cassie was going out, she'd much rather know she was in a car than waiting at the bus stop. 'Text me when you're on your way home.'

'Will do.' Cassie picked up the keys, her mouth almost in a smile. It was the first time Alice had seen her even remotely happy since it had all happened. At least one of them was. She waited until the front door had shut before reaching for the bottle of wine she'd just bought. It wasn't even cold, but desperate times and all of that.

The wine glasses were over on the dresser. As she walked towards it, her eyes fixed on the all-too-familiar sight of Cassie's driver's licence. Irritation went through her. What was it with teenagers and not wanting to carry anything more than their phone on them? And yes, it wasn't a legal requirement, but to Alice it was common sense. More importantly, her car, her rules.

She'd stopped running it out to Cassie after it had happened for a fifth time, and now she simply sent a text message.

You forgot it again.

There wasn't an immediate reply so Alice poured herself a large glass and held it up. Better not to look at the colour. Or smell it. At a fiver, the wine didn't exactly lend itself to careful examination. She took a long gulp and considered breaking into the emergency packet of cigarettes that she'd covered in masking tape to stop her getting to them. They'd probably be stale. But then again, it might go well with the cheap wine. Decided, she bent down to the bottom cupboard where she'd hidden them inside the slow cooker. She rummaged around until she found the packet and stepped out into the back garden.

The overgrown grass danced in the evening breeze, taunting her about her lack of maintenance. She really must hire someone to tidy it up. She lit the cigarette and inhaled. The sharp burn of nicotine, once so familiar, hit her throat and gave her a buzz. God, she'd missed this. The two outside chairs were facing each other, where Cassie had obviously been sitting, using one as a footstool to tan her legs. On the table was a copy of yesterday's *Echo*.

She'd been trying to avoid it but one of her neighbours had handed it to her in case she'd wanted to read the article on Norah, which had managed to slip back to page five. It had been overtaken by a series of drug raids in Birkenhead. She took another drag of her cigarette and flicked through the pages. Crime. Crime. Football. *Love Island*. Drugs. Crime.

The world really was going to shit. No wonder she'd been struggling to get her book finished. How could she paint innocent scenes when there was so much horror everywhere? She continued flicking through it until she reached the sports page. There was a shot of Everton fans celebrating what must have been a goal.

She wasn't into football but had come to accept it as part and parcel of living in Liverpool, and even Mark, who never talked about it much, would still disappear into his study whenever the reds were playing. She was about to fold the paper back up when a single face stood out to her. Most of the crowd were looking away from the camera, their features impossible to see, but this one was face on. He had thinning hair, spiked out, and the slightly puffy face that some drinkers got over time.

God. Where did she know him from? She snatched up the article again and scanned it. It was about a controversial VAR decision from last week's match that had resulted in a goal and a win for Everton. She studied the photograph, but her brain refused to give her an answer. Irritation skittered along her skin.

It had been happening more and more lately. Brain fog. The kind that made her stop mid-sentence because she literally couldn't think what the next word was meant to be. She'd googled it last night and concluded it was because she was over forty and stressed. Which was ironic because not being able to think clearly wasn't helping her stress levels.

She took a gulp of wine as a squeaking noise echoed out. It was the front door being opened. Crap. She put out the cigarette and quickly stood.

'I wondered how long it would take for you to come back and get it,' Alice called out as she waved her hands to help get rid of the smoke. Then she picked up her wine and headed inside.

'It's me.' Mark was standing in the archway between the kitchen and the sitting room. The lethargy of the last three days had left him, and his pupils were dilated, as if some kind of mania had overtaken him. He bounced on his toes, unable to stand still.

'You gave me a shock. I thought it was Cassie. She's borrowed my car and forgot to take her driver's licence. Again,' she said, but Mark didn't laugh with her. Instead, he stalked towards her. He'd always been fit for his age but usually it was hidden behind a veneer of urban politeness. Not now. Electricity seemed to be bouncing off his entire body. Alice instinctively took a step backwards. 'Is everything okay? Have they found who—'

'Who killed my fiancée?' he broke in with a low growl. 'That's rich. Coming from you.'

'I don't understand. Has something happened?' A jolt of fear ran down her spine and the hair on her arms prickled. She'd known Mark for almost half her life, but she'd never seen this side to him before. She didn't even know he had this side. It was one of the things she'd loved about him. That he'd always made her feel safe.

But she didn't feel safe now. Primal rage enveloped him, and Alice took another step back until she was pressed up against the wall.

'Has something happened?' he mimicked before letting out a bark of laughter. 'You always could ignore the obvious.'

His jibe landed and she flinched. Before the divorce he'd accused her of being in denial at the state of their marriage. As if she'd purposely turned away from the giant cracks that he'd assured her were there.

'This isn't funny. Please just tell me what's going on?'

He tilted his head, harsh gaze sweeping over her as he closed the distance. Alice's heart pounded. Was he going to hit her? Was he even capable of doing that? Up until five minutes ago, she would have said no. But now she didn't even recognise him.

Then she thought of Norah. Oh God. Her grip tightened around the stem of the wine glass, holding it out like a weapon. Mark ignored it as he finally reached her.

'I've just been talking with the police and do you know what they told me?' His whisky-fuelled breath brushed across her skin.

'What?' she croaked, her pulse pounding in her ears.

'Cassie isn't mine.'

The wine glass fell to the floor, the glass shattering into a million pieces, but Alice didn't hear it. Nor did she feel the splash of wine as it sprayed against her legs, or Mark's rasping breath.

It was all gone.

She was nowhere. Nothing. Just a tiny collection of atoms floating around in space.

And then Mark's phone beeped with a text message and Alice's trance was broken.

The room came back into focus and with it the terrible, terrible truth.

He knew.

Alice let out a soft wail and slid down the wall, not noticing the glass or the wine. She clutched at her head and tears pricked at her eyes. Oh God, oh God, oh God. It had happened. The one thing that she'd spent the last seventeen years avoiding. Bile churned in her stomach, trying to force its way up her throat but she clenched her teeth together and forced it back down. She couldn't be sick. Not now.

She needed to think.

Mark was speaking to her, but his voice was faint, like he was trapped inside a glass cage. Or was she the one trapped? Yes, definitely her. She was trapped in the cage of her own making. And now that he'd found out the truth, she'd never be able to escape.

'W-why do you think that?' The words scraped along her tonsils.

'I've been with the police. They followed up with the results from the IVF clinic. I'm infertile and always have been.'

'But that doesn't mean Cassie isn't your daughter. You're older now. Doesn't that change things?'

He let out a growl, before seeming to catch himself. 'Don't give me that. Just admit it. For once in your life, just tell the truth.' His body slumped and all the anger seemed to fade away as he slid down to the ground beside her. 'Tell me the truth. Please, Alice. I can't take much more.'

She wasn't sure what was worse, his anger or this total devastation that had now enveloped him. Either way, she couldn't keep it from him any longer.

But where would that leave Cassie?

If Mark wasn't her father, then she had no security. Who would inherit all his money? It seemed callous, but all Alice had ever wanted was for Cassie to have a future.

It was all Norah's fault. If she hadn't been so intent on going for IVF, none of this would have come out. And Mark wouldn't be here with his life in tatters.

'Okay. I'll tell you the truth. But please don't tell Cassie. It would break her heart. She idolises you.'

'I'm listening.' The mania from earlier had disappeared, replaced by stone.

She stared directly ahead. It would be easier if she couldn't see his face. 'After you got the job in Europe and we broke up, I was devastated. It was before I'd sold my first book and that friend of mine, Maureen, dragged me to a writing conference. I hadn't left the house in a week, and she was worried. When we got there, she roped me into pitching my idea to an editor. I was so nervous that I thought I was going to throw up. And then, to my amazement, they asked to see the entire picture book. Things had been so shitty that I couldn't quite believe my luck.

We went out to a nearby pub, and I must've had a few too many glasses of wine.'

Alice swallowed. She'd always imagined what it would be like if she had to tell him. In her vision there had been hysterics and tears, but now she felt strangely calm. Like she was someone else staring down at her own body.

'There was a guy. And we ended up going back to his place. The next morning, I was so embarrassed that I left before he woke up. Four weeks later I found out I was pregnant. I went back to the apartment, but the guy had moved out. My first and last one-night stand. So, I was on my own. The pregnancy, the birth, learning to breastfeed. I did it all on my own, because that's what I thought my life would be from then on. Then you turned up on my doorstep with a teddy bear. A-and when you met Cassie, it was like she was yours and you were hers. I'm so sorry, Mark. You have to believe me.'

She finally looked at him, in time to see the pain that rippled across his face. 'Believe you? You've deceived me for all these years. What else haven't you told me?'

'Nothing. I promise. Cassie's yours. Okay, biologically maybe she isn't, but in every other way. We've raised her together. And now she's growing up, we can't tell her. It would destroy her.'

'Destroy her? What about me? Do you even care how I feel?' His eyes were filled with loathing. 'Who the hell are you? To keep something like this from me for seventeen years. For Christ's sake, Alice. I've just lost the love of my life. And now there's this.'

Alice's body clenched. *The love of his life.* That's how he thought of Norah. What had she been, then? An inconvenience? A duty?

'Please, Mark. I'm begging you—'

They were cut off by the sound of something crashing in the hallway. Hugo, who'd been sleeping in his basket, poked his head up, ears flat as he began to bark. A second later, Cassie appeared. Her face was pale and her eyes wide.

Alice let out a soft moan. The licence. Cassie had come back for her licence. And what? Seen the front door open and walked into the hallway, before discovering her parents having an argument.

'What the actual fuck.' Cassie's hands were shaking, and Alice longed to wrap her in a hug. But that was no longer possible. Her little daughter had gone. The child who refused to leave the house without holding her hand didn't exist.

'I don't know what you heard,' Alice said. 'But—'

'Shut up, Mum. I heard everything. Every. Thing.'

'Sit down. Let's all talk about it.' Alice glanced at Mark, hoping that he wouldn't take it out on their daughter.

'What's there to talk about? That you're a lying cow and that my real father is some one-night stand you had while you were out at the pub, drunk? Have I missed anything?' Cassie snapped before her eyes fixed on the driver's licence, still sitting on the bench. She snatched it up and stormed out of the room, the front door shutting with a thump.

Oh God. What had Alice just done?

17

Cassie slammed the front door and marched down the path and onto the street. Her eyes stung from the tears streaming down her face. She brushed them away with the back of her hand.

Her brain couldn't take it all in. Her dad wasn't her dad. Her boyfriend had been blackmailing her future stepmum. And her own mother? Don't even get her started. The only thing they all had in common was that they were liars.

She was so sick of it.

There was no way she could go back into that house. Usually, she'd go to her dad's, but he wasn't even her father. And she couldn't go to Deb's without having to answer a million questions about Norah and the murder.

How the fuck had this become her life?

Her phone beeped with a calendar reminder about her shift. At least at work no one would lie to her. And considering she didn't want to see either of her parents in a hurry, she could use her wages to pay for a hotel room somewhere.

She reached the car. Part of her was tempted to leave it

there and catch the bus, but she didn't want to bite off her nose to spite her face. Plus, she was already late. Her mind whirled as she drove, oblivious to everything. Her subconscious obviously knew more than she did, and fifteen minutes later she pulled into the car park she always used. The sun had dipped as she hurried along Bold Street.

The restaurant was packed and Felix was at the far end of the counter. The fact he was there at all was a minor miracle, and it was obvious by the dark circles under his eyes that he'd hardly slept since it had all happened. He took one look at her and strode across to meet her.

'Christ. You look worse than I do. I said you didn't need to come in today,' he said in a low voice.

'I-I wanted to help,' she said. 'Besides, you said it's best to keep busy.'

'And look how well that advice is working out for me,' he said in a grim voice as he drew attention to the stain on his shirt and his mismatched socks. 'Has something happened?'

Cassie swallowed. It wasn't fair for her to burden him. Especially with everything else that was going on. 'I'm fine,' she said as a tear prickled in the corner of her eye. Damn. She quickly wiped it away.

'Come with me,' he said, gently leading her past the counter. Tamsin gave her a little wave and a sympathetic look as they went past. He turned to her. 'I'll be out the back. Only come and get me if it's an emergency. Okay?'

'Of course,' Tamsin said before hurrying off to take a tray of drinks to one of the tables. Felix didn't speak until he'd closed the door of the tiny staffroom. It was crammed with empty beer barrels, serviettes, bottles of water and a tray of sandwiches left over from the lunch session, for the staff to eat.

'What's going on? Has there been... any news?' His voice

was filled with hope and fear all at the same time. Cassie winced. She should never have come.

'No. I mean yes. But it's not about Norah,' she whispered. 'I'm sorry.'

He quickly shook his head. 'Don't be. It's becoming painfully fucking obvious that the world keeps turning even when it feels like our hearts have been ripped out.' His voice was so raw and filled with pain that Cassie wanted to touch his hand and reassure him. But she couldn't. Because Felix was right. The world was a fucked-up, shitty place. What was the point of trying to pretend it wasn't?

'I didn't mean to upset you.'

He took a shuddering breath and a mask seemed to settle back on his face. The one where he pretended everything was okay. 'It's not your fault. I'm like this most of the time. I just work through it.'

'I don't get it; why someone would do that to her? She was so... so...'

'Lovely.' He finished her sentence. 'I don't understand either. So, what's going on? What's happened?'

'That day at the clinic. When Norah was getting the IVF results. Turns out that my dad – or should I say Mark – is infertile and has been his entire life. The police told him that he wasn't my dad.'

'Christ.' Felix let out a shocked sigh 'I had lunch with Norah. She wouldn't tell me what the results were, because she needed to speak to him first. Hell, what am I saying? Forget that. How are you feeling? That's a lot to have dumped on you.'

Cassie closed her eyes. How was she feeling? Confused. Pissed off. Devastated. All of the above... and none of them. Her mind was whirling with so many thoughts that she was almost too scared to slow down and examine them.

Felix gave her a compassionate smile but didn't try and fill the silence. It was so different to Alice's approach of pushing and pushing, or Mark's contentment to let her figure things out on her own. The surge of adrenaline finally slowed down and Cassie looked at him.

'It's surreal. Like it's happening to someone else. I can't wrap my head around it. And what does it mean? Do I still call him Dad? Do you think he hates me?'

'He's still your father even if he isn't biologically. He's not going to suddenly turn off his feelings for you.'

'You don't know that.'

He nodded. 'You're right. I don't know, but I've seen him around you. Yes, he's going to be shocked. What man wouldn't be? But he won't take it out on you.'

'You weren't there. The look on his face... it was so bad. And my mum. She's lied to all of us.'

'I'm sure she had her reasons. She loves you just as much as your dad does. I'm sure of it.'

'It doesn't feel like it.' Tears welled in the corners of her eyes, but she didn't brush them away, like she would if she'd been talking to her parents, or even Deb. Maybe that's why she felt so exhausted? Because she was so sick of pretending to be someone she wasn't. 'Nothing feels right. All I want to do is curl up in a ball and forget about everything and everyone. To make it all go away.'

'Boss.' They both looked over as the door opened and Tamsin poked her head in. 'So sorry. But you said only to interrupt if it was an emergency, and this is.'

Felix swore softly under his breath before he stood up. He reached the door and then turned to her. 'Hey, I know everything seems shit right now. But hang in there. You're tougher than you think.'

Cassie swallowed and wiped her eyes. She wasn't sure it was true, but it was nice at least one person wasn't lying out of their arse to her.

* * *

Alice waited until the Uber had disappeared before turning to face the police station. She hadn't trusted herself to drive the short distance after spending the night drinking coffee and trying to get in contact with Cassie. It hadn't worked and her daughter hadn't returned any of her calls.

She'd eventually walked into the house at about three in the morning, ignoring Alice, who'd been curled up on the sofa. And she hadn't emerged from her bedroom before Alice had received the call from the police, requesting her to come in.

The station itself was a depressing red-brick building in the heart of Toxteth. There were a few kids hanging around on the corner, vaping, and they stared as she walked in. She hated the way some kids were so brazen. In the past she'd blamed the parents, but now she realised that she was just as bad as anyone.

She'd lied to Mark, and Cassie.

And now she was about to go into the police station and lie to them as well.

At least that's what she assumed this was about. Why else had they called her in, instead of interviewing her at the house? It was because she'd crossed the metaphorical line in their investigation. No longer helpful ex-wife who might assist with filling in the timeline. Now she was the ex-wife who didn't want her replacement to show anyone the results of a certain fertility test.

Except it was hardly a crime.

She hadn't been anywhere near Norah when she was killed. All she'd done was try and avoid Mark finding out a painful secret. It might be morally ambiguous, but it wasn't illegal.

'What are you here for, love?' a middle-aged woman with poker-straight hair and a heavy tan asked from behind the reception desk.

'I'm Alice Hargraves. DI Day asked me to come in.'

'You'd better take a seat over there, and I'll let her know you've arrived.' The woman pointed to a row of black chairs underneath a large noticeboard. They were as uncomfortable as they looked, and Alice drummed her fingers on her legs while she waited. Then she stopped. Christ. What if someone was watching her. Would they think she was guilty? She pushed her hands under her legs to stop from fidgeting.

A series of people walked in and out of the waiting room before DI Day finally appeared, with DS Walton two steps behind. Neither of them were smiling.

'Thank you for coming in. Please follow me.' The DI nodded for Alice to stand up. It was clear that they were trying to make her as uncomfortable as possible. She wanted to tell them it was wasted on her. There was nothing they could do to make her feel worse than she already did.

Alice followed them to a room down a long corridor. Inside was a table and four chairs. The DI gestured for Alice to sit across from the two of them and started the recording device. Still no smiling from either of them.

'Alice, you're not under arrest but I am informing you that although you do not have to say anything, it may harm your defence if you do not mention when questioned something which you later rely on in court. Anything you do say may be given in evidence. Do you understand?'

'Yes,' she managed to say, suddenly wondering if she *did* in fact need a lawyer. Not that she'd done anything. But even she could see there was a possible motive. And she'd failed to mention that she'd been outside the clinic on the day Norah was killed.

'Where were you between the hours of seven and nine on Thursday the fourth of May?'

'I was at home, working,' she said.

'But no one can vouch for you?' DS Walton said, as if worried she might forget that fact.

'No.'

The two police officers exchanged a glance and DS Walton spoke again. 'We'd like to ask you about your relationship with Norah.'

Same as last time you asked me, Alice wanted to scream at them. Wisely, she swallowed it down. 'I had no relationship with her. She stole my husband, so I wasn't going to go out of my way to be nice to her.'

'I totally understand,' DI Day agreed. 'And would you say that you were angry that this had happened?'

Alice winced. She'd walked straight into that one. '"Disappointed" would be a better word.' *Or 'devastated'.*

'So, you were disappointed enough to confront Norah at the hospital and tell her that Mark didn't want to have a baby with her.'

Alice tensed. 'How do you know that?'

'A porter came forward. He overhead the conversation but he wasn't sure if it was relevant. Then we showed him your photo, and he confirmed it was you. So, I'll ask you again. Were you disappointed enough to confront Norah at the hospital about the IVF?'

'It wasn't like that.' Alice swallowed, suddenly realising how naive she'd been. And for what? It wasn't like her conversation with Norah had achieved anything. 'It just seemed unfair that Norah was making Mark go through it all, when he wasn't even sure he wanted to go back to the nappies at his age.'

'I see.' The detective's face was expressionless. 'And was that why you followed Norah to the IVF Clinic on Rodney Street?'

'It's complicated.'

'That's not an answer,' DI Day pressed. Alice felt like an insect stuck in a web while a spider sat staring at her. Deciding which way to wrap her up in thread. Mark had already told her that the police had the results from the clinic, yet for some reason they wanted her to say it out loud to them.

'Because Mark isn't Cassie's father, and I knew there was a chance that the results would reveal that.'

'And if they did, how would that impact on you?'

'This isn't about me. It's about Mark and Cassie. They're father and daughter regardless of whether it was his sperm. I just didn't want anything to change.'

'Except it would change,' DI Day continued. 'So, you tried to make sure Mark never found out the truth.'

Silence settled between them as Alice finally saw the entirety of the web. There were no other suspects. Not Scott. Not Mark. Just her.

'I swear I had nothing to do with Norah's murder,' she said, her voice getting higher and higher. 'What about the man I saw her talking to at the park?'

'There is no man, Alice.' DI Day's voice was cool. 'But, of course, you know that. You picked a random time when no one could corroborate your story and set it in a place where there were no CCTV cameras.'

No. That's not what had happened. 'That's probably why they *did* meet there,' she said, hating that something so logical was now being turned against her.

'I see. And how do you explain the camera footage that we did find?' The detective pulled out a photograph and slid it across the table. It was of a woman with a ponytail standing outside a high brick wall. Her stomach sank. It was her. The day she'd decided to break into the potting shed so she could spy on Mark and Norah.

It wasn't damning in itself. But it helped create a story. The ex-wife who seemed to be following her younger, more beautiful replacement around. The lies about her daughter's real father. The need to cover up the truth and stop Mark from finding out. It all made so much sense. And the worst of it was that it was all true.

Those things had all happened, and she could tell by the way Belinda's eyes were shining that she believed it could only mean one thing. That Alice had killed Norah.

The whole is greater than the sum of its parts.

Alice's mouth went dry and the truth seeped through her, working its way into her bones until her body began to shiver. This was really happening.

'You don't understand.' She held up her hands, as if to stop the tide from coming in, but it was futile and DI Day stood up and smoothed down her jeans.

'Alice, we're currently obtaining a search warrant for your house. You're to stay here voluntarily until after the search, or we will be charging you.'

* * *

Cassie stared at her phone. She'd sent Scott several more messages, but he still hadn't answered. At this point, she'd probably be more surprised if he did. His mother had filed a missing person's report, but the police hadn't had any sightings.

Had he decided to go to Portugal without her? Probably. It wasn't like their relationship had even been real.

God, he must've thought he'd hit the jackpot with her. And the worst of it was that Alice had tried to warn her, over and over again, not because she was being a bitch, but because she'd seen what had happened to Jasmine. But Cassie hadn't listened.

Her cheeks heated with shame. As if sensing her pain, Hugo, who was curled up in the crook of her arm, nuzzled in closer to her. She ran her fingers through his fur, grateful for the way it anchored her. It was only the warmth of his body and his sweet snuffling noises that were keeping her sane.

Cassie nestled back into the sofa in Alice's sitting room. She hadn't planned to come back to the house last night. But after her shift she'd gone out for a drink with Felix and Tamsin and they'd both pointed out that sleeping in the car or at a park would be a hundred times worse.

At least there was no sign of her when Cassie had come downstairs earlier, not even a note on the bench. She was still furious with her mother for all the lies, but she was also exhausted from trying to manage so many conflicting emotions. If this was adulting, she got why there were so many memes about it.

Because it was fucking shit.

Her phone pinged with a text message and Hugo let out a little bark.

It was from Mark.

Hey, kiddo. I'm outside the house. You ready to talk?

Tears prickled her eyes. How could everything be so different, when he was still exactly the same? He was always considerate. Never came into her room without knocking. Never made her talk about things she didn't want to talk about. And even now, he was still like that.

She carefully lifted Hugo up and settled him on the sofa before going to the window. Mark was standing on the footpath. He looked like shit but at the sight of her, he gave her a wan smile. They were both victims here.

She beckoned him in and then went to open the front door.

'Thank you, love. Is your mum around?'

'No. She was gone before I got up.'

His shoulders visibly relaxed. They might not be related any more, but at least they still had something in common right now. Neither of them wanted to speak to Alice – at least not until they'd had a chance to understand her betrayal.

'Did you want to go out somewhere or talk here?'

'Here,' she said, thinking of ongoing interest in the case. They headed through to the small sitting room in silence.

Her dad sat on the sofa, and she sat opposite on the edge of the overstuffed armchair. She took hold of the hem of her cardigan and wrapped it around and around her finger, until it was so tight the circulation was almost cut off. It was tempting to leave it – the numbing pain preferable to the swirl of emotions she was currently experiencing.

'Cassie,' he finally said. 'I know this is a shock to you. To me, too.' He gave a hollow laugh. 'But nothing's changed. Not for me, anyway. You're my daughter and you'll always be my daughter. I'm sorry I didn't say that to you straight away, but I need you to know it's true. I love you. And I'll always be here for you.'

His head was tilted to one side in that oh-so-familiar way, and a sob caught in her throat. She hadn't realised quite how much she'd needed to hear that.

'Thanks, Dad,' she said, sniffing.

'Come here.' He held out his arms and she went to join him on the sofa. He pulled her closely to him and he held her tight while she sobbed into his shoulder.

'Why did she do it? Why did she lie?' Cassie said once the tears had finally stopped.

'I guess she thought she was protecting you. Me. Us.'

'Well, she wasn't,' Cassie said, her sadness giving way to the underlying panic that had kept her up last night. Because if Mark wasn't her father, then someone else was, and it meant she'd never had the chance to meet them. Again, the gaping hole of Scott's absence filled her. She needed him to come back so that they could go away together. Just the two of them, like she'd planned. They could live in a bubble where it didn't matter who her parents were. Where it didn't matter about anything that wasn't them.

'I know,' he murmured, planting a kiss on her hair, just like he'd always done when she was sad. She leaned into his arms as her lack of sleep started to catch up on her. Her eyelids grew heavy.

Brrrinnng.

The doorbell caused Cassie to jump, and Mark tensed in alarm, as if expecting Alice. For the first time in ages, Cassie burst out laughing.

'Relax. Mum wouldn't ring the bell.'

He flushed. 'Good point.'

Cassie got to her feet and walked to the door, Hugo trailing along behind her. She opened it up and then took a step back. Crowded on the path were the policewoman from the other day, and three more people she didn't recognise. Behind them, several neighbours had crowded around the police car, obviously eager to see if there were any developments. God, but she hated people sometimes.

'Cassie, I'm DI Day. We spoke the other day.'

'My mum's not here right now,' she said, not quite sure why they'd come without calling first. Was that even allowed?

'That's okay. She doesn't need to be here. We have a warrant to search your house.'

'What's this about?' Her dad joined her at the door. He nodded to DI Day, who returned the greeting.

'Mr Hargraves. I was just explaining that we're here to search the house.' She handed over a piece of paper to him. 'It would be helpful if you could go out with Cassie. We don't know how long we'll be.'

'I don't want to go out,' Cassie said, a hint of panic catching in her voice. Why were they here? Surely it should be the house where Norah had been murdered. Not here.

'What if we wait in the garden?' her dad asked.

The DI nodded. 'As long as you don't obstruct us.'

'What are you looking for exactly?' her dad asked, brows furled together.

'It's standard procedure in cases like these.' The DI gave a vague wave of her hand, but it was obvious she was lying. Cassie's stomach dropped and her dad put a calming hand on her shoulder.

'It's okay; I think it's best if we let the police get on with it.' He led her through the kitchen and out into the garden. Alice hadn't wanted to pay for a gardener, which meant the grass had grown and there were weeds poking up between the paving stones. Cassie wrapped the cardigan around her as they sat on the outside chairs, and crossed her legs.

'What do they mean *standard procedure*? It's not like Norah ever came to the house, so what will they be looking for?'

'I don't know.' He ran a hand through his hair.

'Will they make a mess of my bedroom? And put that powder stuff on everything?'

'I doubt it. They're not taking fingerprints, from what she said. Hopefully they won't take too long, it's not like you live in a big house. And—' He broke off as one of the officers walked past them and through to the side gate where the wheelie bin and recycling were kept.

A second one followed him out and the pair of them lifted the lid and tilted it so that the contents spilled out onto the pavers, creating a mess of empty pizza boxes and food scraps. The officers were both wearing gloves as they began to systematically search the mess.

'Why are they going through our rubbish?'

'I suppose they have to look everywhere,' her dad said as one of the officers stood up and stalked past them towards the back door.

'Ma'am, we've found something.'

What the—

Cassie was on her feet before her dad could drag her back down. She hurried towards the remaining officer, who was carefully holding what looked like her mum's disgusting old blue cardigan that she refused to throw away. It was wrapped around something, but it was impossible to see what it was.

'You need to stand back, right now.' DI Day's voice was sharp, and Cassie was herded back to the table as the police huddled together, having a low conversation. Finally, the detective joined them, followed by the two officers.

'Do you recognise this?' DI Day nodded to the cardigan that the officer was still holding in his gloved hands.

'It's Mum's,' Cassie said before catching the smears of dirt all over it. It was filthy. Like it had been buried. The two officers exchanged a look, and too late Cassie realised that something else was going on. Something that involved Alice. Her stomach lurched as if she was walking on a tightrope.

'DC Smith, can you please show Cassie and her father what you found?'

The officer nodded and slowly opened it out to reveal a long knife. It was covered in the same brown stains all over the cardigan, and – oh God. It wasn't dirt. It was blood.

Cassie gasped and her dad let out a soft moan, as his hand reached for hers. His skin was cold. This couldn't be happening. They couldn't possibly think her mother had anything to do with Norah's death. Alice was many things, but she wasn't a killer. She—

'Have you seen this knife before?' the detective asked, her voice almost lost against the roaring sound crashing through Cassie's mind.

'No,' she whispered as bile rose in her throat. She was going to be sick. Everything was happening too fast. Norah's death, Scott's betrayal, and now a knife wrapped up in Alice's cardigan. It was too much.

'Detective, what does this mean?' Her dad pulled his hand away from her as he stood up, his eyes never leaving the bloodied knife. 'You don't think... this isn't...' The words trailed off, as if he couldn't bear to say them. No one spoke and her father let out a guttural moan. 'No. Please. No. You can't mean it.'

'We believe this might be the murder weapon. This house is now a crime scene, and Alice Hargraves is our main suspect.'

18

Belinda finished giving instructions to the rest of the team before beckoning Ryan over. 'I'm heading back to the station. Stay here and make sure the daughter and ex-husband don't try to come back inside.'

'Yes, ma'am,' he said. Not that she was expecting them to. The pair had been silent as they'd gone upstairs so Cassie could pack. The bedroom had reminded Belinda of her own teenage years. Posters covering the walls, clothing on the floor and the stacks of books and knickknacks filling the bookshelf. Except Cassie's face didn't look like it had a few days ago. She was pale and silent as she'd ghosted around the room before finally leaving the house with her father, who'd been visibly shocked.

Clearly neither of them had suspected Alice.

She could empathise with them. No one was ever black and white, and people who committed terrible crimes could still have redeeming qualities. They could also be good at masking their darkness and hiding their secrets.

Was that what Alice Hargraves had done? Belinda still

wasn't sure, but her job was to follow the evidence and see where it led. And right now it was leading to Alice.

Belinda had exchanged a few words with Mark and arranged for the family liaison officer to drive them to the hotel where he was still staying.

It was only a five-minute drive to the station, but she needed to get everything straight in her mind. It had been an easy find. Too easy? But then again, after fifteen years on the job, she'd learned that most people who broke the law weren't that smart. And even if they were, it didn't mean they always made rational decisions.

The real question was whether Alice Hargraves had been smart enough to cover her tracks. Why hide the evidence in her own wheelie bin? It was the first question she'd posed to Ryan. He'd been concerned as well, until they'd door-knocked and spoken to the neighbour. The old woman was clearly rattled by the numerous police cars but had explained that the bins were usually collected on Friday morning, and that her husband would bring in their bin and Alice's. He'd done it so often that she'd given him a key to the entryway so he could put it back.

'Because it stops those little shits at number sixty-eight kicking them about,' she'd added with a sharp nod towards the end of the street. She'd gone on to say the truck hadn't shown up on Friday. Belinda, who lived a few streets over, knew that it wasn't uncommon. So the husband had simply taken both wheelie bins back in and locked the gate for Alice.

In other words, unless Alice had checked the wheelie bin, she probably would've assumed the knife and cardigan were on their way to oblivion in some landfill.

It was plausible, but Belinda would reserve judgement until she'd resumed the interview with Alice Hargraves.

Her phone buzzed and Tim's number flashed up on the

screen. She was half tempted to ignore it, but there was a small chance she'd need to return to the house, so she picked up. 'I'm back in ten minutes. Can it wait?'

'No, ma'am. A body's been found in a flat on Smithdown Road. It hasn't been formally identified yet but the name on the driver's licence is Scott Williams. It's in the same building as the two cousins live.'

Shit. Belinda closed her eyes for a moment and thought of Cassie Hargraves's woebegone face. Then she pushed it from her mind.

'Text me the address. I'm heading over there right now. And make sure that Alice Hargraves does *not* leave the station before I get back.'

The traffic was light and Belinda pulled up outside the apartment block. It was a busy road, and the yellow brick of the apartments was covered in grime. A PC was standing in the doorway of the block. Belinda flashed her warrant card and made her way in. It was on the second floor and the stairwell was a dull concrete that stank of things she didn't want to think about, while graffiti covered the walls. It obviously hadn't been gentrified yet.

She stepped into the flat and almost gagged. It was a sickly combination of rotting cabbage with over-ripe fruit. The forensics team were already there and while Belinda knew better than to get in their way, she didn't have time to wait. She beckoned over a DS who she knew well.

'What have we got?'

'The body was found an hour ago by a couple who have been out of the country for two months. The apartment had been empty while they were away. It wasn't the homecoming they'd imagined. We obviously don't have the official report yet, but it looks like a knife attack.'

'Has anyone rounded up Scott Williams's cousins? They both live in the building.'

'Yes, ma'am, they've been taken in for questioning.'

'And any sign of a murder weapon?'

'Not yet. There was a baseball cap and a wallet and phone. Oh, and in his hands was a strand of blue wool that possibly belonged to his attacker.'

Belinda's eyes widened. 'I need the lab results of that wool as quickly as possible, along with the forensic results. In the meantime, I'm going back to the station.'

'Yes, ma'am.' The DS nodded and disappeared back into the flat. Belinda went back to the car and called Ryan, giving him the update and telling him to meet her back at the station.

'You really think she did both of them?' he said.

Disappointment prickled her gut. It shouldn't always upset her when it was the woman who was guilty. Just because she was a feminist, it didn't mean all women were good and all men were bad. Still, she'd silently hoped it hadn't been Alice. She'd liked the woman she'd first met in the park. The one who'd confessed to being a hot mess, and who'd let herself get covered in mud just to comfort a strange dog. But the evidence was not looking good.

'We'll find out soon enough.'

* * *

'What did you tell the police?' Ben Thomas asked. Alice tried to remember but the words seemed to dissolve in her mouth before she could use them. It was like she was in a surreal play where nothing made sense.

After the police got a warrant to search her house, she'd insisted on calling Wendy, the solicitor that she'd used for the purchase of her property. Wendy had sent along one of the other partners in the firm, who dealt with criminal law.

Criminal law.

So that's what she was now classed as.

It also explained why she was still at the station. It had been almost ten hours since she'd walked through the doors. A lifetime ago. Ben had told her they could hold her for twenty-four hours without arrest. It wasn't comforting.

'I know this is hard,' Ben said in a thick Manchester accent, so different from the scouse ones she heard every day. Shit. She needed to focus. He was looking at her now, watery blue eyes filled with concern. 'But it's important I know.'

Alice nodded, trying to retrieve the threads of the conversation she'd had with the detective. 'I just answered her questions about where I was at the time of the murder, and why I hadn't told Mark the truth about not being Cassie's father,' she said and then winced.

And so you tried to make sure Mark never found out the truth.

She looked up at him. 'They think I did it, don't they? They really think I killed Norah.'

It was meant as a question, but she could see the way Ben folded back in on himself. As if wanting to separate himself from the words she'd just said. As if it was a confession. Her eyes widened.

'*You* think I did it as well.'

'It doesn't matter what I think.' He coughed and smoothed down his suit. 'You're not obliged to answer any of their questions. My advice would be to remain silent. We'll see what evidence, if any, they have against you. Did they read you your rights?'

'They told me I'm not under arrest but that what I say can be used as evidence.'

'And that's why you should remain silent.'

The door to the interview room opened and DI Day and DS Walton stood in the doorway. It had only been several hours, but they'd changed completely. Not their clothes, or their expressions. But there was something lurking just behind their eyes. Anger. Disappointment. Rage. Something had happened.

No. Alice swallowed. She couldn't go there. Dragging in a deep breath, she waited as the officers sat down, without saying anything. DI Day pressed the recording.

'Interview resumed. Joining us is...' She nodded at Alice's solicitor.

'Ben Thomas. Solicitor.'

'Alice, tell us about your relationship with Scott Williams.' DI Day's voice was glacial.

Scott? Alice's brows furrowed together. 'What do you mean?'

'Did you like him? Were you happy that he and your daughter were planning to go away on a gap year together?'

'Of course not. What mother would be?' Alice said before she could stop herself. She took a breath. 'No, I didn't like him. Neither did Mark. He smelled of trouble. And considering what happened between him and Norah, we were right.'

'Why is this relevant?' Ben asked.

'Because three hours ago Scott Williams's body was found. We're still waiting for the results, but it appears to be a knife attack. The same way Norah Richmond was killed.'

Alice let out a reluctant gasp.

Dead?

God. She hadn't liked him, but Cassie had. And the boy had a mother and father. Too late she realised she should have considered that before answering the question. She looked up to see the two detectives studying her. Looking for clues. She shivered.

'Alice, we have been at your house and found something that we'd like to ask you about.' DS Walton opened up a folder and pulled out a piece of paper. He slid it over to Alice.

It was a photo of a cardigan. It was blue and there was a hole in one cuff where she'd ripped it on a nail in Mark's potting shed. It was also covered in mud. She frowned. Had Hugo managed to tug it out of the wheelie bin and drag it into the garden?

'Do you recognise this?'

'Yes. It's my cardigan. But I threw it out the other day because it was beyond repair. Why are you showing this to me?'

'How is this relevant?' Ben cut in as DS Walton pulled out a second photograph and passed it over to them. This one was of a large kitchen knife with a serrated edge, the blade covered in blood and splatters higher up on the handle. Alice's hand flew to her mouth. Good God. Was that Norah's blood? Had that blade been the one to slice into her flesh and drain her of life? Alice's skin prickled and she took a shuddering breath. The two detectives exchanged a glance before nodding, as if pleased with how it was going.

'Detective Inspector, has this knife been identified as the murder weapon?' Ben asked, leaning in to study it with a detached interest.

'It is currently with forensics for examination, but we are working on the assumption that it is likely to be. It was found wrapped in the cardigan that Mrs Hargraves has just admitted to owning.'

'I also said that I threw it out,' Alice said, still trying to plough through the fog in her mind. Ben gave her a sharp look as he steepled his fingers in consideration. Then he turned to her.

'Alice, my advice is for you not to answer the question.'

'But why not? That knife isn't mine. All of my kitchen knives have wooden handles. I've had them for years. They were a wedding present from one of my aunts. You can check in my kitchen drawers if you don't believe me. All the knives are the same.'

'Then why was this particular knife found at your house?'

'That's not possible,' she said, but her voice seemed to echo around the small room, making it sound tinny and insincere. She swallowed and turned to Ben. He raised an eyebrow as if to remind her of his advice. Shit. 'No comment.'

'We appreciate that you're entitled to not comment when we question you, but if you have nothing to hide then why do it? All it means is we will draw our own conclusions regarding what we found. Why don't you explain how the knife came to be at your house?' DI Day's tone was firm.

Did she really want to get at the truth or was she just trying to get Alice to incriminate herself? Except how could she when she'd never seen that knife before?

'Where did you find it?' Alice asked. Ben's shoulders tensed, but she had to get this sorted. She had to make them understand it wasn't her.

'In the wheelie bin at the side of the house,' DI Day said with a challenge to her voice. Alice's heart pounded. The entry down the side of the house had a metal gate across the front that was locked, to stop anyone walking through to the back.

Silence filled the room, and her vision began to blur. How could this be happening? She hadn't done anything to Norah. This was all just a terrible mistake that she needed to clear up.

'I swear that I didn't put it there.' She clutched at the table to stop the room from swimming.

'Officer, my client has had enough. Either you charge her or let her go.'

'Alice Hargraves, we are charging you with the murders of Norah Richmond and Scott Williams. You do not have to say anything, but it may harm your defence if you do not mention when questioned something which you later rely on in court. Anything you do say may be given in evidence. Do you understand?'

No. She didn't understand it at all. The room was silent. All eyes on her. Waiting for her to answer. DI Day and DS Watson were relaxed, as if they had all the time in the world.

This was really happening.

'Yes,' Alice whispered as she turned to Ben. He gave her a grim smile that did nothing to stop the spinning sensation bombarding her. He really needed to work on that.

'Take her to the custody suite.'

'Yes, ma'am.' DS Walton stood up and waited for Alice to do the same. Her legs felt weak, like she hadn't used them for years. As she was taken from the room, Ben lowered his voice and directed something to DI Day, but Alice couldn't hear it. It was wrong. Why couldn't they see that? Then she stiffened. The knife hadn't got there by accident. Which meant whoever *had* killed Norah and Scott was framing her for it. But why?

What had she done to anyone to make them do this?

What had Norah done?

Her mind swirled. Somehow it was all connected, but she had no idea how. A man's face blurred in her mind. The football fan from the *Echo*. It was the man from the park. The one who'd been arguing with Norah. Of course. It was him. She stopped abruptly and turned to the detective sergeant.

'Yesterday's *Echo* had an article about Everton fans. Something to do with VAR. Anyway, I saw him in the photograph. The man who met Norah in the park.'

The detective stared at her as if she'd just sprouted an extra head. 'Please keep walking, otherwise I'll need to restrain you.'

'You don't understand,' Alice said, her voice rising, but it died in her throat when she looked over to where Cassie, Mark and Felix were standing. Felix's eyes were filled with horror and confusion. As if he couldn't understand how she could possibly have done it. But it was her daughter and ex-husband's expressions that destroyed her. Cassie's eyes were wide and her mouth was twisted in horror, while Mark's face was a stony mask of fury.

The fight left her as DS Walton nudged her forward.

The people she loved best in the world thought she was guilty.

And in a way, she was.

19

The session was in full swing. The team had claimed a table in the corner of The White Swan and were having a raucous discussion about their first trips abroad. Belinda balanced the tray in one hand and squeezed between the growing crowd. It was a popular pub for a few of the stations and several colleagues had come past with a drink and congratulations. And rightly so. Murder cases could take years to solve, or remain in the system, gathering cobwebs, as the clues went cold.

They'd found extra evidence after gaining access to Alice's phone, which showed she'd called both Norah and Scott on the day of the murder, and had accessed Mark's cloud-based security footage, which supported the theory that Alice had been stalking Norah – so jealous of her rival, and desperate for her own dark secret not to be revealed, that she'd killed her.

It was a strong case, especially with the murder weapon, and the crown prosecutor agreed, which meant Belinda should be happy. And she *was* happy. She winced. Almost. The only thing missing was that sense of rightness that usually came when all the parts joined together. It was a buzz that usually washed over her, letting her know that it was done.

Except a buzz was quantifiable. It was as unmeasurable as a 'gut feeling', and she'd worked on plenty of cases when she hadn't had that sense of completion. This was just another of those times.

She certainly wasn't going to let it interfere with her team taking a night off to celebrate. They'd worked bloody hard and deserved to soak up the praise and the alcohol. But Belinda was trying to ignore the tension headache building in her skull.

She was too old for this.

A week of no sleep, adrenaline and caffeine was taking its toll and all she wanted to do was walk her dog, take off her bra and have a quiet glass of wine. And perhaps sex with Tara. Heat hit her cheeks as she thought of the message she'd received yesterday from an ex-girlfriend.

I'm in town. Would love to see Hetty again. And you... I miss your face.

Belinda hadn't even bothered to reply at the time. After all, murder and romance didn't really go hand in hand. But she'd finally responded while she was at the bar, and the answer had been immediate.

See you in an hour.

She finally reached the table and put down the tray. Her team let out a roar.

'Cheers.' Ryan held up his pint to her, some of his natural reserve disappearing. 'What a week. Still can't believe we got her. Must be such a relief for the entire family.'

'Let's hope so.' Belinda held up a glass of water. The pair of them still had a long path to healing the trauma of the two murders, but at least they had answers, instead of the many question marks that so many families were left with after a homicide.

'Not that it will be easy,' he agreed, half draining his pint. He looked questioningly at her own empty glass. Belinda almost laughed. He didn't miss much. 'You not having another one?'

'Think I'll call it a night.'

'Please tell me you're not doing paperwork?' Ryan said; there was a slight slur to his voice and even though he could hold his drink, she suspected he'd have a headache tomorrow.

'Definitely not,' she said, her skin prickling at the memory of Tara trailing kisses down her neck. She reached for her bag, pulled out two twenty-pound notes from her purse and handed them over. 'But here's another round on me.'

'Thanks, guv. I think that will go down well with the team.' Ryan grinned and finished his pint. 'Here's to a killer being taken off the street. If her best defence is some random Everton fan in the *Echo*, she'll be in Bronzefield by next year.'

Belinda blinked. 'What Everton fan?'

'Oh.' Ryan gave a vague wave of his hand as he unsteadily got to his feet and retrieved the tray to buy another round. 'She was trying to tell me the guy from the park that the deceased allegedly met was in some photo in the *Echo* on Saturday.'

'When did she tell you this?'

He shrugged. 'On the way to the cells. And don't worry. I checked it out. But it was a photo of a packed Gwladys Street End celebrating a goal. It was clearly a sad attempt. I mean, it could be half the population of Liverpool,' he said, referring to the two football clubs that divided Merseyside into blues or reds. Belinda opened her mouth and then closed it again. Ryan was right. Looking for a random Everton fan in Liverpool would be like sifting through grains of sand.

Her phone pinged with a text message, and she opened it up. It was a photo of Tara wearing only a bra. Belinda pushed her way through the bar; the sooner she got home, the sooner she could try and remember that she was more than just her bloody job.

* * *

'Congratulations, Day, good work. I'll be pleased to put this one to bed.'

Belinda started at the sound of her boss's voice. Heat stung her cheeks. It was an indication of just how much sex she'd had last night, to have not heard him come into her office.

'Thank you, sir.' She dropped her hands to her sides and sat upright.

'I didn't expect you in so early. I was going to leave a note on your desk regarding the next steps. I hope you and the team had a good night.'

'They definitely let their hair down.' Belinda nodded in agreement, Ryan's drunken comment still playing through her mind.

If her best defence is some random Everton fan in the Echo, *she'll be in Bronzefield by next year.*

Just a desperate woman clutching at straws. All the same Belinda had sworn she'd never become one of those coppers who went for the convenient solution rather than the right one. Especially when the niggle that something wasn't right was still with her.

Which was why she was staring at the blurred photo of the

Gwladys Street crowd. Ryan hadn't been exaggerating, and while it was possible to pick out a couple of faces, there were almost one hundred people there.

'I've arranged the press conference for this afternoon. We'll be releasing the name of the second victim at the same time. I'd like you to be with me to answer any questions I field to you.'

'Is it wise to announce we've arrested someone just yet, sir? Shouldn't we wait until we have the post-mortem results and made sure everything's in order?'

Her boss raised an eyebrow, and she wasn't really surprised. Before his rise, he'd had a reputation as a meticulous DI who always let the evidence lead him. It was one of the things she respected about him. And that wasn't something she could say about all her past bosses.

'The CPS have okayed it. You have the weapon, linked the two cases, and have established a strong motive to ensure her daughter wasn't cut out of a will that could be anywhere up to the tune of twenty million quid. There's also the concerning instances of spying on Norah Richmond, including breaking into a garden shed to watch her as well as viewing the security footage from the house. Not to mention she has no alibi. Our part is done, and now it's up to the courts to decide.'

He was right. She knew he was, so it was pointless to explain that she didn't have the buzz of knowing a case was closed. Instead, she nodded her head.

'Sorry, I'm just overthinking it.' From tomorrow her days would be filled with the next case to come across her desk. There was no time or budget to follow clues that would probably lead nowhere.

'Don't be sorry. I'd much rather you think about a case more, not less,' he said, then leaned forward, eyes seeming to land on the photograph. 'Christ, but that's a face from the past.'

Belinda's heart pounded. 'Excuse me, sir?'

He pointed a finger to a face that seemed to be looking up at the camera. 'There. Bloody Roy Walsh. A local loan shark who started life in the adult entertainment industry producing porn, then running the kind of websites you hope your kids never find. He was always as slippery as Teflon. I only got close to nabbing him once. I was hoping he'd retired to a caravan in Wales. Or anywhere so that I'd never have to see him again.' Then he let out a sigh. 'More's the bloody pity.'

Roy Walsh.

Belinda waited until her boss had left her office before picking up her phone. It was safest to do a simple off-the-record search and see what she could find. It wasn't pleasant reading. Roy Walsh was originally from Scotland but had gone to London where he'd run a host of websites that represented the very worst of the internet. But as advertising revenues had fallen, he'd turned up in Liverpool ten years ago where he'd quickly let himself be known to the police by getting caught up in a money-laundering scheme. Somehow he'd managed to avoid prison, but he still seemed to skate close to the edge.

And one of his sites had been notorious for all the revenge porn that people posted.

The hair on her arms prickled as she downloaded a couple of clearer photos of him and rubbed her brow. Part of her longed to go and interview him, but it was pointless. It wasn't illegal to go to a football game. Which meant if she wanted to find out if he was the man who'd allegedly met Norah at the park, she was going to have to ask the only witness there was.

Alice.

20

The prison bed was hard and unyielding, and Alice leaned forward, trying to get comfortable. It didn't work. Maybe that was the point. She wasn't meant to be comfortable. Was prison designed to suck away all the tiny pieces of her until there was nothing left? At least now she had a valid excuse to tell her editor for why her next book was late. Then again, she could always illustrate *Alfred the Rabbit Goes to Jail*. It was sure to be a bestseller.

She gave a hollow laugh, which somehow turned to tears. She didn't bother to brush them away.

Why her? What had she done in her life that was so bad? All she'd ever wanted was to give a safe and secure life to her daughter. Surely it wasn't too much to ask. Any parent would feel the same.

The hatch to her cell opened, but Alice couldn't see anything. 'Stand by your bed, away from the door,' barked a female voice.

In a day she'd learned that it was easier to do as she was

told. It made for a lot less yelling. She stood by the window as the door opened to where the officer was standing.

'You have a visitor.'

'Who?' Her head snapped up as hope filled her chest – the kind that she hadn't allowed herself to feel. Cassie? Mark? Did this mean they knew she wasn't guilty? That they believed her?

As if understanding what the high-pitched voice and breathiness meant, the officer let out a cruel laugh. 'The police. Hurry up, I don't have all day.'

Alice's heart sank. Should she refuse to see them without her solicitor present? And why were they visiting? Ben had called her yesterday to give the grim news. The post-mortem confirmed that Norah and Scott had both been killed with the same knife they'd found in Alice's wheelie bin, and that her prints were all over it.

No. She tried to tell Ben it was impossible. How could her prints get on a knife that she'd never seen before? But he had no answer for her, and instead gave her the timeline of events. She was due in court next week, where the judge would decide whether to take the case to trial. If that happened, Ben had warned that it was unlikely that she'd be given bail.

'Do I have to go?' Alice asked the officer.

'Are you refusing?'

'Yes... No... I don't know.'

'Well, make up your mind. I have better things to do than wait for you.'

Alice chewed her lip. It was a habit that she'd started last week, and it had somehow become a daily ritual. Almost a comfort. Except if she kept it up, she'd probably have no skin left around her mouth. Maybe leaving her cell would act as a distraction? But on one condition. She couldn't allow herself to ask about Cassie or Mark. Because knowing might shatter whatever was holding her together and keeping her tethered.

'Okay,' she finally answered. The officer grunted for her to hold out her wrists. Alice blinked before realising she was going to be handcuffed. The metal was cold and heavy, and rubbed at her skin, but she tried to ignore it as she was shuffled down the corridor, through some locked gates and into a small room. Once she was inside there was a clicking noise that suggested it had been locked again. From one small room to another. Probably not such a great distraction after all.

There was a single table and two chairs and a poster advertising a creative writing course that was three years out of date. Unsure what else to do, she pulled out one of the chairs and sat down. It was several minutes before the same clinking noise rang out and the door opened. DI Day walked in, and the door was once again closed.

She looked good. The dark smudges under her eyes were gone and if Alice was right she had a hint of make-up on. Obviously, her days had improved since putting Alice into jail. She tried not to be bitter.

'Thank you for seeing me. I'm sorry to turn up without any notice,' Belinda said, sinking into the other seat.

It wasn't like she had anything else to do. Or any other visitors. 'What's this about?'

'I want to ask you about the man from the park.'

'The one you said didn't exist,' she said in a snippy voice. It was rude of her, but she didn't really care. After all, no one seemed to care about offending her.

DI Day's impassive mask broke for a second and she frowned. 'You must admit it didn't look good. There was no evidence to prove it was true.'

'Apart from my word.'

'Apart from your word,' the detective agreed before holding up her hands. 'Alice, I'm not here to fight or trick you. I'm just here to talk about the man you saw.'

'I told you everything I know,' she said, the fight going out of her. It had been happening a lot lately. Trying to cope with the events of the last week had become endlessly draining – like a battery that no longer worked properly. Her capacity to stay connected was getting less by the day. And that was before she'd been brought to this place yesterday.

Ironically, she'd always spent a lot of time alone. The endless hours in her studio, painting and working on her books. But there had never been this void inside her before. A nothingness that seemed to be taking over.

Belinda took a piece of paper out of her jacket pocket and passed it over. It was the newspaper article from the *Echo*.

'Can you point to the man that you saw talking to Norah Richmond?'

Alice frowned and looked at the photo. It was a blur of faces – like one of those paintings where if you looked too hard, you couldn't see anything. She shut her eyes and looked again, this time widening her focus, as if she didn't care. The blur morphed into a lined face and a head of thinning spiked hair. She lifted up her cuffed wrists and awkwardly pointed with her index finger.

'That's him, but I don't know anything else about him. He was talking to Norah. It looked like they were arguing. But I was too far away to hear what they were saying.'

'Are you sure?' the detective pushed. 'I really want you to think about it. Is there anything that stood out?'

'I have thought about it. Repeatedly,' Alice said. 'But that's all I saw. Who is he?'

'Roy Walsh is a loan shark who dabbles in money laundering. And some other things. Not a nice person. Can you think of any reason Norah would need to borrow money?'

'Loan shark? That makes no sense. Mark's incredibly rich – and generous. If she needed money, he would have simply given it to her,' Alice said, bitterness rising in her throat. That had been her life once. Free from monetary worries.

'What if it was something she didn't want him to know about? Like credit card debt, or an old student loan that got out of hand?'

Alice stared at her. They both knew the answer to that. If Norah had those kinds of money problems, the police would have found some sign of it. And Alice would be the last person to know about them. Except for the fact she'd spent far too much time following Norah around.

'I never saw anything to suggest she had money problems.'

'Do you think he saw you when he was meeting Norah at the park? Or have you ever spoken to him?'

'Why are you asking me that?'

'I'm trying to establish if he had anything against you,' the detective clarified, and the lethargy that had been enveloping Alice faded. She sat forward with interest. Was Belinda considering the idea she'd been framed?

'Are you reopening the case?'

Colour crept along the DI's neck, and she actually flinched. 'No. I'm just making sure that all avenues have been explored. I... I'm sorry if I gave you the wrong impression. But if you do have any questions or need any help, then please get in contact with me.'

Alice's hope retreated again. God, when would she learn to protect herself from thinking things would work out the way she wanted them to? Wasn't that the whole reason she was here now? Because she'd naively believed she deserved to get what she wanted?

Belinda walked towards the door. There were strands of dog hair on her jeans from where Hetty had brushed against her leg. And suddenly Alice was falling down the painful spiral that she'd been trying to avoid. Her, Mark and Cassie on a Sunday morning in the garden. The air filled with early jasmine as the bees drifted along the lavender bushes while Hugo barked in delight at the ball Cassie kept throwing to him.

It was her undoing. Pain tore at her throat, forcing her mouth open so that the words could spill out. Asking the one question that she'd promised she wouldn't.

'Please. Have you seen my daughter? Or Mark? A-are they okay? Have they asked about me?'

This time it was the DI's turn to be silent. It bounced around the room like a taunt, and the razor-sharp edge of it cut through the tiny sliver of hope that Alice had been holding on to. They hated her. The two people she loved most in the world hated her.

They said the truth hurt, but this was almost painless.

A clean cut. Slicing through the bones and arteries that had been holding her together.

Releasing her.

Once she was alone, Alice swallowed and slumped back into the chair. There wasn't going to be any last-minute rescue. This wasn't a movie. This was her life. And if she was honest, it was always going to end up here.

She'd known that one day she would have to pay the price for what she'd done.

Her karma. Okay, she hadn't killed Norah, but she'd done some bad things. Maybe not intentionally, but that didn't change the fact she deserved to spend the rest of her life in prison.

21

SEVENTEEN YEARS EARLIER

Alice pushed open the door and tried not to gag. The stench of stale beer and mould hit her as she looked around the dark room. She walked over to the window and pulled back the curtains, which were half-hanging from the rail. Pale light tried to push through the dirty windows. If anything, it made the flat appear even worse. There was a table in the middle of the room, with empty beer cans, syringes and white powder littered across it. It was disgusting.

In the corner was a baby stroller, and from the depths came a tiny cry. Alice reached down to carefully lift Lily out. This was wrong. Her tiny, perfect niece was only two weeks old and already her life was at risk. Lily's cries settled as Alice pressed the tiny girl into her own shoulder and began to gently rock.

Her sister was sitting on the sofa.

Alice couldn't believe this was the same Jasmine who'd left their London home two years ago to study art history at Newcastle. When she'd first been accepted, Alice had been thrilled, hoping it would be a new start for her brilliant but sensitive sister. At school Jasmine had started experimenting with drugs and alcohol but had given them up the summer before university.

And then she'd met Skunk.

Who would call themselves that? Jasmine had met him in their first year and within eight months had developed a serious drug habit. She'd soon been kicked out for non-completion of work and had moved in full-time with him. And while Jasmine swore she hadn't touched any gear since finding out she was pregnant, she was still jumpy and way too thin.

Alice stared at her now. Jasmine's arms were wrapped around her legs as she gently rocked back and forth. A dark purple bruise covered her cheek, and there were red welts in the shape of fingerprints on both of her arms. Christ.

It explained why Jasmine had called Alice last night, begging her to come back and get them.

Alice had made the long journey from London to Glasgow to see Jasmine and meet her new niece but had only been able to stay a few days before heading back to work. In that time Skunk had only put in one appearance. His hair was matted into unkempt dreadlocks and his cheekbones almost jutted through his narrow face, while his eyes were dilated. Definitely wasted. She wasn't even sure he'd seen her as he'd crashed around the place looking for money. It was only when he couldn't find any that he turned to Jasmine, mouth set in a sneer.

'Where the fuck is it?' His voice was raspy and slurred.

'I-I don't have any money,' Jasmine stammered, but he ignored her as his eyes finally found what he was looking for. A grimy handbag that Jasmine used to carry her wallet and Lily's nappies. He upended it and snatched up the tattered wallet, which Alice knew contained five twenty-pound notes that she'd given her sister earlier that day.

She opened her mouth to protest but Jasmine's terrified expression had stopped her, and she'd been forced to watch Skunk tear out the notes before flinging the wallet down on the floor. Then he'd stumbled out the door. It had all happened in less than five minutes.

From that moment Alice had tried everything she could think of to convince her sister to go with her. But Jasmine had refused to leave him, saying over and over that she loved him.

And so Alice had climbed on the train and started the journey back home but had only got as far as Newcastle when Jasmine had called, begging Alice to come back and save them.

So here she was.

Exhausted from travelling and worry, but here all the same.

Jasmine, scared that Skunk might find out, had made Alice promise not to come to the flat until after he'd left. Alice had dutifully caught a bus from the station and waited around the corner until Skunk climbed into a beaten-up old Fiesta and disappeared down the road.

'Did he see you, Letty?' Jasmine looked up; her eyes were clear, but her long fingers were knotted together, and her nails were bitten down to the quick. Her sister was the only person who still called her Letty. Alice hated the nickname. It made her sound like a servant girl from a Victorian novel. But Jasmine had never managed to remember.

'No. I was careful,' Alice said in an urgent voice as she picked up the tiny baby jacket she'd brought Lily as a gift. It was already grubby, and Alice realised that it probably hadn't been washed. Still, once they were safe, she'd buy Lily all the clothing she needed. And for Jasmine as well. 'Come on. We need to go. Once we're in London, everything will be okay. I can take care of you both.'

Well, she'd try.

Alice's own life hadn't exactly been going that great either. Mark had decided the lure of a job in Berlin was more important than their relationship and hadn't even considered trying to make it work long-distance. While her work at the graphic design firm was basically making cups of tea and answering emails.

She pressed the now sleeping Lily closer to her. The sweet scent of baby filled her as a familial bond roared to life. She tightened her hold on her tiny niece and swallowed back her guilt. Lily had been born two weeks early and Alice hadn't been able to change her days off at the agency, meaning that Jasmine and the baby had been living here... like this.

'Are you sure? What if he finds me? I'm scared of him, Letty.' Jasmine shook, her voice weak. She'd always been quiet and sensitive, the first to cry if an animal was hurt or injured. But there was another side to her as well – hidden behind the sensitivity was a bright, shiny girl who was smart, strong and impulsive, eager to try new things. But as she'd grown up, it was almost like the entire world was too painful for her to live in, and the impulsivity had led to addiction, burying the other parts of her beautiful sister. 'You don't know what he's like.'

That wasn't true.

Alice knew exactly what he was like – their father. And even though he'd died when she was eight, he'd inflicted enough damage on them both to remind Alice that every day spent with a psychopath was a day too many.

'I promise it will be okay.' They could move somewhere else. Change their names if they had to. Besides, with his emaciated frame, pinpoint pupils and scarred face from all the scabs he'd scratched, she wasn't sure how long Skunk would even live for. 'We need to go. Please, Jasmine. It has to be now.'

'Okay.' Her sister stood up gingerly, making Alice wonder

what other injuries her sister had. Jasmine fetched a jacket from the back of the chair. As she struggled into it, something slithered off from around her neck and fell onto the floor. Jasmine let out a low moan, like a wounded animal. 'No, no, no. Not this. It can't be broken.'

Alice instantly recognised the delicate gold necklace. It was the one their mother had given to Jasmine when she'd passed her GCSEs with amazing grades. It had all seemed so perfect back then. Before their mother's cancer had taken its toll and Jasmine had retreated from the world.

Alice carefully put the sleeping Lily back into the pushchair and retrieved the necklace. 'Hey, it's going to be okay. Look, the clasp was just stuck. Let me put it back on and then we can go. The train to London leaves in two hours.'

'London,' Jasmine echoed, as if it was the name of a long-lost lover. Her bony fingers clutched at the necklace that was once again sitting on her wasted collarbone.

'That's right. We're all going back to London,' Alice said in a soothing voice as she buttoned up her sister's jacket, just like she'd done many years ago. Jasmine didn't protest and seemed happy for Alice to steer both her and the baby stroller out of the apartment. 'I'll arrange for a cab to meet us a couple of blocks away.'

'Wait. Can we go down to the water one last time? To say goodbye?'

Alice frowned. Jasmine had thought Skunk would be out all day, but it still worried her. The sooner they were gone, the better. But Jasmine's lower lip was poking out, in a way Alice knew well. Her gentle sister had a stubborn streak that sometimes appeared.

'Fine. We'll go down to the water and walk along the front.

We can get a taxi from further along. It might be better that way.'

Jasmine nodded and started to walk. The apartment was in the middle of a rundown estate that was flanked by disused fields where houses and factories had once stood. Beyond them was a series of docks and then finally the River Clyde. They made their way down, pushing their way through the neglected grass, which was littered with bottles and takeaway containers.

The pushchair bumped across an old wooden bridge that acted as a pathway but the sleeping Lily didn't stir. The sun was leaking through the clouds, and despite the years of disrepair, there was something beautiful about the disused docks. The water was a dull brown but at least the air seemed a little fresher, bringing some colour into her sister's cheeks.

There was a steep bank with a low white wall between the path and the river below. She knew from her last visit that the path went on for over a mile, and once they were away from the estate she'd call a taxi, and then they'd be free.

The breeze picked up and dark clouds appeared, bringing with them a sudden burst of rain. Alice blinked as the rain intensified, leaving her dripping wet in a matter of seconds. Too late she remembered the old saying. *There's no such thing as bad weather. Just bad clothes.*

She yanked up the hood of her jacket and bent down to retrieve the plastic cover from under the stroller as Lily began to cry.

'It's okay. Good girl,' she crooned as she fumbled with the cover, trying to pull it over the hood so that the rain couldn't get in. There were only a few people in the distance and as the rain became heavier, they all disappeared. She couldn't blame them. 'Hey, Jaz, we need to go—'

Alice broke off as she turned around to see Jasmine

standing on the wrong side of the white fence. Her hair was plastered to her face and her bones jutted out against her jacket. In her arms was a bundle wrapped up in the soft baby blanket that Alice had brought with her as a gift.

For one terrible moment Alice thought Lily was in the blanket.

But she couldn't be. Lily was in the stroller. As if on cue, the baby let out another cry and Alice swallowed as she peered through the rain cover to see her tiny niece. Whatever Jasmine had in the bundle, it wasn't Lily.

'I can't do it,' Jasmine said, her voice almost lost in the wind as she let go of the fence and stepped closer to the riverbank. Her eyes were wide and manic. A look Alice knew all too well. Jasmine had taken something. 'I'm sorry, Letty. I'm not as strong as you. I want to be, but I'm not. Promise you'll look after Lily. You're the only one who can make sure she has a good life.'

'No,' Alice screamed, trying to push the stroller closer to where her sister was standing. She put out her hand. 'Jasmine. Please, you need to climb back over. It's not safe. Lily needs you. I need you. I have money and plenty of room. I can get you everything, and—'

'Promise me.' Jasmine cut her off, her voice suddenly urgent.

'Of course, I promise. I'll keep her safe. Always. But please. Just take my hand.'

Jasmine's face suddenly relaxed, making her look fourteen again. Back when she was so full of promise and life. Before the world had started to chip away at her. Before things had become too hard. 'You are such a good sister. I know you'll love her like I never could.'

And then she stepped off the side of the bank and down into the dark brown water of the river.

No.

Alice's screams were lost in the pounding wind and rain. She peered over the barrier. But the sudden storm had made it impossible to see anything as the swirling water swept everything away. She clutched at the railing with one hand, part of her desperate to jump in after her sister, but she couldn't leave the baby.

'Help,' she screamed but there was no one to hear. She fumbled with her phone. She had to call someone. The ambulance. The police. Someone. With shaking fingers, she stabbed in the emergency number. A voice answered but Alice could hardly hear.

She opened her mouth to speak as she stared at the roiling water below. Lily began to cry in earnest. Huge racking sobs that cut through the storm.

Promise me.

Jasmine's words echoed through her mind as the rain pounded against her skin. Lily continued to cry. What was she meant to do? Would they be able to find Jasmine? Save her? And if they couldn't, what would happen to Lily? She'd go to Skunk. To the father who was so addled on drugs that he couldn't speak.

Promise me.

The person at the other end spoke louder, but Alice didn't answer.

She could either try and save her sister, even though she knew the chances of Jasmine surviving were slim. Or she could save her niece.

Lily. So tiny. Only two weeks old. Who deserved a better start to life than a filthy apartment without a mother. Alice turned off her phone as her mind spun. Why had Jasmine jumped? It made no sense. Especially after she'd finally agreed to leave Skunk and move back to London to start a new life.

And then it hit her. Jasmine had never intended to go to London. She'd only called Alice back for one reason. To make sure Lily was safe. That's why she'd waited until Alice had left Glasgow – so Skunk wouldn't know she'd come back. Oh God.

Alice ended the call and then she peered down at the tiny baby in the stroller. Her cheeks were red from crying and her lashes were clumped together, glistening. She was so beautiful. So innocent.

And now she was hers.

She'd promised Jasmine that she'd raise Lily and give her a good life. Keep her away from Skunk and his violent temper and addiction. Still, that shouldn't be hard. He didn't even know her real name, and she'd make sure that he couldn't find Lily either.

'Oh, sweet baby girl. It's just you and me now. But I guess we need to find a new name for you. What about Cassie? Do you like that?'

The baby stopped crying and Alice's heart filled with love.

She was a mother, and from now on Cassie was her daughter.

22

FIVE MONTHS BEFORE THE TRIAL

The Eagle was an ugly concrete and brick pub that had been built in the sixties at the top end of Smithdown Road, and while it had survived the Liverpool 8 riots, it didn't appear to be prospering. Still, she'd been in worse places. Ryan was waiting in the silver Hyundai, which had been the only car left in the police pool. The DCI hadn't been pleased about her pursuing the case.

If Norah really had borrowed money from Roy Walsh, then where was it?

A careful examination of her bank records hadn't flagged anything suspicious, but the fact she might need it for something unspecified was plausible. He'd eventually approved it, while at the same time handing her a new case to work on. No such thing as a free lunch. And so she'd left most of the team door-knocking for the second case, while she and Ryan had stepped out.

It was two in the afternoon, and she had to squint as she stepped into the dark gloom. The seductive clang of the fruit machines played in the background and the yeasty stink of stale beer hung in the air. On the wall was a poster with a photograph of Scott Williams's face. Underneath, it said: *An evening to remember, from someone who was taken too soon.* The font was florid, like something from a wedding invitation, and the five-pound cover charge was to help raise money for his parents. She belatedly realised this must have been Scott's local.

The same place where Roy Walsh operated from. Interesting.

She walked past the poster and scanned the room. Roy Walsh wasn't hard to spot.

He was in his early forties, but the broken capillaries and bloodshot eyes made him appear older. He was wearing an Everton replica shirt and had his arm in a sling, as if he'd recently strained it.

Belinda made a beeline towards him, but before she'd even pulled out her warrant card, he'd held up his good arm in mock surrender.

'Well, what a nice way to break up an afternoon. Hello, Officer,' Roy said in a thick Scottish accent that hadn't been watered down since his move to England.

'It's "Detective",' she corrected with a smile as she held out her warrant card. 'DI Belinda Day. I was hoping to ask you a few questions.'

'Ah, hope is a wonderful thing, is it not?' He picked up a half pint of bitter and took a sip. 'As it goes, I'm a busy man.'

'Then I'll be quick.' She sat down opposite him and put a photo of Norah Richmond down on the table. 'Do you recognise this woman?'

'But of course. Such a terrible tragedy. Taken too soon, if you ask me.'

'I meant before the murder,' Belinda corrected, giving him a sharp glance. It bounced off him like a rubber ball.

'I'm sure you did,' he said. 'But I meet a good many people and can't recall.'

'Does Sunday the twenty-third of April at Sefton Park ring any bells? You were seen talking together.'

'I'll have to get my secretary to check my diary,' he said in a maddening voice, while his shrewd eyes studied her to see if he'd scored any points yet. He hadn't.

'You do that, and we'll arrange for you to come and give a statement in a more formal capacity.' She mirrored his tone. She was rewarded by a slight flinch, and his lips thinned in response.

'That won't be necessary. I don't recall ever meeting her, or going to Sefton Park. Too many scallies there.'

'So if we were to get a forensic accountant to go through your books, there wouldn't be any mention of Norah Richmond in your records?'

Again, he smiled. 'Most of the books on my shelf are by Lee Child. But if I did have any other kind, you wouldn't find that name mentioned. I give you my word.'

Belinda ignored his needling. 'What about from somewhere else? Like, say, from a revenge porn website?'

'Detective, it appears your tastes are more salacious than mine. Can't say I visit places like that.'

'Not even when you were a co-owner of one?' she snapped, her patience finally starting to wear thin.

'Was I? I have many business interests,' he said in a smooth voice that made Belinda long to strangle him. The site in question had been linked to several suicides and seemed to be a breeding ground for incels – the involuntary celibates who blamed women for not having sex with them. The fact that Roy profited from those kinds of sites, let alone could be so blasé about them, made him pond scum in her books. Belinda decided to move the interview along before she said something she might regret.

'How well did you know Scott Williams?' To her surprise a flash of annoyance darkened his features and then it was gone. She hadn't expected to get a hit.

'Only in passing. I know you shouldn't speak ill of the dead, but most of the kids today are skivers. Bloody Gen Z. Too busy thinking they're in a reality TV show with their bling and big gobs. Think they deserve the coin without getting their pretty little hands dirty.'

'What kind of coin?'

'Nothing to make you lose any sleep. Him and his cousins weren't that bright. A bit of arson and tagging. No finesse.' He let out a weary sigh, as if it was a heavy burden for him to shoulder. Belinda hadn't had a high opinion of him to begin with, but now she'd be happy if she never had to see his face again.

No wonder her boss had been so disgusted to learn Roy was back in Liverpool.

'When did you first meet Norah?'

He gave her an eye roll and picked up his paper. 'We're done here. The fact you already have someone in the nick, and you're questioning me here instead of at the station, makes me think you're pushing your luck with the guv'nor. Say hello to Big Jim for me.'

Belinda didn't bother to reply as she stood up, pausing only to drop a card by his beer. 'If you think of anything else, please call me.'

Then she walked back out into the daylight. She hadn't really expected Roy to give her any answers, but it did give something to speculate on. Because if Norah really had borrowed money from Roy, and Scott frequented the pub, it might explain where he'd got his leverage from.

The question was, did Roy Walsh know about it? She couldn't imagine he'd appreciate having his clients blackmailed by an elementary Gen Z-er like Scott. But if Roy was behind it, why frame Alice? Was it because she was a middle-class picture book illustrator who'd come out on the wrong side of a divorce and was looking for revenge?

Belinda rubbed her brow and walked back to the car, where Ryan was waiting.

'Did you get anything?'

'Only a headache. He swore he'd never met her before. But I did find out that Scott Williams drank there, which does give us a connection. Call the prison and make an appointment with Alice Hargraves again. I think we need to go straight to the horse's mouth.'

'Yes, ma'am.' Ryan made the call while Belinda checked her emails, and listened to her messages. She was only halfway through them when Ryan finished the call. His face was grim.

'Sorry, ma'am. Alice is refusing to see you.'

Belinda swore softly under her breath. It had been hard enough to convince her boss to let her keep going, and without Alice's cooperation she doubted he'd agree. Unfortunately, that was the nature of the job. Most cases didn't get neatly wrapped up with a ribbon. All the team could do was collect the evidence and piece together the story as best they could.

So why did Belinda feel that they'd told the wrong story?

23

PRESENT

Alice waited until the jury had been ushered out before gesturing for her solicitor, Ben Thomas, to come over. It hadn't been a good day. His shirt was covered in sweat and his face had taken on a chalky colour that didn't fill her with confidence. This morning, that hadn't been a problem. She'd accepted her fate and was ready to pay the price for her crimes.

But it was different now, and the zen-like bubble she'd been floating in for the last few weeks had disappeared as soon as she'd seen... *him.*

He'd only stayed in the court for another ten minutes before disappearing. But then he didn't need to stay, did he? Just seeing her in the courtroom, facing trial for a double homicide, was probably reward enough. And it was also enough time for him to convey what he'd wanted to convey.

That he was back. And wouldn't stop until he got what he wanted.

She knew this because Jasmine's necklace was around his neck. The one she'd been wearing when she'd stepped off the wall and into the swirling waters below. The necklace hadn't been returned after Jasmine's body had been recovered, and Alice assumed the clasp had snagged and that it had ended up on the riverbed. Lost forever.

Except that's not what had happened.

She wanted to scream at her past self. The one who hadn't even tried to help when Belinda Day had visited her in prison, trying to keep the lines of enquiry open. And now... oh, God. She had to stop him.

'I need you to give DI Day a note from me. Can you do that?'

Ben, who probably wanted nothing more than a beer and a night on the couch, gave her a cautious look. 'Will it help the case?'

No. But it might prevent someone else from being killed.

'Definitely.' Alice plastered on what she hoped was a persuasive smile. She probably looked like she was drunk. But for whatever reason, Ben's shoulders slumped in agreement.

'Fine. I'll see if I can find her,' he said as he slid a piece of paper across to her and she began to write.

'No. You have to find her,' she said as the court officers arrived to transport her back to the prison. 'Please. You have to,' she repeated as she was led away, her mind still reeling at the fact he'd finally found her.

Skunk was back.

* * *

Belinda's temples were throbbing. It had been a long day and all she wanted was to go home and have a glass of wine and fall into Tara's arms. Not necessarily in that order. Instead, she stared at the envelope that had been delivered to the station courtesy of Ben Thomas. It was accompanied by a text message, telling her to read it immediately.

While she wasn't in the habit of letting solicitors tell her what to do, her curiosity had been stirred. She'd purposely stayed away from the first day of the trial, though she would be called to give evidence soon. Sighing, she opened the envelope. There was a single page of text. All neatly handwritten and signed off at the bottom with Alice Hargraves's signature. She read it once, then a second time before the reality of it hit her.

Shit.

Should she believe what Alice had written? Except Alice had nothing to gain by lying. And while there was a good chance it was yet another false lead, could Belinda really take the chance?

'Ryan. With me,' she said, standing up with a such a start that half the office turned to stare at her. 'We need to talk to Roy Walsh. Put on your stab vest,' she said as she reached for her keys and phone. Her own vest was in the locker room, and she'd grab it on the way out. She turned to where Amy, Cheryl and Tim were waiting for any orders. 'Find Cassie Hargraves right now. Don't say anything to alarm her, and if she won't come into the station, then keep watch on her until I call. And don't let anyone come and go without informing me. Understood?'

'Yes, ma'am,' they said in unison, but Belinda hardly heard as she turned to Ryan. His phone was up to his ear and while his hand showed that he'd heard her, the conversation continued. Belinda raised an eyebrow and was about to repeat herself when Ryan finally put down the phone.

'Something to tell me, DS Walton?'

His face was grim as he gave a slight nod. 'Roy Walsh is

dead. His body was found half an hour ago in his house. His throat was slit, and he bled out on the spot.'

Belinda sucked in a sharp breath.

Alice had been right. She'd been right about it all. 'Amy and Cheryl, go and find Cassie Hargraves and bring her in. I don't care if you need to knock her over the head. We need to find her and keep her safe.'

'Yes, ma'am.' They hurried off and Belinda and Ryan weren't far behind.

'Who the hell do you think did it?' he said, face perplexed. 'Alice is in jail. Is it an accomplice?'

'Worse. Much worse.' Belinda thrust the letter at him. 'Read this.'

Detective Day, you once asked me about Cassie's father, but the real question is about her mother. My sister was twenty-one when she gave birth to Lily Rose Masterton. Jasmine had her demons. The drugs and alcohol and the abusive relationship that I tried to rescue her from. I think she could've beat them in the end, but we'll never know because two weeks after Lily was born, Jasmine begged me to make sure her daughter was safe, and then she took her own life.

I know it was wrong. But how could giving a tiny baby back to a drug addict of a father be right? So I took her and changed her name to Cassie. Mark heard about her and, thinking she was his daughter, he proposed. I said yes for two reasons. Because I loved him and because I wanted to keep Cassie safe. And as for her real father, I'd only ever known him by his street name. Skunk. At twenty-two he was a violent addict who thought nothing of hurting a pregnant woman and dealing drugs. It was impossible to keep track of him, and based on his life choices, I assumed he'd died.

But today in court I saw him. I'd only met Skunk once and he'd been vastly different from the man he is now. I dread to think what kind of monster he has become. But now it all makes sense. Why someone was trying to frame me for two murders and destroy my relationship with my daughter and ex-husband. It's because Cassie's real father is back, and I think he'll stop at nothing to get what he wants. My daughter.

But at least now I know his real name, and I hope you'll be able to stop him and protect my daughter. Please, Belinda. You have to help me.

You have to stop the monster that is Felix Richmond.

24

TWO YEARS EARLIER

'Thanks so much for letting me hold our engagement party here,' Norah said. She was dressed in a plain black dress and her hair was hanging in long curls. She looked radiant. And that made him happy. They'd had such a fucked-up life that they both deserved a little bit of happiness. And for his sister, that seemed to be in the form of Mark Hargraves. Felix had been slightly surprised when she'd first introduced them. Mark was older and looked like he'd grown up knowing exactly how to eat kippers and use an oyster fork. But he seemed to adore Norah, and she was crazy for him.

Plus, he was loaded.

That certainly didn't hurt.

'It's my pleasure. You know I'd do anything for you.' He put an arm around her. He was five years older than her and when she'd first rushed into the restaurant to show off the ring, he'd immediately offered it up as the venue. Might as well get in good with the in-laws.

'And I don't want you staying out the back supervising.

You've got a great chef working for you, so you must join in. I want you to meet Mark's daughter, Cassie. She's a lovely girl.'

'So you don't intend to play the wicked stepmother role, then,' he said, grinning.

'You know me better than that.'

He took a few minutes to survey his restaurant. His pride and joy. But life hadn't always been like that. He was living proof that someone could turn their life around.

Once he'd been a university drop-out, so strung out on drugs that everyone thought he'd be dead by twenty-two. He hadn't blamed them. Especially since it had happened to so many of his friends back then. Including Jasmine. He tensed at the thought of her name. The drugs had turned him violent. Made him do things he regretted. Nothing like he was now. The only good thing that had come from her death was that it had been the catalyst for him to turn his life around. He'd cleaned up his act, moved away from Glasgow to Europe and trained to be a chef. He now ran a successful restaurant in Liverpool and, if he ever indulged, it was on his terms. The odd line of coke. A joint or two. It didn't matter because he had it under control.

If only Jasmine and Lily were still with him. He'd never forget them. That was why he hadn't settled down with anyone and started a family. The scars were too deep from what had happened in the past. He'd messed up and missed out on a chance to have a family. He didn't deserve a second go.

'Earth to Felix. Are you in there?' Norah raised an eyebrow.

'Yeah, sorry. What is it?'

'The guests are starting to arrive.'

'Okay. You join Mark and do your royal duties and I'm going to take a quick look in the kitchen.'

Norah rolled her eyes. 'I told you it's going to be a laid-back night. No royal duties.'

'Yes, Your Majesty.' He grinned and disappeared into the kitchen. His sister was right, everything was under control, but he spent some time out there just to make sure. The buzz of conversation greeted him as he went back out and wove his way through the crowd to where Norah and Mark were standing.

'You've really pulled out all the stops tonight,' Mark said and shook his hand. Felix liked that. It made him feel refined and important. He returned Mark's grip just as a teenage girl beelined for them. She was about five foot five with long caramel hair that had been straightened to within an inch of its life. Her head was bent down as her fingers flew across the screen of her phone with the speed that only people under thirty could manage. 'And here's my daughter, who might bless us with some direct conversation.'

'I can hear you,' Cassie said, still not looking up. She hit a button on her phone and then finally put it into her back pocket before looking up. 'Hey, I'm Cassie.'

'Pleased to meet you, Cass—'

The words stuck in Felix's throat as the world stopped spinning.

No. It was impossible. Felix rubbed his eyes and opened them, but nothing had changed. The girl standing in front of him was Jasmine. But that was impossible. Jasmine was dead. And even if the police hadn't dragged her body out of the River Clyde, she wouldn't still be sixteen.

'Everything okay?' Norah said, the nurse in her never far away. She'd try to take his temperature if he wasn't careful. He faked a cough.

'Sorry, shouldn't have eaten peanuts before. They always get stuck in my throat. Pleased to meet you, Cassie.'

'You too.' She gave a tentative smile. Just the same as Jasmine's. He had to get away from there or he'd lose it.

'I'm sorry, looks like they've forgotten to bring out the good champagne,' he said, in what he hoped was a calm voice.

'Felix. You promised.' Norah stuck out her bottom lip.

'I won't be long.'

He squeezed his way through all of Norah and Mark's guests, and straight up to his office on the second floor of the building. It was a tiny thing, just enough for him and a desk, but it was better than nothing. He dropped down into the chair and pulled out a bottle of Scotch from the bottom drawer of his desk.

It was the good stuff. The kind he only drank when he wanted to impress someone. But right now he just needed to calm his nerves. It had to be a coincidence. Or a doppelganger. He'd flicked through enough of Norah's gossip magazines to know about similarities. But this was a whole other level.

The alcohol burned his throat as he downed it in one, and then picked up his phone. He knew the mother's name. Alice Hargraves. Norah had mentioned her enough times. He keyed it in and went to images.

There she was. A photograph of her holding a children's book in her hand. Another one with an arm around Mark, and a younger Cassie at her side. On and on they went.

And in every one she was still the same.

Letty Masterton.

Jasmine's bitch of an older sister, who'd come and visited for a couple of days when Lily had first been born, with her holier-than-thou attitude, trying to convince Jasmine to leave him. It hadn't worked, and she'd headed back to London, like the stuck-up bitch that she was.

But he'd lost his rag all the same and taken it out on Jasmine. He knew he shouldn't have, but she'd driven him to it.

If she'd really loved him, she wouldn't have let her cow of a sister into the apartment to talk shit about him.

Jasmine had killed herself the next day. It hadn't been on purpose. He knew that. The stupid bint had found his stash and had fallen into the fucking river, along with Lily. The divers had found some of her clothing and the baby blanket but not Lily herself.

She was so small, and probably got carried further down river. That's what they'd said.

But they were lying. Because here was living fucking proof that his daughter hadn't died. But how? Had Letty pushed Jasmine in and taken Lily for her own?

The answer was obvious. Otherwise, why had she changed her name? And Lily's? Not that it mattered now. The important thing was that he'd found his daughter and he was going to make up for lost time. But first Letty... correction... Alice was going to pay. However long it took. No question about it. And then he could be a proper father to Cassie.

25

'Crafty little git.' Belinda let out a long whistle as she finished going through the data on Roy Walsh's cloud storage accounts. The moneylender hadn't been lying when he'd said they wouldn't find Norah Richmond's name on his ledger.

Because the person who owed him money was Felix Richmond.

It was for eighty thousand pounds, and it wasn't until he'd missed several payments – and no doubt even more aggressive reminders – that Norah had started servicing the debt. But the worst of it was the email that Felix had sent Roy, along with a copy of the grainy video. Belinda had only looked at two frames before her stomach had churned and she'd been forced to stop it.

How could he do that? How could he hand over that kind of leverage to a man like Roy Walsh, just to ensure his sister helped pay his debts? Belinda suspected the money had been used to set up the restaurant. As soon as she had enough evidence, she'd request a warrant to go through Felix's books and see his financials.

There was no mention of how Scott Williams fitted into the picture, but Belinda's best guess was that he'd speculated on Norah not wanting Mark to know about the debt. As to whether Scott knew about the video – it was hard to say.

But the real question that Belinda couldn't answer was: why would Felix kill his sister?

From everything they'd collected, Norah and her brother had been very close, and she was paying for his loan – not to mention that she was marrying into a lot more money. It would be like killing the golden goose.

She turned back to the report the DI in charge of Roy Walsh's homicide had sent her. Despite Roy Walsh's preference to do business out of a shitty pub in Smithdown, he lived in a detached house in Woolton, and that was where he'd been killed. He'd been found at six thirty at night by his wife and the body had still been warm. The early report suggested he'd been knocked unconscious, and his throat had been slit. Very cold and calculated.

I dread to think of what kind of monster he has become.

She scanned the rest of the report. A neighbour had spotted a black Fiat parked across some double yellow lines outside his house. Apparently, it was an ongoing problem and he'd started taking note of the plates. It was registered to Felix Richmond.

It wasn't enough to tie him to the crime scene, but it did mean they could go back over their old CCTV footage to try and connect the car to Norah or Scott. A limited amount of overtime had been approved by the DCI, but it wouldn't last long. She had to move quickly.

'Excuse me, ma'am.' Ryan's cheeks were red and his denim jacket soaking wet. Another fine day in Merseyside. She'd sent him out to speak with Mark Hargraves and try and find Cassie, who they still hadn't tracked down.

'Please tell me you found her?'

He grimaced. 'No. She's been sharing an apartment in town but moved last week. Mark's also moved out of the house, but he spoke to Cassie yesterday morning before the trial. He'd asked her to go with him, but Cassie refused. They talked again briefly on the phone yesterday at around five in the afternoon. She was staying with her friend until she found a new apartment. He hasn't heard from her this morning and we're still trying to track down the friend.'

'Have you tried her social media accounts? It might give you a location,' she said.

'Ma'am, I've got something.' Tim called them over to his computer. He'd been going through the hours of footage, looking for the black Fiat. 'I've found the car on the day of the first homicide.'

Belinda raced over and studied the screen. 'Have you been able to identify the driver? Is it Felix?'

'Yes, ma'am. We caught his face on a camera as he went through the lights on Aigburth Road at 7.05 at night.'

Belinda rolled her shoulders. Murder investigations always brought with them a complex sense of emotions. And while it was a relief to get the physical evidence they needed to build a strong case, the fact that Felix Richmond was still out there meant she couldn't relax.

'That's excellent work. Can you track where the car goes after that?'

'I'm working on it. I've already checked the footage from the cameras on North Road, but there's nothing. It's likely, if he did kill her, that he parked several blocks away. Probably doesn't think we have the manpower to cast a wide net.'

They might not have the manpower, but her entire team had the tenacity and not one of them had protested when

Belinda had called them back in last night. 'Better to be tired than have the wrong person go to prison' was what Ryan had said and they'd all nodded in agreement.

'What motive did he have, ma'am?' Ryan asked. 'She was his sister. The only family he had. No one who was interviewed mentioned any bad blood between the two of them. Not even Alice, in whose interest it would be to find another culprit. If anything, she believed that it might have been her ex-husband.'

'I don't know,' Belinda was forced to admit. 'But something isn't right. Felix didn't mention being at Norah's house. In fact, he said he was at the restaurant the whole time. Who checked his alibi?'

'I did, ma'am. His chef vouched for him being there,' Amy chimed up.

'Well, someone's lying, since he couldn't possibly get back to Bold Street in time for his alibi to be valid. We need to pick up his car again.'

'Working on it,' Tim said, his fingers flying across the screen. His whole body was tense as he leaned forward, like he was playing a video game. But it was with someone's life. 'Damn. Here he is coming back up Aigburth Road towards town. Time is 8.13.'

'So he could've had time to murder his sister and turn around,' Belinda theorised. 'The real question is: where does he go next?'

'Bear with me,' Tim said as he kept flicking to different camera feeds. 'Got him. Woah. He's turning off towards Sefton Park.'

'Towards Alice Hargraves's house?' Ryan pondered, leaning closer as Tim worked.

Belinda's heart pounded. 'It's possible that he went straight there to plant the evidence. Did we do any checks in the area to see if anyone was spotted close to her house at the time?'

'No, we didn't. But if it was Felix, then how did he manage to get hold of Alice's cardigan and wrap the knife in it? And do all of it without being seen?'

'We don't know why he wasn't seen. Although I expect it was because Alice was very involved in her painting. She mentioned having a deadline that she was working towards. As for the cardigan, she claims to have thrown it away. Could he have just planned to put the knife in the bin and then saw the cardigan already there, covered with her DNA?'

'It fits,' Ryan agreed. 'So now what do we do?'

'I'm going to get in touch with the DCI and explain what's happened. If he agrees that we have additional evidence, then he will speak to the CPS and they'll decide next steps. While I'm doing this, I want you to gather as much as you can on Felix Richmond. And Ryan, get to work on Cassie's socials. See if she's got a geolocator going. Until we know for sure about Felix, we need to find her. And keep her safe.'

26

Felix took a final drag on his cigarette and then flicked it towards the black Fiat before walking away. The accelerant would burst into flames and soon the car would be gone, probably taking some of the empty houses as well judging by the piles of orangey-brown autumn leaves that were piled up around it. He could've paid someone to write it off, but it was pointless to bring in a middleman. Besides, he preferred to keep his money for himself.

He'd driven it to a rundown estate that some housing agency was waiting to plough down and start again. A couple of kids paused to stare at him, as if trying to decide whether he was worth robbing. He gave them a bemused smile and they darted off. Probably for the best. He much preferred talking to fighting, but he had no problem defending himself.

Or whatever else needed to be done to ensure he got what he wanted.

And he already had. Seeing Alice Hargraves sitting in court yesterday had been worth every miserable minute he'd spent suffering because of what she'd done. Divine retribution for being a stuck-up bitch. And Roy Walsh had almost ruined the moment. Felix's mood darkened. How dare Roy send thugs after him? Like that would work. Still, they wouldn't be needing the ten thousand pounds he'd found in their pockets. It would help fund the new life he was about to step into.

His phone buzzed with a text message. It was from one of the chefs. He hadn't bothered to tell them he was leaving. The restaurant was about to tank anyway. Better that he was far away from it when it happened. He'd only been hanging around until Cassie had turned eighteen anyway. So much easier when someone was an adult.

It was all going just as he'd planned.

Well, apart from the killing. He hadn't minded slitting Scott's throat. The little prick. How dare he mess around with Felix's daughter. The kid had to be taught a lesson. That's what a good father did. And Roy and his thugs... well... that was just business.

But Norah. That hadn't been on the to-do list.

He'd loved his sister. Of course he had. After all, he was the one by her side when that fucking prick had posted the video online. She'd been devastated and he'd helped her through it. So yeah, it had pained him to pass it on to Roy when Felix couldn't come up with the loan money, but Norah was about to be married to a goddamn millionaire. She could afford to help him out.

It's what family did.

His mouth flattened into an angry line. What family *didn't* do was talk about what a shit father you were. But that's what she'd done. At lunch she'd told him about Mark's infertility, and how devastating the news about Cassie would be for him. And she wouldn't stop talking about it. Going on and on about what a great father Mark was, how he and Cassie had a special bond, and how being a father was more than just blood. It was about turning up each day – and that's what made his relationship with Cassie so special.

She just wouldn't stop. It had all been Mark, Mark, Mark. And when she'd referred to Cassie's biological father she'd said several times that he must be a no-hoper if he'd never tried to see his daughter in seventeen years.

It wasn't true. He was a good father. An excellent one. He'd stopped Scott from harassing his daughter, hadn't he? And the only reason he hadn't been around when Cassie was growing up was because Letty Hargraves was a bitter whore who'd stolen something precious from him.

The world began to spin then, and his vision blurred. The sea of red would come next, sweeping through his mind, making him forget anything but pain. He didn't want that. He wasn't a bad person; he was good. And so he'd pushed away his half-eaten lunch (it was shit anyway, and the chef should be ashamed of himself) and had stumbled to his feet, stopping only to put some notes on the table. He had to get out of there, right now.

'Sorry. It must be something I ate,' he'd managed to say as he staggered away. Once he was out of sight, he leaned over a flowerbed and was violently sick. It had helped, but not enough, and by that evening he'd known there was only one thing he could do to make it go away. Plus, he had to admit that it had helped solve his problem of how to make Alice Hargraves pay.

And now it was done. Everything had worked out properly and the life that had been stolen from him all those years ago would once again be his.

The Uber he'd ordered had pulled up around the corner

and he strolled towards it. He still had some assets to dispose of.

'Hamish?' the driver said.

'That's right. I need to go to Stockbridge Village.' He climbed in and held his phone up to his ear until Cassie picked up. 'Hey. How's my new restaurant manager doing? I'm just sorting out some paperwork but will collect you in about three hours. Then we'll go straight to Gladstone Dock and catch the nine p.m. ferry. And don't forget that Barcelona will be warmer than Liverpool this time of year.'

He didn't bother to tell her about the new passports and the name change. No point making things more complicated than they needed to be. Besides, it wasn't really a name change. She was just getting her old one back. Lily. Then he closed his eyes as the Uber headed towards town. Soon they'd be in Dublin and could assume their new identities, and finally people would know that he was a good father.

* * *

'I still can't believe you're not waiting for the trial to finish.' Deb picked up a red bikini and held it against her chest. Cassie, knowing just how casual her friend could be when it came to clothing ownership, plucked it out of her hands and added it to the overflowing suitcase. Not that it was the right weather for bikinis, but this was a long-term plan. Summer would come around eventually, just like it always did.

'What's the point? It's not like I'm going to speak to her ever again. She's a liar.' And that wasn't even the worst of it. Alice had become the most notorious woman in England. Her mother was a killer. She'd murdered Norah and Scott. Cassie couldn't even think about it without gagging. And yet it was impossible to get her brain to connect the mother she'd known and the woman in the newspapers. It was why Cassie had refused to go to the trial or even follow the case.

It just hurt too much.

Cassie picked up the sunhat she'd bought last year and then put it down again. Every time she'd worn it, Scott had called her the cutest Boy Scout he'd ever seen. Tears stung her eyes. It wasn't getting any easier. Which was another reason why she couldn't stay in Liverpool.

It had almost been six months since he was killed, but everywhere she looked, all she could remember was him. There was nothing to stay for. Mark seemed to be having his own version of a breakdown and had moved into a two-bedroom apartment, but it was clear there wasn't room for her. And even though he called to check in a couple of times a day, she could always hear the slur in his voice from the booze.

Besides, she was eighteen and the money she'd made at Felix's restaurant had been enough to pay her half of the rent with Tamsin from work, and so she'd taken Hugo with her. It hadn't quite been how she'd planned to spend her gap year, but she'd been as happy as was possible, under the circumstances. Then Felix had dropped his bombshell. He was going to set up a new restaurant in Spain and he wanted her to come.

After everything that's happened, staying in Liverpool is unbearable. Plus, I've found some new investors who are giving me a huge opportunity out there to build the brand into something bigger. I want you to join me. I've been impressed with how much you've grown in the last six months. Especially considering...

He'd trailed off after that, and Cassie was almost pleased. Getting up and cleaning her teeth and going to work she could do. But talking about Norah and Scott was just too raw. It was another thing they had in common. A shared grief that let them speak in a way that others around them couldn't understand.

She'd moved out of the apartment two days ago and had planned to stay with Deb in her place above a betting shop in Old Swan, but that had changed when the landlord decided to try and fix the broken toilet himself and ended up flooding the place. And so she'd ended up going back to Alice's house.

It wasn't like it was being used. And besides, once the trial was over, her mum would have to sell it, so it might be the only chance for Cassie to take everything she wanted. Not to mention it was a bolt hole. With the start of the trial, the reporters and dark tourists had all come out again, looking for anything connected to Alice.

But soon it would be over. She and Felix would be getting on the night ferry and leaving. Deb had thought it was weird they were sailing to Dublin and then flying to Spain from there. *It's the other direction*, she'd said. Which itself was impressive since her friend had failed geography, but Cassie had explained that Felix's new business partners were over there, and there was paperwork to sign.

'Yeah, but don't you even want to talk to her?' Deb said, her complete lack of ability to read the room on full display. Not to mention it was the same conversation they'd had every day since the arrest.

'No. Never,' Cassie assured her. 'That's why I'm leaving to start a new life. I don't want any of this.'

'Yeah, well, don't forget about me. As soon as you find a nail bar out there, you let me know.' Deb held up her hands to display her long acrylics, each one a clash of stripes, colours and diamanté. Her friend had been training as a nail technician ever since finishing school and was working part time at a place in town.

'I promise,' Cassie said as Deb's phone beeped. She looked at the screen and let out a low growl. 'Are you actually kidding me? That prick... I swear I'm going to kill him. Sorry, I've got to go.'

'Remember, violence is never the answer,' Cassie said as she hugged her friend. Deb rolled her eyes but didn't promise anything. The ongoing drama between her friend and her boyfriend was the stuff of legends. 'And please tell your mum not to give Hugo too many treats. It's not good for him.'

'He'll be okay,' Deb assured her before kissing her cheek and hurrying away as fast as her platform heels would let her. Cassie waited until the front door shut before sitting down on the bed. The only thing she'd really miss was her dog. They'd already dropped him around to Deb's mum's house, and she'd sworn to send weekly reports. It wasn't ideal but once the restaurant was up and running, she'd be able to fly him over.

She turned her attention back to the room. There was a layer of dust, and the entire house was cold. The gas and electricity weren't working so Cassie had just thrown an extra coat over her jumper. It seemed weird to think she'd never see it again. Maybe never even see Liverpool again. It was for the best. She bit her lip to push back the threatening tears just as her phone rang. It was the only number that she hadn't blocked.

Felix.

'Hey,' she answered. 'I can't believe it's finally happening. Spain, here we come.'

27

Alice's temples were throbbing as she lay down on the hard bed
in her prison cell. The second day of the trial had been even
worse than the first and her barrister, Cameron Lyle, had developed a nervous tic that didn't bode well for the rest of the week.
Nor did the fact that Ben hadn't given Belinda Day her note. All
he'd done was leave it at the station with an explanation. And
so Alice had spent the entire day scanning the room, hoping to
catch a glimpse of Felix. *Keep your enemies closer.* Because if he
was there in the courtroom then he couldn't be anywhere near
Cassie. But there hadn't been any sign of him.

Hence the headache. A rattling sound came from outside
her door and the scraping click of the door being unlocked. A
different officer appeared in the doorway. Her mouth was set in
a sullen line, as if she'd just eaten a lemon.

'Stand up.'

'Why? Where are we going?' Alice said, though her legs still
complied, and she got to her feet.

The officer's face darkened. 'There's been a discontinuance.'

Alice had no idea what a discontinuance meant, but the

officer's dour expression told her it was better not to ask. However, she found out soon enough when Ben greeted her. He looked equally bewildered but relieved.

The case against her was being dropped, which meant the trial wouldn't be going ahead and therefore she was free to go. Free. Just like that. Alice blinked as she was shuffled through the process, filling out paperwork and finally being handed back her measly possessions before being pointed in the direction of the exit.

As they walked, Ben talked to her about her options. Did she want to lodge a complaint? But Alice hardly heard. The last six months had been such a surreal experience, deprived of liberty and everything she'd thought she needed to live her life. And now, just as suddenly, it was being given back to her.

They stepped outside. It was late October and despite only being five o'clock, the sharp wind reminded her that winter was on the way. She tugged at the lightweight jacket she'd been wearing back in May when she'd first been remanded in custody.

Ben finally seemed to notice her confusion as he guided her towards his late-model BMW. 'I know it must be a lot to take in. But this is wonderful news, Alice. You're free.'

'But how? What happened? Have they found evidence that Felix killed Norah and Scott? Do Mark and Cassie know? I-is my daughter safe?'

There was silence as he started the car. 'I don't have the full details, but they've issued a warrant for his arrest. He's disappeared so they're currently hunting for him.'

'You didn't answer my question. Where's my daughter?' she said, but as his face drained of colour, it was all the answer she needed. Oh, God. No. Not Cassie. Razor-sharp blades sliced through her heart, as something immense pressed down on her chest, making breathing impossible. The pain of watching Jasmine jump to her death and Mark leaving her had been nothing compared to this.

Ben kept his eyes on the road, as if not daring to look at her. 'The police are still trying to find her, but I-I'm sure she's okay.'

Except that was a lie.

She'd seen first-hand what kind of destruction Felix could do. There was nothing he wouldn't do to get his daughter back. And to destroy Alice for what she'd done.

A kind of rage swept through her then. Dark and angry. Felix could do what he wanted to Alice. She didn't care. But he couldn't have Cassie. He hadn't been good enough back then, and he certainly wasn't good enough now. She'd promised Jasmine that she'd keep her daughter safe. She wasn't going to break her word now.

Belinda Day. That's who she needed to speak with. Her phone was still in the paper bag that they'd given her, and she fumbled to retrieve it, only to discover it wasn't working. Probably because the battery was flat. Alice swore.

'I need to charge my phone so I can call DI Day.'

'I strongly advise against that. You've just been released. This is a police matter, and you need to leave it to them,' he said as he turned onto the motorway. Then, as if realising how harsh he sounded, he pointed to the USB slot. 'You can plug your phone in there. And, Alice, I think it's probably best if you check into a hotel tonight and wait until the media interest has died down. Give yourself time to adjust back to having a normal life.'

Alice wanted to laugh. Prison had taught her that normal didn't exist. It was all an illusion. Someone else could come along and change her life in a second. And the sooner she stopped pretending otherwise, the better. Also, her income had dribbled to a halt while she'd been in prison, so she couldn't afford a hotel even if she wanted to.

'I'd rather go home.'

Ben opened his mouth, as if to argue, but finally shrugged. 'Sure. Would you like to stop and get some supplies first?'

'No. I have a few non-perishables in the cupboard. I just want to sleep in my own bed and forget this ever happened.' It wasn't quite the truth, but he seemed to accept it and forty minutes later she was back inside her small terrace. It was thankfully free of the press and either the reporters hadn't been informed about the new development, or they'd simply lost interest in her.

She could hardly blame them.

The electricity had been turned off while she was away, and she draped a heavy coat over her shoulders as she went in search of a candle and matches in the bottom drawer in the kitchen. Once she had retrieved them, she went in search of the hideously ugly silver candlestick holder Mark's parents had given them for a wedding present.

Alice managed to screw the candles into the base and soon she could at least see again. Her phone had enough charge in it from the trip home, and she called Cassie's number. It went straight through to voicemail.

'This is Cass. You know the ropes. Beep. Beep. Beep.'

Alice's heart lurched. It was the first time she'd heard Cassie speak in six months. And she'd changed her message. It was cute and sassy. Just like her daughter.

A lump formed in her throat. 'Hi, Cassie, it's Mum. No... that's not right. It's Alice. And I know you're mad at me. I don't blame you. I should have told you the truth. Given you the opportunity to know about your real father. And your real mother. Please, sweetheart. Just tell me where you are so I can come and find you. I just want to see you—' Alice cut herself off. Was it too much? Yes, definitely.

Though she didn't have the energy to cancel it.

Actually, she wasn't even sure she *could* cancel it. That was the sort of thing Cassie did for her. Eyeroll added for no charge.

Sighing, she rubbed her neck and reached for a pad and pen. At the top she scribbled down Cassie's name and then put a little X against it. Then she picked up her phone and this time called Mark. If she'd been hoping for a reunion, she would've been disappointed. His voice was slurred, and he seemed to think Cassie was at work. A sliver of rage went through her. She'd been in prison for six months and had assumed Mark was keeping an eye on their daughter. Making sure she was okay.

She ended the call and moved on to the next person on her list, but half an hour later she was no further ahead. No one seemed to have any idea where her daughter was. Despite Ben's advice, she'd left several emails for Belinda Day, as well as Cassie's friend Deb.

The flames began to flicker, and Alice stood up. Her legs were cramped, and fatigue tugged at her senses. It was only six thirty at night, but she'd hardly slept since the trial. She walked over to the sofa and was about to lie down when there was a creaking noise and the front door was pushed open.

Alice immediately tensed. Her time in prison had made her hypervigilant and she quickly blew out the candles and clutched at the candelabra.

'Shh. Someone might hear us.'

'Like who?' a male voice replied. 'No one's here. Didn't you say that your mate had legged it to Dublin?'

'Seriously, do you *ever* listen to me? I said she's going to Spain with her boss. They just need to make a side trip to

Dublin. On the ferry,' the girl said, and Alice widened her eyes. It was Deb. Was that why she hadn't answered the phone earlier? Because she didn't want to risk telling Alice what she really knew? 'And what's that smell?'

'Wasn't me,' the guy protested. 'Come here and I'll prove it.'

Deb let out a little squeak and then it went quiet, apart from the sound of teenage kissing. Old Alice would have charged in and broken them up before calling Deb's mother. But now she couldn't care less what two eighteen-year-olds were doing. Her mind was whirling.

Dublin.

Cassie was taking the ferry to Dublin. With *her boss*. Did she mean Felix? Or had she got another job that Alice knew nothing about?

No. It had to be Felix. He's taken his daughter.

Alice had to stop them before the ferry left or she might never see her daughter again.

Alice had only made the trip to Dublin once and had thrown up the entire time. But she did recall that it had been a night crossing. Still clutching at the candelabra, she slipped out of the back door, quietly picking up her bag as she went.

A quick internet search told her that the ferry left at nine p.m. Alice didn't waste another minute as she booked an Uber and unlocked the side gate to wait for it. At least she now had a chance.

* * *

Alice gave the driver a twenty-pound tip for getting her there so quickly. His eyes were bright with excitement, and she suspected he wasn't often told to speed. She thanked him again and hurried over to the terminal. Her lungs burned from lack of exercise and the light rain had already soaked her clothes.

She finally reached the booking office and gave her name. She'd booked the ticket on the trip over, and suspected she'd paid far too much.

She didn't care. All that mattered was Cassie. She'd left another message for Belinda Day, wishing the detective was with her. She'd just be able to flash a warrant card and demand to be told which cabin Felix Richmond was staying in. But there was no sign of her, and Alice was forced to go on board alone. The ferry was huge and there were people milling around everywhere. Some were laughing while others beelined straight for the bar.

Alice's stomach roiled despite the fact the ferry was still moored. Please don't let her be sick. Inside there were three bars and numerous chairs and sofas dotted along the glossy wooden floor. What if Deb was wrong and Alice had boarded the ferry for nothing?

No. She couldn't think like that. She just had to focus on where her daughter might be. A voice spoke out over the tannoy. 'Can Rita Pattison and Charlie Boyden please come to the reception area. I repeat, can Rita Pattison and Charlie Boyden please make themselves known to the staff.'

Alice hurried over to where a hostess was handing out information about the journey.

'Excuse me, I've lost my daughter. Her name's Cassie Hargraves. Is there a way to have it announced?'

'Oh, you poor thing.' The hostess patted her arm. 'Let's get some details and we'll get the notice up immediately. And try not to worry.' Alice wished that was possible as she followed the woman over to the reception. She told them that Cassie was five and had darted off when she'd seen another girl her age playing with a doll.

A minute later another announcement sounded out.

'Could Cassie Hargraves please come to the reception area. Your mother is here and waiting for you.'

Her nerves were shredded as she peered around. Now that she'd committed herself, she had no idea what to expect. Would Cassie turn up, or Felix, or neither of them? The hostess who'd brought her over was summoned away, but she gave Alice a supportive smile.

Alice tried to return it, but her heart was pounding.

She checked her watch and continued to scan the crowd, which was why she didn't even notice the man walking up behind her, until a hand was over her mouth, and an iron grip pressed into her arm. Then she was violently yanked back until she was pressed up against a wiry body.

'If you scream, she dies. Now walk. You and I need to have a little chat, Letty.'

'Let me go.' Alice tried to break free, but Felix was too strong, and he twisted her arm tightly behind her back, sending pain into her shoulder.

'Move,' he growled, giving her a sharp shove in the back.

'Where's Cassie?' she gasped as he gave her another push.

'Sleeping. I gave her a sedative. I doubt she'll wake up until Dublin. And by then it will be too late.'

Too late for what? Alice tried to control her breathing as Felix continued to thrust her forward. Her legs were aching from lack of use and by the time they stepped out onto a deserted deck, she was winded. The sky was covered in dull grey clouds, the moon only just giving enough light to see the drizzling rain.

'You won't get away with it,' she said. 'The police are looking for you.'

'They can look all they want. Tomorrow I'll be untraceable. And so will my daughter.' As he spoke, he pushed her across the deck, until they reached the railing. Then he spun her around, and she saw him properly for the first time.

His dark hair was dishevelled, and his eyes were bright. His mouth was twisted at one side, and it was something she recognised from when Jasmine had first started using. He was high, and the traces of his old persona seemed to settle on his face like a shadowy mask.

How had she not seen it sooner?

'You won't get away with this,' she said as the rain pounded against her skin.

'I beg to differ. So far, I've done an outstanding job of getting away with it. Now, climb over the rail.'

'What? Why—' The words died on her lips as understanding hit her. Jasmine had climbed onto a railing and jumped into the River Clyde. Was this his revenge? By getting her to re-enact it by drowning in the Mersey?

She tried to slip from his grip by spinning around him, but he yanked her back, almost pulling her arm out of the socket. Pain exploded through her, and her vision blurred. He thrust her back against the rail before lifting her up.

'Why? *Why?*'

His calm had gone and the Skunk she'd first met reappeared. Sullen, belligerent and very angry. 'You know why. You stole them. Jasmine. Lily. They were mine and you took them away from me.'

'I didn't steal them. I saved them. I couldn't help Jasmine, not after what you did to her. Do you think I didn't know how you beat her black and blue? How you forced her to take drugs so she'd be dependent on you?' she said as her stomach churned and nausea swept through her.

'She loved me,' he snarled, lifting her higher. The ferry lurched and Alice's legs kicked out, but there was nothing but air. He slammed her against the railing, the backs of her knees burning as she hit the metal. She wriggled and managed to drop back down to the deck. It was wet and she slithered against the wood.

'She hated you,' Alice said as her stomach heaved, and her vision blurred. She bent over and was violently sick. Acid burned her throat as Felix's hands grabbed her arms again. 'She made me promise to take care of Cassie.'

'Lily. Her name is Lily.' He hauled her up as the rain continued to beat against them. Alice panted, limp and worn out.

'It's Cassie and if she'd been left with you, she'd be dead. Because you destroy everything. You're not fit to be a father.'

His face contorted into fury, the last of his control leaving him. 'You know nothing. You and your waste of space ex-husband were happy to stand by while Lily ruined her life with that shithead. I was the only one who knew what to do. I stopped him. Because that's what a good father does.'

His hand had moved up to her throat and his strong fingers tightened, blocking the air from her lungs. Her head began to spin as he lifted her higher again. This was it. He was going to strangle her and throw her overboard. And Cassie. Her beautiful daughter would be—

The grip loosened and Alice dropped back onto the deck. She gripped the rails to steady herself as she faced him. But his eyes had lost their feral anger as he stared at her in confusion.

'What the fuck?' he spluttered before suddenly lurching to one side. As he moved, a trail of blood fell onto the deck before being washed away by the rain. And then he tumbled to the ground, a knife sticking out from his back.

She wiped the rain from her eyes as a figure hurled itself at her.

Cassie. Something broke in Alice's chest and she let out a sob as she wrapped her arms around her daughter.

'Mum. Mum.' Cassie's wails were muffled against the wind and rain as Alice stroked her hair, wanting to make it right. Then Cassie's body went limp, reminding Alice of when she was a toddler, and had worn herself out from crying. She cradled her daughter, like she'd done so many times before.

'Hey, it's okay, sweetheart,' she whispered. 'Everything's okay.'

'No, it's not. I killed him. All this time I was mad at you. I didn't know how you could be a killer. And it turns out I'm one.' Cassie stared at the unmoving body. Her face was white and her body was shaking.

'Shh. It doesn't matter.' Alice gently turned Cassie's face away from Felix's corpse. 'Just look at me. I'm here and together we'll sort it all out. I promise. You saved my life, Cassie. You saved my life.'

'I heard what he said. That he's my father, and Jasmine's my mother. And... he killed Norah, and Scott. All this time I thought he was nice. But he lied about everything and I fell for it.'

'He's had a lifetime of manipulation,' Alice said as the rain finally began to ease. She wiped the strands of wet hair away from Cassie's face. 'He fooled us all. Even his own sister. But how are you even awake? He said he gave you a sedative.'

'He gave me a glass of wine, but I was already feeling queasy from the boat, so I did what I do with Deb. Just took a sip and tipped the rest of it out. I didn't think anything of it until I went back to the cabin to rest and I got your message. I – I didn't want it to be true.' Cassie began to cry again, this time in earnest. 'I was such a bitch to you. I never even visited. I-I wanted to, but it hurt to think about it.'

'It's okay,' Alice said truthfully, her fingers linked with her daughter's. A noise sounded from the other end of the deck and Cassie's hand went cold.

'They're going to find out,' she whispered, suddenly sounding so like Jasmine that Alice's heart squeezed with pain. Jasmine. The sister she'd loved but couldn't save. And now there was Cassie. Her daughter. Her niece. So young, so much life ahead of her. Alice had failed her sister, but she wouldn't fail Cassie.

'It's okay, my love. I promise you.' Alice let go of her daughter's hand and dropped to her knees. The knife was still protruding from Felix's back, and Alice wrapped her fingers around it, making sure that every part of her fingerprints was pressed onto it. Then she pushed her hand into the blood that pooled around the knife.

Cassie let out a pained cry. 'No, what are you doing?'

'I'm doing what any good mother would do. I'm giving you the life you deserve,' Alice said as footsteps sounded out around them.

Then a woman appeared. She was tall with short, cropped hair and a grim expression on her lips. DI Belinda Day. Two more officers flanked her.

Alice was pleased. She liked the detective and how she took pride in her work. Alice stood up, rubbing Felix Richmond's blood into her own shirt, just in case there was any confusion.

The inspector walked towards Alice while the two officers dropped down to inspect the body.

'What happened?' She stared directly at Alice.

'It was me. I killed Felix Richmond.'

The DI opened her mouth as if to protest but then shut it again and stared directly at Cassie, whose entire body was shaking, making her look twelve years old. Then she nodded.

'Okay, then. Alice Hargraves, you are under arrest...'

ACKNOWLEDGMENTS

No book is ever written in a vacuum, and we'd like to say a huge thank you to everyone at Boldwood Books for their input and support, especially: Emily Ruston (one of the best editors we've ever had the pleasure of working with); Amanda Ridout; Nia Beynon; Claire Fenby; Becca Allen; Arbaiah Aird, and the rest of the team. Being Boldwood authors has been a wonderful experience for both of us.

We'd also like to thank Christina Phillips, our long-term critique partner and friend.

Finally, to our families. Thanks for your continued support.

MORE FROM SALLY RIGBY AND AMANDA ASHBY

We hope you enjoyed reading *The Ex-Wife*. If you did, please leave a review.

If you'd like to gift a copy, this book is also available as an ebook, hardback, large print, digital audio download and audiobook CD.

Sign up to Sally Rigby and Amanda Ashby's mailing list for news, competitions and updates on future books.

https://bit.ly/SallyRigbyAmandaAshbyNews

Explore more psychological thrillers from Sally Rigby and Amanda Ashby.

ABOUT THE AUTHOR

Sally Rigby and Amanda Ashby are a writing duo who live in New Zealand. They have been friends for eighteen years and agree about everything (except musicals). They decided to collaborate on a psychological thriller which they then entered into a competition, run by Boldwood, and which they won!

Visit Sally Rigby's website:
https://www.sallyrigby.com/

Visit Amanda Ashby's website:
https://amandaashby.com/

Follow Sally and Amanda on social media:

 twitter.com/AmandaRigbyNZ
instagram.com/amandarigbybooks
facebook.com/Amanda-Rigby-111632041134381

THE

Murder

LIST

THE MURDER LIST IS A NEWSLETTER DEDICATED TO SPINE-CHILLING FICTION AND GRIPPING PAGE-TURNERS!

SIGN UP TO MAKE SURE YOU'RE ON OUR HIT LIST FOR EXCLUSIVE DEALS, AUTHOR CONTENT, AND COMPETITIONS.

SIGN UP TO OUR NEWSLETTER

BIT.LY/THEMURDERLISTNEWS

Boldw⊕d

Boldwood Books is an award-winning fiction publishing company seeking out the best stories from around the world.

Find out more at www.boldwoodbooks.com

Join our reader community for brilliant books, competitions and offers!

Follow us

@BoldwoodBooks

@BookandTonic

Sign up to our weekly deals newsletter

https://bit.ly/BoldwoodBNewsletter

Printed in Great Britain
by Amazon

26483245R00175